Edna Gray

One Woman's Life

the steppings of faith - Edna Gray's story

Edna Gray

One Woman's Life
the steppings of faith - Edna Gray's story

ISBN/EAN: 9783337284442

Printed in Europe, USA, Canada, Australia, Japan

Cover: Foto ©Andreas Hilbeck / pixelio.de

More available books at **www.hansebooks.com**

ONE WOMAN'S LIFE.

THE STEPPINGS OF FAITH.

EDNA GRAY'S STORY.

ATLANTA, GA.:
The Franklin Printing and Publishing Company.
GEO W HARRISON, State Printer, Gen. Mgr.
1898.

ONE WOMAN'S LIFE.

Scenes Laid in the Mountains of Western North Carolina,
Near Round Knob and Asheville.

———

A TRUE STORY OF A WOMAN'S LIFE.

HER ROMANTIC, TRAGICAL, AND FATAL MARRIAGE.

WAS BEDRIDDEN AND BLIND SIX YEARS.

REMARKABLE RECOVERY.

YOUNG CHILDREN HIDDEN AWAY MANY YEARS.

THE MOTHER'S FRANTIC AND
FRUITLESS EFFORTS IN THEIR BEHALF.

THEIR FINAL EXCITING ESCAPE AND RESTORATION.

———

This Story Sets Forth the Wonderful Answer to Prayers
of Faith and the Triumphs over Trials and Tempta-
tions Through Christ and Faith in God.

EXTRACTS FROM LETTERS.

ONE WOMAN'S LIFE, OR STEPPINGS OF FAITH.

By Mrs. William King, of the Atlanta Constitution:

The above is the title of a book soon to appear before the public, by Edna Gray. Having seen and known the author and having a synopsis of the book, we can safely say that it will prove very interesting reading. It is a true history of a very eventful life, so sensational and dramatic as to keep up the interest through the entire story.

The author has gone through various and dark trials, ill health and blindness, but her implicit faith has sustained her, and even when nearly through her work and her blindness caused her to desist, in a most unexpected way a friend was raised up to her who finished the work. So it has been by steppings of faith that at last she will soon present it to the public. It is truly a strange and interesting history of one woman's life.

———

From the Atlanta Journal:

A book which will shortly appear is written by an Atlanta woman and called "One woman's Life" and "Steppings of Faith."

Edna Gray is the authoress and tells in a clear and interesting manner of this woman, who as a blind and bed-ridden sufferer for six years, struggled with herself to overcome her weakening of faith; and the book admirably portrays her triumph over self and the return of faith, which came to her through direct answer to prayer. The book will be out in a short time and will be a sweet story of religious struggles and trials, which were all swept away by that divine peace which comes to all who have perfect faith.

———

Mrs. Lollie Belle Wylie's Letter:

November 6th, 1897.

My Dear Edna Gray:—I have read your manuscript, One Woman's Life, and find the story full of dramatic action and interest. I think the story will find a ready sale if published, and its idea "to do good" result as you hope it will. Wishing you much success and all life's blessings, I am, Sincerely your friend,

LOLLIE BELLE WYLIE.

From Mr. H. T. Phillips, Atlanta, Ga.:

"Edna Gray's book, One Woman's Life, is the most remarkable personal history I ever read. Her powers of endurance were wonderful and beyond anything I ever heard of."

I have not had an opportunity to examine the book called One Woman's Life, but wish to commend it as a token of my faith in its author. I knew her well in 1883, a suffering, blind invalid of radiant Christian character, whose sweet spirit and beautiful example of patience and joy in suffering shed a hallowed influence upon the entire community in which she lived.

EDWARD L. BELL., Clergyman.
Richmond, Va.

From the Mountain Voice, North Carolina:

The many friends of Edna Gray, who has been blind and helpless for six years, will be glad to hear that she has entirely recovered the use of her eyes and spine and can see and walk as well as ever. Below is an extract from her last letter:

Providence Hospital, Washington, D. C., Oct. 12th.

Dear Father and Mother:—Our many prayers are being answered and I am getting well. I can walk around the room and can see nearly as well as ever.

My trust is still in God and I pray daily that we may meet again. We have the best of physicians and all are very kind to me.   Your loving daughter,

EDNA GRAY.

The book called One Woman's Life, I heartily endorse and recommend as being all it purports to be, a reality, and not mere fiction. With my prayers for its success, I am,

Very truly,   W. B. REESE,
Pastor M. E. Church, South, Bakersville Station, N. C.

I hereby certify that I believe the story, One Woman's Life, to be a true history of the life of Edna Gray.

J. B. DAVIS., D.D.,
Pastor Holy Trinity Lutheran Church, Mt. Pleasant, N. C.

ten under the greatest difficulties, failing sight the chief trouble, so I ask my readers to forget the author in the glimpses of Christ and his-love that at times filled my soul, lifting me above the unhappy surroundings to worlds of light, love, and beauty. The poems inserted without quotation marks were composed when sick and blind, and are not supposed to be the product of a poetess, but only the cry of a breaking heart—praying that through my weakness and sorrow Christ's light and life may shine.

I dedicate my book to all who are seeking more of Bible truths, Bible promises and fulfillments in answer to the written word: "If ye abide in me, and my words abide in you, ye shall ask what ye will, and it shall be done unto you." John xv.

CONTENTS.

PART II.

CHAPTER VIII.

CHAPTER IX.

CHAPTER X

CHAPTER XI.

CHAPTER XII.

CHAPTER XIII.

CHAPTER XIV.

CHAPTER XV.

Oh! What will become of you, my poor little girl?

One Woman's Life.

THE STEPPINGS OF FAITH.

CHAPTER I.

CHILDHOOD.

"Childhood's days now pass before me,
Forms and scenes of long ago,
Like a dream they hover o'er me,
Calm and bright as evening's glow."

THE story of my life begins with my seventh year, in the town of Windsor, situated on the banks of the Connecticut river, in the State of Vermont. Our family consisted of father, mother, four brothers and myself, a sensitive, bashful child, happily surrounded by loving friends and all the comforts of life. My parents were of Puritan descent, though French blood flowed through my mother's veins, her mother being a descendant of a French marquis.

My father was fair, with deep blue eyes and dark curling hair. He was mild, practical, fond of literary and scientific pursuits; and being in comfortable circumstances, as he was a manufacturer of sewing machines, and naturally indulgent and generous, took an active

1

part in all good and moral works. My mother was a brunette, tall, stately and beautiful. She possessed much literary and musical talent, a proud spirit, and a warm and generous heart. Unlike my father she was sensitive, imaginative and impulsive; inheriting, I suppose, a deep love for the beautiful in nature and art. My eldest brother, Sias, was a strong, robust youth of seventeen, with dark, earnest eyes and a heart so brave and true that he was esteemed by all who knew him. Uncle John, my mother's youngest, and favorite brother, a gifted artist and musician, with three of my father's nephews, made our house their home, and added their full quota of enjoyment to our happy family circle. I being the only girl in the house was petted to my heart's content, especially by my father and uncle, both of whom I loved devotedly.

At this period the war between the North and South broke out, taking in its yawning jaws, brother Sias, Uncle John, and my cousins. My father was a Canadian and also being too old to engage in active service, was left to comfort and care for his family. Moving us to his farm in Canada, his boyhood's home, he built a pretty white cottage, with French windows, on a plateau two hundred feet above the still, deep waters of the Massawippi lake, which lies about five miles east of the celebrated Memphremagog. Our view extended across this beautiful lake, and many miles beyond, taking in valleys and rivers, in visions picturesque and sublime.

Well I remember the night of the departure of my soldier brother, uncle and cousins. The sleigh stood at the door, the prancing steed impatient to be off.

Aroused at midnight the novice soldiers bravely bid farewell to all that was dearest to them in life, all but their country.

I crept from my father's overcoat where I had been asleep in the wood box, to say the sad good-bye, with heart choking with emotion. Though only seven years of age I beheld that scene with mind and heart of older years. Never shall I forget it. My brother, only sixteen years of age, brave, noble, kind like a dear father to me, now saying farewell to his dear home forever, for no "return" came to that loving mother. It is only repeating the "old, old story" of vain hopes, secret longings and heart aches so common during that bloody war. More than a year of hard service for his loved country and he stood one day serving at his post of repairing a bridge which was necessary, though so dangerously near the enemy ; but it must be done, and several of the bravest and best were selected for the dangerous post. With the courage of a Napoleon they faithfully performed their duty ; but alas ! alas ! to human life ! The enemy was upon them ! My brother was shot through his foot, killing his horse under him, and was of course captured. His brave young friend, Orange Ayer, galloped to his aid only to receive a like fate ; and to the cold prison walls they were sent. Oh! the sad, sad tales prison walls could tell, alike both for North and South. Only the mother hearts of both countries know full well the keenness of the poisoned arrow that broke their hearts. Sisters in sorrow indeed they are. May they now truly be sisters in the peace that is Christ-like and forgiving. How many sad tales of woe. Ah, who can tell them!

> " Under the sod and the dew,
> Waiting the judgment day,
> Under the roses—the blue ;
> Under the lilies—the gray."

Anxious and weary with waiting, my mother longed day by day for news of her eldest born. Suspense that could scarcely be borne. Then it came of how he died in prison, so weak and worn. Merely a shadow of his fine noble form, crawling about on hands and knees, no strength to walk, untold suffering, only known to the prison, life. The overwrought brain and full heart waiting at home for him, could not bear up under the rod that was chastening her, and the mother's heart broke at the sad, sad end of her noble, proud boy. Not now possessing the perfect hope in Christ, the burdened brain fell into melancholy, gradually brought on by the dwelling on the fate of her loved boy, buried away without care or tears in an unknown grave.

> "Will it matter to him who may sorrow,
> For the loved one we tenderly miss?
> Since our voices can never more bring him
> Back again to our presence and kiss?"

Almost heart-broken, my parents were robed in garments of despair. My father, always frail, was now completely broken down in health and spirit : while a great sorrow shone from my mother's dark eyes, as she sat by the window watching and waiting for the loved one who would never return. While I, too young to comprehend their grief, romped as usual over the meadows and hills, with my playmate and constant companion, brother Bradley, a gentle, delicate lad, nearly three years my senior. Together we roamed the woods in search of flowers, while our little hearts were cheered by the songs of merry birds. When tired of outdoor sports we would ransack garret and closet for old relics to add to our numerous treasures. Then at last we would separate, he going to his room to read or draw—drawing being his favorite pastime—and I to amuse myself with my sweet, black-eyed baby brother Harry, or to visit my pets, which consisted of eight white rabbits, with pink eyes and soft, downy fur; "Skip" an ugly little dog, but, nevertheless, good and dear to me; "Topsy," a darling cat ; six pigeons ; a tame crow ; four pet lambs ; a cage of canaries, and numerous others.   My chief delight was with a book perched upon the back of a favorite cow lying in the yard, where I would sit and read, no fear of harm from any of my pets.   Another favorite spot was up in the third loft of the barn; with my book near a window, I would read and watch the sheep in the "bay" below.

Books and love of nature early formed a solid foundation of character, and at the age of ten my mind was deeply impressed upon the subject of religion, and hours were spent each day with some favorite pet, or watching the birds in some sequestered spot or shady nook, reading the Bible, or Pilgrim's Progress, or some other good book.   Laboring under the mistaken idea that I was too young to be a Christian, I determined, when I became a woman, to embrace religion and devote myself to the cause of Christ.

Naturally affectionate and impressionable, this rural life directed by reading good books and pure influences gently nurtured by nature's wise hand, early developed in me a strong character, craving wisdom and usefulness and love. Eagerly seeking a noble life, not yet, however, knowing the "Way" perfectly and the frailty of human strength.

During this year, Charley, a chubby, blue-eyed baby

was added to our family. I was greatly dissatisfied because I had no sister, and succeeded in winning a reluctant promise from my father that he would at some time make up the deficiency, from an orphan asylum, in the shape of a sister, with large black eyes and long black curls. How I longed for this event that never happened. Years passed and no sister gladdened my heart, as my mother would never consent to a stranger being admitted into the home circle.

At the age of twelve I was an accomplished romp, and spent a large portion of my time skating, coasting, riding horse-back, or roaming over hills and vales with my father, holding his hand and listening to his tales of bygone days; but frequently enjoying these sports alone, being too independent and bashful to even speak to the opposite sex, thereby keeping them at a respectful distance, while girls were too timid to engage in my daring adventures.

Two years later my father's business called him to Guelph, a large prosperous town near Toronto. This trip was very interesting and made a vivid impression on my young mind. We traveled a portion of the night, and arrived at the famous Victoria bridge about dawn; the wheels of our coach being considered unsafe we were compelled to change; entering the tunnel we were surrounded by midnight darkness, only broken occasionally by gleams of light through very small windows in the bridge. We spent two days in Montreal and visited many points of interest. The stone buildings, so dark and gloomy, presented a decided contrast to the ones in our former home.

We traveled up the lakes and spent another day sightseeing in Toronto. Here and at Quebec, and other places my father was appointed judge of the machinery exhibits in the provincial fairs in that country. At Guelph, I was placed in a Young Ladies' finishing school. In this school there were about one hundred girls, all of whom were over twelve years of age. Miss Walker, the senior teacher, was an accomplished lady, capable of instructing in the languages, arts and science. Our outside pleasures were numerous compared with those allowed school girls of the present day, we being permitted to attend festivals, celebrations, picnics, concerts, sleigh-rides, etc. Thus a year of my life went merrily by, when my father, whose health was still declining, determined to exchange our cold northern climate, our snow-clad hills, for the sunny South, and save himself, if possible, from that much dreaded disease, consumption. Previous to this Edgar, my oldest living brother, imbued with a roving disposition, and a desire to see more of the world, forsook home and friends for distant scenes. He was a handsome, impulsive, black-eyed boy, and in my childish sight he seemed a hero. Letters in which he spoke of his love for his little sister were treasured until worn out by repeated readings. One of my chief regrets upon leaving Canada was the thought of being separated from a dearly loved aunt, my father's noble and sainted sister Mary. Her heart was ever open to the wants of the poor and destitute, and so beloved was she, for her charity and goodness, that those who knew her, styled her "the orphan's friend." Every spot and corner of her home possessed a charm for me, her favorite niece, from the room where dwelt the aged grandparents, to the old garret so dear ; but I must leave it all and say good-bye. To the old-fashioned farm-house, groves and meadows, schoolmates, scenes of childhood, and even childhood forever—good-bye, good-bye.

> "Still in my sorrow, my childhood's dear home,
> Oft in deep sadness its memories come,
> There with the beings on earth I loved best,
> I lived, but too happy, too happy to last."

"O beautiful dead past, too fair and bright to stay,
Too much like Heaven to last. gone like the rose-crowned May,
Yet the beauty that it cast still lingers round my way."

CHAPTER II.

MAIDENHOOD.

"My heart is like a lonely bird,
That sadly sings,
Brooding upon its nest unheard,
With folded wings."

"The smiler with the knife under his cloak."

S we left our Canadian home, a new and strange feeling stole over me, "A feeling of sadness and longing," such as I had never before experienced. Instead of the wild romp of twelve I was now a quiet maiden just entering my sixteenth year,

"Standing poised with eager feet,
Where womanhood and childhood meet."

So I stood a slender figure, of medium height, round face, blue eyes, a fair complexion, scarlet lips, pink cheeks, long dark eyelashes, and hair of a peculiar shade, varying in different lights from a bronze brown to a bright golden. My character was composed, as was human, of faults and virtues. I was proud and ambitious; while on the other hand, truthfulness and systematic and industrious habits had been taught me by my noble mother, and I naturally had a deep thirst for knowledge; a mind that loathed the coarse and unrefined, and longed for the artistic and beautiful.

My heart, not yet purified by Christ, was filled with conflicting emotions. My temperament was nervous and excitable, and impatient for improvement and growth. Sensitive and diffident, my manners were not always agreeable to strangers, and I was often called cold and haughty. "Every heart has its secret sorrows, and oft-times we call one cold when he is only sad."

My father having business to attend to in the province of Ontario, carried us by a circuitous route to our new home.

Niagara was the first and principal point of interest. With bated breath we viewed the sublime grandeur here displayed.

New York was the next point of any note, where was found humanity of all classes. We spent two days here, finding new delights each hour. We passed very slowly through Washington, but had only a glimpse of the city. Passing the cultivated lands of wealthy farmers, and the squalid huts of the poor, our impressions varied between the wild and grand, the lowly and lovely. Arriving at Lynchburg, Va., weary and dusty, and learning that we must "change cars," we concluded to rest. Our hearts sank as we noticed the change in the soil and the general aspect of the country, and the car that would carry us to the end of our journey. At that time that portion of the South had no handsome palace coaches, such as we had rested so comfortably in during our trip. It would be difficult to describe my feelings, as, once more on our way, I sat silent and alone (a gentleman having appropriated my usual seat by Brother Bradley), my face pressed against the window pane, watching, with awe and dismay, the changed appearance of the scenery. Instead of green fields, groves and smoothly flowing streams, wild gorges, dark ravines, and rocky cliffs met our gaze. Reaching Wolf Creek, Tenn., after sunset, we were informed that there was no stage leaving for Warm Springs, N. C., our future destination, and not finding any suitable accommodations for remaining over night, we adopted the only course left, that of traveling in wagons, into which our lady companion, my mother and the boys were snugly "tucked." Little Charley was ill, which added greatly to our discomfort. The road looked so dark, rocky and precipitous, I decided to walk with my father and the other gentlemen of our party. The impressions formed during that moonlight journey will never be erased from my memory. The tall trees, rendered gigantic by the moonbeams, reaching their long arms heavenward, cast dense shadows in the distance ; the solemn "hoot-te-hoot" of the owls, together with the distant roar of falling waters, created an effect both weird and ghostly.

Late that night a disconsolate little party drove up to the Warm Springs Hotel. The sleepy porter, being aroused, prepared us refreshments and showed us to our rooms, where all but I sought rest in the land of dreams. Homesick, I could not sleep, and spent the night in tears. Refusing my breakfast next morning, I sat like "Rachel, weeping and refusing to be comforted." At last I ventured from my room when there was no one present. I met a girl about my own age, who informed me that her name was Ada Howell. Her sweet, artless manner, chestnut hair, and dark blue eyes completely charmed me ; while her kind cordiality cheered and lifted the gloom from my heart.

Warm Springs at that time was largely patronized by

the aristocracy of the south. This summer, there were, in addition to our family, a large number of northern visitors, who, like ourselves, were in search of a warm climate in which to locate. I soon became acquainted with a number of ladies and gentlemen, and passed the summer pleasantly playing croquet, dancing and taking long rambles through the romantic forest surrounding the Springs. Everything was strange and new to me; the mountains and people who lived among them; especially the women with their large frames, their tanned, leathery complexion, rendered so by exposure and hard work, and their peculiar habits of speech; the wide yawning fireplaces in the houses; and the southern negro, of whom I had read, I now beheld with wondering eyes. A huge black negro, attempting to shake hands with baby Charley, broke out into an uproarious peal of laughter when Charley drew his hand away and examined it to see if it was smutty.

My father and some other gentlemen purchased some property, known as Old Fort, and prepared to settle. We traveled by private conveyance from Warm Springs, up the French Broad, a wide, rapidly flowing river, with steep, rugged mountains on either side, between which and the river winds a narrow romantic road. Overtaken on the way by a heavy rainstorm, we were completely drenched before we reached Asheville, a highland town, now a wealthy, flourishing summer resort. Entering the public room of a hotel to dry our dripping garments, I noticed a gay party at the further end of the room, one of whom, a pale cripple, immediately aroused my sympathy by his sad appearance: but pity soon turned to anger, as he glanced significantly toward me and drew at-

tention to my now flushed face. Indignation kept me
silent, though I inwardly hoped that at some time they
might feel ashamed of their rude conduct. I presume
their merriment was due to our foreign and draggled appearance. I never forgot the little incident, and years
later under peculiar circumstances, I was gratified by
meeting a lady who had taken a conspicuous part in the
fun-making.

The next morning we left Asheville, and crossing the
silvery Swannanoa, we saw in the distance the huge summit of Black Mountain, which looms up dark and grand,
above all others east of the "Rockies."

We stopped at a house on the way for refreshments but
were told that "Major D——,"who lived a short distance
ahead, would accommodate us. We wondered at a major's selling edibles, and our wonder grew into astonishment when we drove up to the squalid little hut surrounded by tumble-down out-houses, which was very like
most mountaineers' homes in any country, yet not a "Major's" home. After some difficulty, a dirty looking girl supplied my little brothers with bread and milk, and the rest
of us concluded to wait a more suitable opportunity to re-
fresh ourselves. Gaining the top of the Blue Ridge we were
again caught in a violent storm, and afraid to ride I decided to walk down the mountain, a distance of six miles. The
rain fell in blinding torrents, the vivid sheets of lightning,
followed by terrific peals of thunder, reverberated from
hill to hill, and made a picture fearful in its wildness and
sublimity. About half way down the mountain, we saw
the stage which had preceded us, lying, bottom up, at
a distance of sixty feet down a cliff ; torn bushes and
harness told of a terrible accident. We shuddered as we

remembered how near we came taking seats that morning in the fated coach and we hurried on, to find its former occupants in a tumble-down hut close by, moaning with pain and awaiting relief. Entering the dismal hut, we found one lady lying on some planks, her head bound in a handkerchief, fatally injured. Several ladies and gentlemen were standing around, wet, chilled and seriously hurt by the fall. They were without matches and could not light a fire, so begged us to hasten on and send them aid. My father telling me to keep the main road, took a near path through the woods, hoping thereby to find someone to relieve the suffering strangers. As I flew down the mountain road through the falling sheets of water, I met several horsemen ; I forgot everything but the distressing scene in the hut above and hastily exclaimed, "Will you please give me some matches ?" They smiled, and as I remember the picture I made, I do not wonder, though at the time their smiles puzzled me no little. Dressed in the Canadian style of short skirts, high boots and gypsy hat, with my yellow hair hanging in disheveled masses around my face, which glowed with excitement and unusual exertion, standing in the road, ankle-deep in mud and water, I must have presented a ludicrous spectacle.

After telling them of the catastrophe, they said they had matches and would do all they could to assist the distressed party. Joining father again, we found shelter in a tunnel and waited for the wagon. When we arrived at Old Fort, great was our consternation to find the house we had expected to occupy torn from its place and standing about sixteen feet from its chimneys, the kitchen crushed by a large tree, and the ground strewn with fallen trees,

SCENE NEAR ROUND KNOB, N. C.

"What a premonition of the stormy life in store for me!"

loose timber and remnants of a coach that had been caught in the cyclone and shattered by a falling tree. We were informed that two men were carried some distance by the cyclone and injured seriously.

There we were joined by several families, who proceeded to erect dwellings ; my father built a Gothic cottage where I lived until my marriage.

Old Fort was built during the revolutionary war, and has retained its historic name. It is a lovely valley enclosed by heavily timbered hills, and mountains covered with dense growth of laurel, rhododendrons, and many other handsome flowers and shrubs, besides a great variety of medicinal plants. A clear crystal creek runs through the valley shaded by magnificent trees, walnut, poplar, maple, chestnut, etc. There was the terminus of the Western North Carolina Railroad, and travelers were compelled to continue their journey across the Blue Ridge in the old-fashioned stage coach. Many were the adventures, accidents, hair-breadth escapes of those days.

Illness, brought on by exposure while crossing the mountain, confined me to my room for several weeks after arriving at our new home. By the time I had recovered, the news had gone out through the surrounding country of the Northern settlers, and many were the curious spectators who flocked to Old Fort to see "the Yankees," as they termed us. They gazed in amazement, and considered us curiosities in every sense. We, too, gazed at the queer "country folk," who thronged the place. This class lived in small houses daubed with red clay, their food consisted of corn-bread, baked by an open fire, muddy coffee, with an occasional scanty allowance of rusty bacon. They were coarse and ignorant, many of them not being able to read or write, while their children were addicted to the habit of eating clay and chewing tobacco. Of course there is a class of farmers far superior to these, who own large farms, live in comfortable houses, and keep their tables supplied with substantial food. They are hospitable, also shrewd and intelligent. The aristocracy of the south I found composed of cultivated, wealthy people. Some of them were prosperous, and vainly proud of their superior advantages and high social position, but the majority of them were courteous, kind and chivalrous, true ladies and gentlemen. Our earliest southern friends were Dr. McCoy and wife, an intelligent Christian couple, residing at Old Fort. In our darkest days of trouble we received comfort and sympathy from these faithful friends. There existed in many hearts a bitter feeling of animosity towards northern people, and we were exceedingly troubled when we heard of threats against my father who had been appointed mayor, made by a company of roughs who came to town to disturb the peace and convert the new town into a den for gamblers and drunkards. Many acts of violence were being committed throughout the country by a disguised band called the "Ku Klux Klan," and although my father was a Canadian and not a Yankee, as they thought, so anxious was I that often I would follow my father unseen by him, determined, should they attack him, to do all in my power to save his life, even at the risk of my own; but the days passed without a call upon my bravery or muscle, and there was no excitement save the capturing of large bands of "Ku Klux" by the United States officers. They talked very pleasantly with my father, and one of them gave him the disguise, horned

"Great was our consternation to find the house torn from its place and standing about sixteen feet from its chimney."

mask with red eyes, mouth and nose, a frightful looking thing. There were many innocent looking boys among them, and we could not help but feel sorry that they were engaged in this business. In the days following these exciting troubles, I spent many hours rambling through the beautiful woods so dear to me, building air castles and gathering flowers and mosses. Often I joined Bradley's sad, rich voice in song accompanied by the plaintive notes of the guitar. Later becoming acquainted with some young persons of Marion, a neighboring town, I accepted a kind invitation and spent a few happy weeks there.

Like other girls, I had my admirers, perhaps more than my share. Among others, was one in particular, Mr. Ray, handsome, intelligent, gentlemanly. His devotion was marked, and though appreciated as a friend, no tender sentiment was awakened in my heart. I was too young and inexperienced. That devotion was afterwards very kindly remembered, and at one time longed for as a protection from the awful evil about to engulf me. One day, some young ladies of my acquaintance planned a walk, giving me for escort their uncle Charles, and passing conveniently (?) by Mr. Ray's place of business that his jealousy might be aroused. Accidentally I walked by him without speaking, which was instantly noticed, and the heart of love offended, the beginning of many misunderstandings, originated by persons desirous of the estrangement of our friendship. Thus I lost a friend whose kind heart might have saved me and turned the tide of an awful future.

I had fully determined to secure an education, and soon after gained admittance to a good thorough school, flourishing under the fostering care of Mrs. Grovesnor.

On entering her school I was charmed by her kind, motherly manner and striking resemblance to my much loved Aunt Mary. In her were embodied all the Christian virtues; her presence inspired within me a longing for something holier and better than I had ever known. Assisted by her intelligent, interesting daughter, and our kind friend, Mrs. McCoy, a successful system of religious and moral training was established. The long walks to and from school were made pleasant by Ada's company, my friend of Warm Springs, her father having joined our colony. At first we were treated with suspicion by some of the larger pupils, their thoughtless conduct causing me many tears. Arthur Grovesnor, my teacher's youngest son, now proved a kind and helpful friend. So intelligent and studious, his aid in my studies was invaluable to me, and his kindly protecting friendship won my highest esteem. He, too, would have proved a brave defender of his little friend in the severe trial that soon came into her life. But it was not to be.

About this time there entered into our house one whose cruelty and deception cast over my life the darkness of midnight and the gloom of the grave. One evening during my father's absence, he having returned to Canada on business, answering a knock at the door, we were surprised at the entrance of Mr. Roderick, a merchant who had recently located in our little town. Making some trivial excuse for calling, he entered into a spirited conversation with my mother. I continued my studies and was soon lost to his presence, little dreaming that *I* was the object of his visit.

Mr. Roderick was a bachelor of uncertain age, six feet high, large muscular frame, dark piercing eyes, and soft brown hair. His appearance was not attractive or calculated to inspire confidence or love, in a youthful nature like my own. During the frequent calls which followed, in which he professed tender affection for me, I paid him little attention, and was often uncivil, although, to my discomfort, he was quite indifferent to my indifference; and, continuing his calls, succeeded by acts of kindness and interest in their affairs, to win the regard of my family. As time went on, my mother's health failed. She labored under great nervous and mental strain, having never recovered from the sad fate of her eldest son, and owing partly I think, to our feeling of friendlessness and insecurity. Bradley, who was a kind son and brother, having never seemed happy since leaving his boyhood home, now grew pale and sad, spending most of his time in solitary confinement, dwelling on the studies he loved. Enjoying good health myself, I felt a tender sympathy for my delicate brother, and the interest and sympathy shown by Mr. Roderick for him and my mother, finally won my deepest gratitude. My younger brothers, Harry and Charley, taking advantage of my father's absence and my mother's indisposition, exposed themselves to all sorts of danger, causing me great distress, which was alleviated somewhat when I found that Mr. Roderick was keeping a watchful eye on them, even defending them from assaults of rude boys on the streets. He seemed a faithful and staunch friend of the family instead of a suitor for my hand.

My parents had organized a Sabbath-school at our house for the benefit of the neighborhood and upon one occasion, walking home with a friend from the school, Mr. Roderick joined us. After seeing her safely home we returned together. "So you are determined upon going off to school to finish your education?" remarked Mr. Roderick. "Oh, yes," I said, "it will take me just four years more to graduate in all I wish to study. My music just begun too. I shall be happy indeed when I know all I desire. I love study and want a thorough education. Going away to this school I shall obtain all I wish."

"Sorry you insist upon these things. I do not want you to go away, I want you to marry me." Like a frightened fawn, I sprang from his side, startled, surprised. I darted forward, hastening home without another word, Mr. Roderick keeping near me, though I almost ran. Into the house I hastened to my mother's side. The bachelor friend of the family, as my suitor, had never occurred to me. I had never thought of such a thing and then a feeling of distress possessed me. "Oh, mother," I exclaimed, in a frightened undertone, "Mr. Roderick wants me to marry him." To my great astonishment and distress my mother replied, "Well, my child I think it would be well for you to become the wife of so good a Christian man; I would die happy if I left you in his kind care." Surprised, disappointed, I turned away, my heart sinking with many doubts and fears. I see now, but did not then, that the melancholy, overburdened life my mother led, together with a diseased body, had affected her reasoning, for she was not herself to consign her only daughter to such a fate. Often I had heard her say, that a daughter of hers should not marry young. Was I not only sixteen years of age? What could it mean! Mr. Roderick's great pretensions to religion and extreme kindness and devotion to our family,

and my mother's weakened condition had entirely changed
her. True, I respected Mr. Roderick, because I thought
then his pretensions were sincere. I was filled with surprise and wonder when he spoke of his love for *me*, such
a frivolous child! I could not understand how such an
elderly, quiet Christian, one almost sanctified in his saintly
devotion, generally carrying a Bible in his pocket, and
conversing freely on religious subjects, could love me!
He was, apparently, so thoughtful of others, and so unselfish, that he soon won the esteem of the people. I
felt flattered, and quite inferior in virtues. Lacking confidence in myself, I soon began to rely upon his strength,
will and judgment, thereby drifting unconsciously into
the channel his will had determined upon, for I learned in
after years, that on seeing me the first time, he registered
a vow that I should be his wife, saying, that if not his
wife, I should never be the wife of another.

One evening, returning home from an entertainment,
Mr. Roderick accompanied me, having been left to his
care. I stood near the center of the room, waiting for
him to go, but he was not to be gotten rid of so easily.
"You do not love me? Tell me only that you care for
me," he pleaded. "I love you so devotedly I cannot live
without you. You are the only one I have ever loved,
and shall never love another. Will you consign me to
such a lonely, unhappy existence?" My tongue refused
to speak, my heart replied only in silence of vexation and
aversion that he should force his presence upon me.
Go, go, was all I wished, and I said nothing. Finding
his words in vain, he finally left me, remaining away one
week; then he returned more persistent than before, and

laid siege with a determined will to succeed, and I felt myself growing weaker.

Our family, innocent of hypocrisy and unsuspicious, trusted too much to outside appearances, all ideas of deceptive treachery being foreign to their natures; therefore I was an easy prey to Mr. Roderick's artful plans, and almost before I was aware of it, was his promised bride. My father and brother Edgar having returned in the meantime, were also won; at least my brothers were, and congratulated me on the prospect of marriage with one so noble and good. My mother thinking her end near, wished to see her only daughter secure from the possibility of marriage with a dissipated or cruel man, and placing implicit confidence in the honor and apparent tender heart of Mr. Roderick, strongly urged my marriage with him—provided I could love him. Ignorant of the affairs of the heart I mistook—a very common mistake—feelings of friendship, and gratitude for his kindness to my parents and brothers, for love, and thus made the fatal blunder.

My all absorbing devotion to my parents and brothers urged my obedience to their wishes. Any sacrifice I would make for them. Though not accustomed to sacrifice in little things, yet greater ones were readily made for their dear sakes, even to this, the fatal step that crushed all happiness for me and ruined my life. Oh, God that human hearts could be so blind, so easily deceived! Marriage without the guidance of prayer, and that too wanting the judgment of maturer years. What a mistake! O, ye mothers and daughters, let my life-story be a warning to you! Starting to school one morning I stopped in the room where sat my mother and brothers; knowing that Mr. Roderick would be there that day for his answer, I said to them, "What shall I do about it ? Shall I marry this man?" My mother said, "My daughter, if you can love him, I think it would be the best thing you could do, for I do not think I can be with you long." Brothers both advised me to marry him, saying he was a gentleman, and a good man and worthy of any woman. My father was abroad and was not consulted. It was the general opinion of the town and neighborhood that Mr. Roderick was a thorough Christian gentleman, and my mother and brothers only fell in with the estimation of all others regarding him. My heart sank in utter despair—more than ever before. I felt the fatality of my circumstances. Standing upon the railroad crossing on my way to school, my mind ran over it all in feverish despair, as I realized that to remain under my present circumstances was to marry that man. To run away, I would gladly have done it, if I had known how, and where to go. Ignorant of the world and inexperienced, where could I turn ? I thought of Mr. Ray and Mrs. Grovesnor and her son Arthur, and oh, how I longed to tell either of them my troubles and solicit their aid!

I was too timid to tell my own people, in the face of their different opinions, or it might have ended very differently, for they were far too good to have forced me into it, and not aware that my love for them caused me to make such a sacrifice; but they did not know my heart, and I could not tell them. Unaccustomed to seeking help from a Higher Power, I knew not how all could have been righted, and wisdom given to guide me right, but I did not go to God. I had not yet enlisted under his banner, but was a stranger, entering upon one of life's severest, fiery trials to bring me into that fold.

Since my tenth year I had cherished the desire to possess the hope of eternal life; and I now trusted with Mr. Roderick's strong arm to lead and guide me in the right way the hope of this blessing would be sure.

School ended with the usual ceremonies. Becomingly dressed in white with blue ribbons at waist, neck and hair, I went through the last exercises. I read my composition; the subject, "Twilight," suited my mood on that occasion. I spoke of the twilight of the soul when we pass from innocent pleasures into the power of sin and darkness, and from happiness to the depths of despair. A vein of deep sadness was notable throughout, seeming a presentiment, as it were, of the great sorrow in store for me. The ill will entertained by some of the pupils for Ada and myself, had gradually vanished, and we were now treated with consideration and kindness, making our last weeks of school life only too pleasant. Accompanied home that last day of school by my beloved teacher, Mrs. Grovesnor, and sharing her room with her that night, we talked into the "wee sma' hours." I wished in my heart to speak to her of Mr. Roderick, and the promise I had made him, but the words died on my lips. Many times in after years did I regret the want of courage that kept me silent. Two o'clock found us pleasantly chatting, when suddenly our window became brilliantly illuminated. Hastily arising, we found that Mr. Roderick's store was burning to the ground. This incident only bound me more firmly to my promise, as I thought it would be cruel to forsake him in adverse circumstances.

Some time after this in passing him on the street, I experienced a strange sensation, wholly unexplainable. His face wore an expression that I had never noticed before. Sudden fear took possession of my senses. Hastening home, almost bewildered, I stood in the doorway several moments, trying to resist the inclination to fly and thus escape the coming union. Silently the day passed, and the evening brought, as usual, the destroyer of my peace. Watching him closely, I saw nothing in his appearance resembling what had caused my alarm. Attributing my fear to a foolish, overwrought imagination, and believing my plighted word too sacred to be broken, Mr. Roderick having often impressed upon me that it would be a crime to break an engagement, I dismissed the unpleasant thoughts, and for the time they were forgotten. One day while attending a camp-meeting, in company with him and my mother, the same feeling of fear overwhelmed me with an irresistible force that left me weak and trembling. Looking around I saw Hattie Grovesnor and her brother Arthur and Mr. Ray. My impulse was to flee to them and solicit their aid in escaping the impending evil that oppressed my heart. But the thought of exposing my inward feelings shamed me into silence, rather than endure the publicity of my affairs. I succeeded in stifling, what I persuaded myself, was a weak and foolish idea, and afterwards felt ashamed to mention it. For the benefit of my readers who have never visited a camp-ground, I will describe one. They are in the country in a spot of cleared ground, surrounded by wood. In the center there is a large arbor, and near the edge of the woods, is a circle of huts or tents, in which the tent-holders cook, eat, sleep and entertain their friends and strangers, in a truly hospitable way, during the two or three weeks of the meeting. Large crowds gather here from far and near, and everything dates from camp-meeting time. Several ministers preside, and by their eloquence or persuasive powers, many are converted. A great display of dress is generally noticeable; some combine elegance and good taste, but the majority unite the colors of the rainbow, with their dresses cut after the fashion of our grandmothers. The scene, by torch light, is solemn and weird. Many of the ignorant scream, shout and laugh, groan, clap their hands, stamp their feet, embrace each other, jump up and down, and do all manner of absurd looking things. The hymns, ringing out on the night air, echoing through the forests, from hill to hill, sound sweet and mournful; while to me, the effect is sad and depressing.

Yielding to Mr. Roderick's appeals for a speedy marriage, I was soon busily engaged making the necessary preparations which are to most girls so delightful, but which to me now only seemed a sad duty.

The warm sultry days of summer had given place to the gentle breezes of the autumn, laden with the odor of dying flowers which had yielded their last sweet breath to the departing season. The Indian summer had come and gone, carrying with it the hazy veil in whose misty folds all nature had been softly sleeping. The day which was to make me a bride dawned with a dark threatening sky, the rain falling drearily down; the very earth seemed shrouded by a dismal pall as if all nature wept at the approaching sacrifice. Mr. Roderick's brother and sister had arrived the day previous, and when I saw them my childish heart felt a keen disappointment. However, we had been informed that they were worthy people and descendants of the best families of the State, and I did my utmost to make everything agreeable to them. A few intimate friends had been invited and were now assembling, with the venerable clergyman, Rev. Mr. Paxton, of the Presbyterian church, and his amiable wife. The rain ceased falling, and I was bade make ready for the wedding ceremonies, white being chosen for my dress. I was soon enveloped in its soft clinging folds, with rich lace falling over neck and arms. Mr. Roderick looked better than I had ever seen him, his face wore a serenely pleasant expression, and I was led to the altar with a trusting heart, believing that I had won one of earth's noblest and best ; little dreaming that a cloud, fearful in its blackness, would soon overwhelm me. The words were pronounced " man and wife," and at this moment the sun burst forth in radiant splendor, flooding the room with dazzling light, and sending a bright gleam full upon my face. " A good omen, a good omen," sounded amidst the congratulations of our merry friends ; but no thrill of joy pervaded my heart, as I quietly received their good wishes for our future happiness. There were two others present who seemed sad and thoughtful, my little brother Harry who retired to a secluded spot and wept bitterly, and my bridesmaid and faithful friend, Ada. Running to my room about ten o'clock to rearrange my hair, standing meditatively before the glass, I again saw the face of Mr. Roderick wearing a wicked and repulsive expression. I was seized with uncontrollable fear and horror of the man I had married, and obeying a sudden impulse, I hastily turned with the determination to leave the house and seek protection and refuge in the motherly arms of Mrs. Grovesnor, when a voice called pride urged, "You will be laughed at. What will your friends say?" Discretion sighed, "It is not safe to go several miles alone at night," while judgment plainly said, "You are his wife and cannot escape; you must yield to the inevitable." Regaining strength and self-possession, I quietly rejoined the merry circle in the parlor, and spoke not of the fearful foreboding that had troubled me. Thus ended the bright hopes and happy days of my girlhood, when seventeen summers only had passed over my head.

> "A hungering look cast backward,
> Into the days gone by,
> A turning to the future
> With a sad and anxious eye."

MEMORIES OF EDNA.

My thoughts are of Edna, a slender young girl,
With round happy face framed about in curl,
Cheeks rosy and fringed by dark lashes long,
Lips ready to scold, or to ring with song;
With ribbons and frocks, e'er matching eyes blue,
Complexion was fair and teeth pearly hue,
With heart loving truth and honor and friend,
E'er dreaming of joys that heaven might send.

While books were to Edna a source of delight,
"No, no," to her suiters she ever would write,
When they questioned "why" oft merrily she said,
"Long years in the future perhaps I may wed;
For all arts so useful I first must acquire,
To mount wisdom's heights my soul doth aspire;
Your hearts then for me, sirs, pray no more break,
At some fairer shrine your love may awake."

" I was seized with uncontrollable fear and horror of the man I had just married, and hastily turned with the determination to leave the house."

3

But fortune's strange freak with many a wile,
Brought one to Edna with dreary cold smile,
Her age he had doubled, had gray sallow skin,
A gloomy, stern visage, 'twas both gaunt and thin,
Resolving that Edna his bride he would make,
This object to gain, false steps he would take;
Her mother's kind heart he won by shrewd deed
On which her trustful approval did feed.

Her mother was ill, on a couch she reclined,
Delusive sad fancies infusing her mind,
Her fancies were these, that she could not live,
To him it were wise, her Edna to give;
She talks oft of death, of dark troubles drear;
The tall gloomy man poor Edna did fear.
Despondently, Edna doth oft lonely weep;
A sad timid child, with courage asleep.

A young tender heart its first sorrow knew,
A frail slender form—still more slender grew;
The pale silent lips did nothing but sigh,
And sadness shadowed the wistful blue eye;
In white bridal robes at length Edna stands,
Her bright golden curls a white forehead fans,
With frightened wild looks she turns round to flee;
But alas! alas! it is never to be!

Her bonds are now sealed—forevermore sealed;
What else then could this strange marriage yield?
But most bitter woe a future life long,
And sorrow too sacred to mention in song!
That dearest friend, mother, always at hand
Lies sick unto death in' a far distant land;
And the beautiful castles she built in the air,
Had flown like mists, leaving naught but despair.

CHAPTER III.

WIFE AND MOTHER.

"Like Niobe, all tears."

THE first ten months of my married life were spent under my father's roof. During that time I was frequently shocked by the strange fits of rage indulged in by Mr. Roderick, whenever he found me enjoying the innocent pleasures to which I had been accustomed. Greatly distressed I made every effort to please him, seldom leaving his side during his leisure moments, as he seemed unhappy in my absence. My life was robbed of its brightness when he objected severely to my books, music and friends. It was with reluctance that he allowed me to attend Sabbath-school, church, and the benevolent societies to which I belonged. I thought very strange of this, but my faith in his superior judgment, and confidence in his professed piety being yet unshaken, I thought he must be right and I wrong.

We had been married nearly a year when he gave up merchandising and moved to his farm, twenty miles from Old Fort. He had given me glowing descriptions of the comforts and luxuries of farm life, and excited my youthful ambition to secure pleasures not attainable elsewhere. When I began housekeeping in our new home, my zealous energies could not be excelled. "Lonely Retreat," was the name Brother Bradley gave our farm, on account of its loneliness and quiet beauty. Surrounded by trees and hills, it was indeed isolated ; the silence in the evening being broken only by the " Whip-poor-will's " plaintive cry, and the dismal hoot of the owl. Though lonely and isolated, there was a charm in its green fields, clear brooks, and tall trees, in whose lofty branches many joyous birds sang, "from early morn till dewy eve."

A short time after we were established in our country home, a change came over Mr. Roderick's spirits. On returning, after a short absence from home, he announced his presence by slamming gates and doors in a furious manner, often screaming loudly in his anger. At other times he returned moody and silent, especially until his appetite was appeased, when he became talkative and pleasant. His fits of weeping were changed to violent bursts of temper, often using abusive and threatening language to me, and against members of my family, who had never wronged him by thought, word or deed. Upon meeting them, much to my relief, his manner would change and become affable and pleasant. His parents, bachelor brother and sisters, lived within a few miles, and paid us frequent visits. I found them very poor, ignorant and coarse, and without any mental or social training. They were hard working, and I believed, honest people in their way, which called forth my respect and pity for their ignorance and hard lot in life.

Three of his sisters were widows with small children, two spinsters, ages unknown, and one married. They informed me that Mr. Roderick had been afflicted in boyhood, and being the first son after so many daughters, had secured some advantages of education, from which they had been debarred. He had been allowed to domineer over, and control the entire family, his every whim and caprice being gratified. One sister also warned me never to act contrary to his wishes, as he had a strange disposition. I received this intelligence with some surprise, it being given before I had discovered the whole truth. Naturally affectionate, my heart had to lean upon and trust some one, and now I was fond of my husband, eagerly awaiting his homecoming, and hurt and disappointed when I perceived the great change in him. Dropping the gentlemanly guise of speech, manner and dress he had assumed, he soon fell into the old rough habits of former days. Having no regard whatever for personal appearance, he allowed his hair and beard to grow to an unusual length, and wore garments that a beggar would blush to look upon. All this was very humiliating and distasteful to me, especially when he objected to any system or order in our house. On becoming acquainted with the inhabitants of our settlement, I found them, with few exceptions, poor and uncultivated; many of the women being compelled to perform rough labor, such as ploughing, hoeing, chopping wood, etc., while their husbands and masters spent the greater portion of their time hunting, or loafing in the nearest town. As I did not and could not work in this way, many of my neighbors united with Mr. Roderick's sisters in calling me "lazy and stuck-up." They considered Mr. Roderick a remarkably kind and indulgent husband because he had not as yet required it of me, though I did all of my household work without the help of a servant.

It was a common sight to see a thinly clad, worn-looking mother following her husband to the field, one infan

in her arms and two or three clinging to her skirts.
Leaving them under some tree, or in a fence corner, she
would plough, or follow the plough, planting or hoeing
until noon. Then while her husband is resting on the
bed, or under some shade tree, she carries bark and
water and prepares their frugal meal. After dinner,
before she has had time to rest, they trudge to the field
again, and work until dark. Then with the baby in one
arm, and a load of bark in the other, she goes home—
prepares supper, makes up the beds, puts the little ones
to sleep; and when she ought to be at rest, finds a day's
work before her. She sits up far into the night spinning
and weaving, and piecing quilts. These poor women
look old and faded long before their prime. They are
deprived of every comfort and pleasure that is calculated
to keep "roses on the cheek, and brightness in the eye."

"Work, work, while the cock is crowing aloof,
And work, work, work, 'till the stars shine through the roof;
It's oh to be a slave along with the barbarous Turk,
Where woman has never a soul to save, if this is Christian work:
Oh men with sisters dear, Oh men with mothers and wives,
It is not the linen you are wearing out, but human creatures lives:
Stitch, stitch, stitch, in poverty, hunger and dirt,
Sewing at once with a double thread, a shroud as well as a shirt."

Under the influence of a mild southern climate, my
father's health rapidly improved, enabling him to engage
in active business again. Not wishing to return North,
he joined a company formed at Shelby, N. C., an
attractive town situated south of us, level and beautifully located, and with the assistance of my two oldest
brothers, built the " Carolina Sewing Machine," the first
sewing machine ever manufactured in the South. Think-

ing it best not to move my mother and little brothers until the venture was tested, he concluded to leave them with Mr. Roderick and myself. Mr. Roderick seemed very desirous for such an arrangement. I knew that my mother was not aware of his changed condition, and felt greatly troubled over the possible discovery and the manner in which she would receive it. Already the seeds of disappointment and wounded pride rankled deep in my heart. But my mistake was irrevocable; he was my husband, therefore I jealously guarded his imperfections from my friends. My mother had been with us about three months before he gave vent to his latent passion. Many violent scenes followed the first outbreak; yet no comments passed between mother and child. My secret was revealed, and I waited in fearful suspense my mother's opinion; yet dreading and avoiding a conversation on the subject, I determined not to speak first. My father was paying the expenses of his family, but suggested that Charley and Harry assist Mr. Roderick on the farm. He believed it would foster habits of industry, strengthen the muscles, keep them from mischief, and at the same time aid and please Mr. Roderick. Harry, who was twelve years old, was kind, obedient and willing to do his full duty. Charley was nine years old, fond of books, but less willing to work. His studious habits and enthusiastic zeal often caused remark. Finally Mr. Roderick's anger turned upon innocent Harry, when my mother could no longer hold her peace. She spoke freely of his cruelty and strange conduct. I could not deny what was so evident ; and when Mr. Roderick became harsh and unkind to Harry during an attack of whooping-cough, imposing heavy tasks upon him, doubting his illness, our hearts filled to overflowing and we mingled our tears while we consulted what was best to be done. Soon after a violent outburst of temper, with terrible threats against myself, a pretty blue-eyed daughter was given me. When the dear little form, with dimpled cheeks, was placed in my arms, the long yearning for a sister was gratified.

> One of my childhood's fondest dreams,
>   Was for a sister kind and true.
> None was given me; yet it seems,
>   God answered in the gift of you.
>
> Now mayest thou prove a precious gem,
>   And may no sorrow thy life mar,
> A gift from God, my prayer is then,
>   Bright may thy life be, Stella, Star.

Though happy in the possession of such a treasure, in my weakness I could not repress the bitter tears of anguish over the unkindness of its father, and my hopeless mistake.

Stella, the name given baby by my mother, was but one month old when my father came for his family. Mother's health had been restored, and her mind was in its normal state again. Her distress at leaving me was great, for her perceptive mind saw further than mine, and understood the danger I was in of being violently stricken down by Mr. Roderick. On her departure she begged me not to do or say anything contrary to his opinion, and repeatedly warned me of every danger. I could not believe that he would strike me, so I made no promises. Sorrow had crushed the feeling of anger and resentment I might have cherished under different circumstances; but my pride and self-respect cried out, " Am I to suffer a life of martyrdom ? No, a thousand times no! I will defend myself." So my mother left me with a troubled heart. Standing in the door, I could see her anxious face looking back until a bend in the road hid her from my view. I was left lonely and friendless in a strange country. In justice to my father and older brothers I would say that they were yet in ignorance of what had happened, and were very angry when they learned the truth.

My servant remained one week, when she left without a word of warning. Sunday morning found me trying to perform my household duties, and care for my infant. My morning work finished, and baby laid in her crib, I sat by a window to rest, feeling lonely and desolate for pleasant, congenial society, from which I had been deprived for so many dreary months. Though not a professed follower of Christ, I had always received comfort and consolation from the clergyman's holy teachings, and enjoyed the sacred hymns of praise. Memories that had lightly slumbered were disturbed, and glowing pictures of former days, contrasting strangely with the bitter yearnings of the present, arose before me. While thus occupied, a scene transpired so fearful that even now I cannot recall it without shudderings of horror. Mr. Roderick having returned from a walk over the plantation, sat down on the steps and dilated upon the advantages of farming. My attention was attracted, and I could but notice his slovenly appearance. Coatless, long, straggling hair, rough beard, torn hat and shoes, he presented a picture not calculated to inspire one with pleasant thoughts. I could not repress a sigh and a feeling of aversion which forced its way into my heart. Noticing my silence, he asked, "What ails you?" "Nothing," I replied, "only that I am lonesome." "Lonesome," he said, while his face turned white with rage. "You ought to have some of your charming people here, then you wouldn't be lonely." The sneer implied in his words stung me, and I hastily retorted, "I only wish they were here." "For me to wait on?" he said. I replied, "Why, Mr. Roderick, how can you say such a thing when my mother and brothers helped you so much?" "It's a lie," he thundered. Then followed a volley of imprecations filled with threats against them and myself, and finishing his accusations by charging me with pride, deceit and every form of hypocrisy, he said, sneeringly, "Haven't I got a a pretty wife?" His brutal language roused the anger that had lain dormant under its covering of sorrow; mimicking his words and tones, I replied, "Yes, and haven't I got a pretty husband?" The words had scarcely left my lips when a horrible apparition arose before me. Stricken speechless, I could only watch in terror the approaching form, which seemed inhuman in its fearful loathsomeness. A figure, drawn double with rage, livid face, eyes blazing with a fearful demoniac glare, white lips, drawn back, leaving the large, glassy teeth and gums exposed, with a peculiar jumping or jerking step, he approached. Clutching my arm, he raised his hand to strike me. Instinctively I felt that calmness was my only hope of escape. I looked firmly into the murderous eyes, now leering close above mine, and bade him leave me alone.

My composure kept the cruel blows from falling. In a few seconds, which seemed ages to my excited fancy, he obeyed my command. Though still bent and moaning with rage, he crept to the bed, threw himself, face downward, while he screamed, groaned and ordered me to leave the house. Fear more horrible than I had yet experienced thrilled through every nerve as I realized that I was alone and in the power of a cruel madman. Conscious that my life was at stake, that self-possession was my only hope, though nearly paralyzed with fear, I quietly and steadily passed the bed where he lay writhing and groaning in a way sufficient to strike terror in a much stouter heart than mine. Clasping my infant close in my arms, I paused at the door, not knowing where to go or what to do. My first impulse was to flee to my nearest neighbor, Mr. Holland, who lived a half mile distant. But I argued, " Perhaps they will not believe this wild story; I am a stranger, he their countryman, and always kind and courteous to them and to me in their presence." These thoughts flashed rapidly through my mind, and taking the only course left, I ran rapidly down the hill, over the creek and meadow, until I reached the dark woods. They presented a new terror, and, seating myself on a fallen tree, I wept bitter, scalding tears of fear, sorrow and disappointment over the helpless little creature nestling so close in my arms, and gazing at me, as it were, in silent wonder.

" What will become of you, my poor little girl ?" were the thoughts and words flitting through my tortured brain. I had been sitting some time absorbed in my grief when I noticed Mr. Roderick coming toward me. I could not escape him, and as he approached, I saw with joy that he was walking erect and quietly. Every trace of anger had left his face. He drew near and mildly bade me give him the child and go with him to the house. Trembling, I hesitatingly placed Stella in his arms and returned with him, neither of us speaking on the way. During the succeeding weeks a deep gloom settled over my mind. The fear, anguish and despair I suffered submerged my whole being in blinding tears which fell on the work and books in which I fruitlessly tried to forget my great sorrow. My dear little babe looked in vain for smiles while her eyes followed me pathetically, I imagined sadly, as I carried my uncontrollable grief. My nervous system had received a shock from which it never recovered, and as the days wore wearily away, my sorrow became more overpowering; but I stifled every appearance of distress when in the presence of Mr. Roderick, and lived in mortal dread of his displeasure. I had no way of communicating with my parents, as he carried all letters to and from the country post-office. I also labored under the impression that I had not a friend in whom I could confide, as Mr. Roderick had repeatedly told me that I was disliked by every one in the neighborhood, and I was also mortified by the unwomanly words I had given utterance to causing his fit of passion, and had always entertained feelings of disgust and shame for husbands and wives who could not agree, and had promised myself never to be guilty again of conduct so disgraceful. The above reasons combined, sealed my lips, while a strong desire filled my heart for the old home life. Could I ever again join in the pleasures of the home circle it seemed that my joy would be equal to the bliss of entering Paradise. The deep solitude around filled my soul with dread, while the mountains looked bleak, dismal and gloomy. Twice in my rambles I encountered a huge poisonous snake lying coiled with head raised, mouth widely spread, from which protruded the forked tongue. This only added to my alarm and utter helplessness and hopelessness. I also suffered from the want of suitable food. That which was provided was so coarse and unlike any I had seen that my appetite refused it; consequently I frequently felt the pangs of hunger.

One day, late in the autumn, while sitting alone with bedewed eyes, my ears caught the sound of carriage wheels. Drying my tears hurriedly I hastened to the door, where I recognized the kind benevolent face of my father. Never was a sight more welcome. And when he told me that he had come to take me home, and I felt that the prison bars were broken, I could scarcely realize my happiness. I waited with fainting heart and abated breath the answer Mr. Roderick would give to my father's request. Finally a reluctant consent was granted, and I was seated in the carriage homeward bound; but I was afraid to look back and nervous when the horses slackened their speed, for fear that Mr. Roderick would change his mind and call me back. Every hill we crossed and every mile we gained enabled me to breathe more freely, as it placed a barrier between me and his dreaded face. I could not tell my father what had happened for want of courage. But I remarked many times that I could never again cross those lonely, dreary hills. "Why do you dislike them so much?" he asked. I could only answer that I had been so lonely among them. Then he tried to cheer me by giving a description of his boyhood's home, his courtship and marriage with my mother, a pleasant account of their new home in Shelby, their bright business prospects and the kindness of the Shelby people.

Home at last! Oh, that sweet word—Home!

> "Home is not merely four square walls,
>   Though with pictures hung and gilded;
> Home is where affection calls—
>   Filled with shrines the heart hath builded;
> Home, go watch the faithful dove,
>   Sailing 'neath the heaven above us,
> Home is where there are those to love,
>   Home is where there are those to love us."

Home at last and safe within those sheltering walls surrounded by kind sympathizing faces and pleasant associations, one would think that my happy youth would be renewed. But not so; I could not smile and often crept away to some lonely corner to hide my tears. One day while trying to conceal my emotion from my mother she suddenly said, "Edna, what ails you? Why do you weep so much?" These questions forced the truth from me. Trembling and in broken accents I tried to tell her of the terrible scene I had passed through. She expressed little surprise as she had a foretaste of it during her stay with me previous to that time. She said I must not return to him. But I replied, he would kill me or some of my people if I dared to leave him and would probably steal my little girl. She argued that I should be sent to my aunt in Canada where he could never find me. But in my blindness, weakness and despair, I said, "I cannot go and leave you and father to bear his fury. Everyone will believe and help him. What can you do against so many?" My mother made my unhappy condition known to the rest of my family, and all united in saying I should not return. My parents had advised me to marry Mr. Roderick. I was afraid to trust to their judgment again, fearing they might be mistaken and I had not as yet gained the wisdom from my heavenly Parent to guide me "through all trials." Blind child that I was, all these years of misery might have been spared me. My mind seemed to me under a pall so dark and dense that I could not throw off its enshrouding folds and be my natural self. I could not endure the thoughts of Stella being torn from my arms, and carried to a fate pictured so fearful by my imagination. My father was delicate and weak. I could not go away and leave him to be murdered, as I anticipated he would be. No, I would not sacrifice him, my kind, dear father to save myself. They failed to discover the true state of affairs—for I could not paint it as black as it was, and—after much pleading on my part, allowed me to have my own way and go with him again to the gates of misery and woe.

LONELY RETREAT.

In a lovely green vale, called "Lonely Retreat,"
With bright blossoms filled both fragrant and sweet,
The mocking birds' song rings out o'er the hills,
Tall trees, shading brooks, green meadows and rills.
There stood a dwelling, so gloomy and drear,
Ungainly it stood, in appearance no cheer.
My story will tell of a bright Sabbath morn,
A young wife who sat so sad and forlorn.

With small girlish figure robed daintily neat,
The sun kissed the bronze head and played at her feet.
A far distant look in the dreamy blue eyes;
And misty her future—for curtained it lies—
A footstep she hears, from reveries she's drawn,
The form of a man appears on the lawn,
Whose strange hidden ways bring sighs for her wrong,
Her face betrays naught, though weak, she is strong.

Betrays not the pang from sorrow's fierce dart,
At sight of his face, that entered her heart,

She watched him in sorrow, this husband, her fate,
As he sat on the step, talking o'er his estate;
Her silence was noticed. "What is it?" he cried.
"Not anything much, but lonely," she sighed.
Then quickly she starts, her cheeks and lips pale,
A sight met her gaze, that made her strength fail.

Cold, speechless she sat, all fainting with fear,
The frightful object toward her drew near;
Figure drawn double with short jerking step
His head thrown backward, he moaned as he crept;
Lips drawn from the teeth, left gums red and bare;
A face livid with rage, then o'er her did glare,
In wild lurid eyes shone a dangerous light,
One hand caught her arm, one lifted to strike.

Grasped by a wild man, far from a friend!
God saw her danger while strength he did send,
And no outward sign of fear did she show,
Quiet, possessed, bade him from her to go;
Then turning he crept, still moaning with rage
To a bed standing near, like a wild beast in a cage,
Gave vent to loud moans, to strange and harsh cries,
To reach her dear babe she must pass where he lies.

Her safety she knew, in instant flight·lay,
Her life was in peril, she must haste away;
Quickly she passed, where he lay screaming wild,
And clasped in her arms her one little child.
She paused at the door one instant to see
What course to pursue, oh! where could she flee?
Down hills and o'er streams the frightened girl flew
With heart throbbing wild, with steps fleet and true.

Approaching the wood, her strength failing fast,
She peered through the gloom the foliage cast.
To enter their depths, her infant would die
With hunger and cold, oh! where could she fly?
Then fainting she sank, while sobs her heart rent,
Homesick and weary to grief she gave vent,
When coming she saw so dimly through tears
Him she had fled from, which strengthened her fears.

4

Too exhausted to rise; for her he would seek,
'Twas useless to fly, he was strong and she weak;
Nearer, still nearer, her heart turned to lead,
In amazement she saw what lessened her dread.
He walked quite erect, was quiet and mild,
Spoke kindly and said, "Come, give me the child."
Then anxious she glanced straight into his face,
Saw nothing to fear, of anger no trace.

Weeks and months followed, the lonely wife wept,
Shades of a drear future around her heart crept;
With needles and books she'd drive away fears,
Yet vainly she tried so blinded by tears.
Her babe's small face now oft to her turns
For mother's fond words, for mother's smile yearns;
No fond word is spoken, not a smile nor a song,
For the frail sweet babe for them waiting long.

Leaves of autumn now fall, twilight shadows cast,
The sound of a carriage sets her heart beating fast.
Her father was coming, she brushed back a tear
His face seemed never to her half so dear.
In the carriage seat now, so close by his side
To mother and home, o'er the mountains they ride.
"My father," she said, "I can never here stay,
These cold, dismal hills fill my soul with dismay."

Horror came o'er her, she spoke not again,
Her lips pressed firmly revealed not her pain.
Voices of loved ones now fall on her ear,
Familiar home faces sought her to cheer,
Promised protection, home, comfort and love;
In every direction one face glared above,
His cruel threats sounded and lurid eyes gleam
The extent of her grief her friends never dream.

Her dear father's life he had threatened to take
Her father was aged, in strength could not mate,
He'd follow and steal her one little girl.
Oppressed by the darkness, her brain seemed to whirl.

She'd sacrifice, never those friends she loved well
Preferring to suffer whatever befell,
"We're strangers," she said, "and no friend is near,"
Then to their entreaties she turned a deaf ear.

A wistful sad look shone from the blue eyes,
Her smiles and her songs were replaced by sighs,
While deep in her soul and over her face
Dark sorrow had laid its withering trace;
Her hopes were blighted forever more still,
In silence and pain she returned o'er the hill.
So cold neighbors said, "pride ruined her life."
They knew not the grief of the unhappy wife.

Mr. Roderick seemed to understand that he had gone too far, and was now more kind and pleasant, and promised me in a year's time to move back to Shelby, the home of my parents. The year passed without serious disturbance. The presence of his cousin Henry, who joined in farming, afforded a shield against violent acts, and I was visited frequently by members of my family, who always brought nice presents, consisting generally of wearing apparel, Mr. Roderick having failed to supply me with suitable clothing. About this time brother Edgar brought me a present which I had so craved—a dear sister. Having fallen in love with a gentle orphan girl in the city of Charlotte, he married and brought her to see me. Never will I forget the sweet picture she presented when I eagerly hastened to meet them. A small slight figure, graceful in every outline, with a pure delicate face framed in masses of dark waving brown hair, while her expression was peculiarly sad, sweet and spiritual. Again Edgar urged the necessity of my leaving Mr. Roderick, saying that he was a lunatic, and that sometime I would have to leave him to save my life.

My reason was ruled by the demon fear for my child
and my people, which took my strength, and shook my
frame like a reed. I had not as yet asked God to help
and direct me, but was depending on my own judgment,
and I replied that it was impossible. In his fearless
strength he could not understand my weakness, and believing that affection for Mr. Roderick caused my non-
compliance with his wish he allowed the subject to drop.
Shortly after they left, my mother paid me a visit, accompanied by Mr. Wills, an intelligent pleasant northern
gentleman, who was traveling in the South for his health
and pleasure. He seemed delighted with everything, especially with Stella, and gave us brilliant descriptions of
his Philadelphia home.

On one occasion about this time I met my former
teacher, Mrs. Grovesnor, and all of my Old Fort friends;
but no word passed my lips of my unhappy life. Doubting the friendship of everyone (for Mr. Roderick had
made me believe that no one liked me), surprised when
spoken kindly to, I usually appeared cold and silent,
keeping at a distance those who might have been my
friends. This was caused by the poison Mr. Roderick was
constantly dropping into my ear.

Our first year in Shelby was spent with my parents.
Mr. Roderick's moods during this time were as "variable
as the shade by the light quivering aspen made." Part
of this time he was pleasant, courteous and kind, and then
again quarrelsome, gloomy and morose, destroying the
hopes which sprang in my heart during his peaceful
hours. His gloomy face, and his watchful jealous eyes
followed me every moment, preventing me from enjoy-

ing the music, cheerful society, and comforts by which I was surrounded, and kept me sad and silent.

Soon after the birth of Earnest, my second child, my eyes became seriously affected, confining me to a lonely darkened room for months, and I was finally thrown into typhoid fever, which came near ending my life. Baby Earnest and brother Harry were also dangerously ill at this time, with fever, which caused great distress in our family. Mr. Roderick was very attentive during this illness, but distressed me much by his harsh language and threats to whip little Earnest, whose wailing cries annoyed him. When I recovered sufficiently to notice the wasted little form, with pale, sunken cheeks, I thought my heart would break.

The second year of our stay in Shelby we kept house in a new home purchased by Mr. Roderick, and for several months I lived alone with him and the children. During this time I was frequently terrified by the prolonged and unreasonable manner in which he chastised our little girl, Stella; although for some reason, he was really kind to me. During my illness I had been alarmed by my near approach to death with my sins unforgiven, and had resolved to join Christ's church and try to live nearer to God. The way seemed dark and I blindly groped for light that did not come, though I united with the church and tried to learn my duty. My parents had been members of the same church for years, but had grown cold and worldly indeed, neglecting their Christian duties, and Mr. Roderick had long since dropped even the semblance of Christianity and was melancholy, jealous and quarrelsome. My health was failing visibly under the frequent and violent shocks to my nervous system and with the hard work, keeping boarders, taking in sewing, and doing all of my household work that I might help provide for my children. The bright spot in the cloud of sorrow which had driven all smiles from my face was the solicitude, the tender sympathy and constant help of my father's family. Even affectionate brother Harry seemed almost intuitively to understand my unhappiness, and his tender thoughtfulness seemed unusual in a boy so young and was never forgotten. One night after my father and mother had spent the evening with us quietly and pleasantly, and had departed home, I was utterly stunned by Mr. Roderick's change of manner and the wild language he used. He raved about them in a fearful malicious and vindictive way, using terms and threats that I cannot repeat. My mind filled with dread for their safety. I exclaimed, "Is it possible that you have joined against them?" "Yes," he hissed between his clenched teeth, "and against you too, for you are all nothing but a set of black-hearted Canadians." Unable to longer bear the mental strain, I entered my own room and throwing myself on the bed wept aloud convulsively. His rage only increased, and coming towards me after shutting the door, he bade me in a loud, threatening voice to "shut up." His fierce screams of madness aroused Stella, who began to cry. Fearing his rage would fall on her, I crushed my grief and was on the very eve of calling for help when he became more quiet. Another evening accompanied by a sister of my brother's wife and her brother we attended church near by, Mr. Roderick permitting me to go, as I had gone to church so little during our stay in Shelby. Returning, we said "Good-bye" at the gate, and I entered the house and found Mr. Roderick so

sullen and jealous he would not speak to me. I endeavored
to amuse him by pleasant conversation, but he only raved,
saying all the hard things he could. Oh! how I longed
to show him the true state of my heart, that I would be
so happy, indeed, to love him if he would only be what I
had thought him, and let me, by acting so I could. But he
was so jealous and cruel, even of my brother's attentions to
me. What could it all mean? I had a high ideal of a wife's
and mother's responsibilities, and longed, oh, so greatly, to
fully perform mine. A dark foreboding of some new
trouble weighed heavily upon me which I fruitlessly tried
to shake off. I often wondered how the people, who passed
our doors, could be so happy and gay when I was so
miserable, and oh, how I wished for Mr. Roderick to be
what I had thought him, that I might respect and love
him, and be as happy as I dreamed and hoped to be in
youthful days.

> "They came and went like shadows,
> The blessed dreams of youth,
> They left behind no impress,
> Nor record of their truth.
> Then the future was all sunshine
> In gorgeous robes arrayed
> But ever as I've reached it
> 'Tis sunshine turned to shade."

CHAPTER IV.

BLIND AND HELPLESS.

"Father before thy footstool kneeling,
Once more my heart goes up to thee ;
For aid, for strength, to thee appealing,
Thou who alone canst succor me.

"Hear me ! for heart and flesh are failing,
My spirit yielding in the strife ;
And anguish wild and unavailing
Sweeps in a flood across my life.

"Help me to stem the tide of sorrow ;
Help me to bear thy chastening rod ;
Give me endurance ; let me borrow
Strength from thy promise oh, my God.

"Not mine the grief which words may lighten,
Not mine the tears of common woe.
The pangs with which my heart strings tighten,
Only the All-seeing One may know."

THREE weeks after Mr. Roderick's last burst of passion, described in the last chapter, Marie, a second daughter, was added to our family. She was but five weeks old when the chastening rod of sorrow was laid more heavily on my shrinking form, and I was robbed of earth's greatest blessing, my sight. Crushed in the spring of my life, cut down by the sword of affliction, helpless, powerless to escape, I could only sit tearless and almost dumb in my new sorrow.

One day while sitting alone with my litt'e ones, Stella

and Earnest playing near and Marie sweetly sleeping in
a cradle close beside me, I must have received a premonition of coming blindness, though unconscious of it at
the time. Glancing at the mirror hanging on the wall at
my side, I surveyed my face and figure with unusual interest, even noting every article of dress I wore, yet not
aware at the time that I was taking my last and farewell
look for years. The face I saw reflected there was thinner and paler than the one that had looked at me years
before ; the mouth being slightly drawn with lines of sorrow on either side, while the eyes looked hopelessly sad.
Short clinging curls replaced the long ones lost during the
illness of the past year. Sighing at the change, I turned
away. My gaze resting upon Stella observed her with
the same marked interest, noting the round fair face, the
flaxen hair, clear bright eyes, and sweet expression; three
years old, innocent and happy. What would happen before I would gaze upon her dear face again God alone
knew. With a deep sigh, I turned my eyes from her to
Earnest—wistful, earnest face with its large laughing
eyes of deep blue—an affectionate baby of eighteen
months, ever clinging to his mother for love and sympathy, but destined to be cruelly torn from her arms. My
darling boy, what thy fate was to be, thy heavenly Father only knew. Lifting the cover from Marie's face, I
watched her lying in beautiful sleep, the dimpled, waxen
hands folded as if in prayer, the round little head covered
with soft dark rings of hair, while the long dark lashes
drooped upon the tender cheeks waiting to be kissed.
Sleep on, sweet little one, in peaceful unconsciousness of
the heart which bled for you and of the eyes above your
face that would be shut for years—long, dreary years..

Sadly I replaced the cover while my eyes wandered to
the window where I saw my mother coming down the
lane. Watching her closely, as I had myself and children, I
noticed she was looking unusually well, the dress and walking hat being tastefully and becomingly worn; while I admiringly thought, that she was, as many said, very attractive and fine looking; with her soft dark eyes, dark brows,
heavy coils of black hair slightly silvered by time. She
entered my room and occupyied the chair I had vacated
for the sofa, and was soon joined by my brother Bradley,
who entered into conversation with her, while I lay silently and sadly listening, my eyes seldom leaving their
faces. Bradley was now a young man of twenty-five
years, with a slight delicate figure, pale face, large, deep
blue eyes, black hair and mustache. Many times in
after years did I recall the picture they made that memorable evening. After their departure Mr. Roderick
came in and asked me if I would like to take a drive.
Declining on account of my eyes paining me, I stood in the
door-way watching him employed in the yard, vainly wishing he would always be kind and cheerful as he was at present. I looked up the lane and saw father approaching and
observed that his hair and beard were turning gray, his
form thin and slightly stooped, while the truth forced its
way impressively through my mind that he was rapidly
growing old, and ere many years I might be left without
his tender care; and the feelings of sorrow and pity I felt
for him were strong.

Walking down the yard I gazed thoughtfully upon
the portion of the town within the range of my vision;
taking a lingering look at the blue sky and mountains in
the distance, and of the trees, flowers and birds around

...ne, even hesitating and looking back several times before entering the house. The last thing I saw was my father's face, on which my eyes rested for an instant as I passed into my room. Twilight with a gentle hand was now softly drawing a dark mantle over the face of tired nature.

Early next morning on waking and attempting to rise, I found that my eyes were unable to bear the light without severe pain. Binding a handkerchief over them I groped my way to a chair, and, calling the children to me, I dressed them without seeing. Believing like the person who wrote, "Happy is the child who has its own mother for a nurse," I had never trusted my children to the care of thoughtless servants, except when compelled by illness; knowing the evil influence of ignorant nurses upon the pliant young natures of children, impressions are often implanted that are lasting and hurtful—often faults of speech that can never be erased, as well as those of manner, besides the neglect of health through carelessness. Not realizing my sad condition, I went to the breakfast table and moved the handkerchief from my eyes, not thinking but that I could see, what was my horror and dismay to find I could not. I rose hastily without speaking, and returned to my room in no enviable frame of mind, as the fearful truth flashed upon me with overpowering force. I was followed by Mr. Roderick, who urged me to return and eat my breakfast. "No," I replied, "I do not want to eat when I cannot see." He remained with me several moments and attempted to persuade me not to be discouraged, while I sat mute and tearless, trying to resist the hopeless tide of sorrow which was fast taking my strength. The light shining through the bandage over my eyes now became intensely vivid and painful, forcing upon me the necessity of having the doors and windows darkened. Two weeks of suspense and anguish followed, when one night, attempting to open my eyes, I found they were tightly closed, and I was powerless to raise the lids. Alarmed at this discovery I awoke Mr. Roderick, who soon dropped to sleep again, leaving me to bear my new sorrow alone. For a few moments I was nearly frantic with grief, wringing my hands and even tearing my hair, as I was compelled to realize the sad truth. I was blind. Blind and only twenty-two years old. Blind and the mother of three little children. Blind and in the power of one who seemed a maniac in his fits of rage ; blind! blind! oh, what would become of me and my helpless little ones? I could not even conjecture. These thoughts were maddening, while the intense, lancinating pains through my eyes were intolerable. My physician had given me some hope, but I was rapidly growing worse under his treatment, he having added greatly to my suffering by drawing a large cord through one of the leaders in my neck and poisoning it.

Previous to this, serious trouble had arisen between Mr. Roderick and my father and brothers. They had been transacting business together, and on coming to a settlement, difficulties had sprung up, which could not be agreeably settled, as Mr. Roderick had been acting dishonorably with their money. Some weeks previous to this, I had accidentally discovered the fraud he was guilty of towards them, and had suffered severely, thinking myself and children disgraced by a dishonorable husband and father. Father and brothers were very angry, but on my account let the matter rest, while Mr. Roderick constantly abused them to me in their absence, distressing me with malicious and vindictive threats, regardless of my unhappy state. About this time Mr. Roderick carried Stella to his own people. Little Earnest missing her and my care seemed unhappy and dissatisfied, refusing to play, and cryed piteously. My mother, who visited us three or four times a day, carried him home with her, where he was very happy and contented.

It was my first separation from my children and I sorely missed them, but was compelled to submit, for I was now scarcely able to sit up.

When Mr. Roderick returned he brought with him his eldest sister Rachel, who was a widow. Her small, treacherous black eyes, sharp nose and chin were true indications to her character, although her long, flattering tongue had deceived me. She added greatly to my sorrow by joining with Mr. Roderick against my people, neither of them showing any sympathy for my physical sufferings, and even seemed to doubt that they were as great as I declared them to be. They seemed so cold and heartless that I entirely suppressed all mention of the mental and physical anguish I was laboring under. Deep convictions of sin, my neglect of God, and every thoughtless word and act of my life now arose before my excited mind, so largely magnified that I felt my hope of heaven was entirely lost, while my prayers for mercy seemed useless and unavailing.

I had about lost all hope of recovering my sight, when my parents received a letter from Mr. Wills, urging them and Mr. Roderick to send me to Philadelphia for treatment, promising them all the assistance in his power.

My parents and brothers were very anxious to accept his kindness, proposing to assist in any way that would be acceptable to Mr. Roderick, also offered to help bear my expenses and take care of the children in my absence. A hope of regaining my sight was kindled in my heart that was soon cruelly destroyed. I was fearful of a refusal, but showed the contents of Mr. Wills' letter to Mr. Roderick. He angrily refused the assistance offered, calling my friends meddlesome villains. In vain I tried to show him the benefit I might derive under the treatment of skilled physicians. He would not wait to hear, and madly raved about my extravagant ideas, and my friends' interference in his affairs. His sister Rachel joined him in opposing my request. My friends, unwilling to give up all hope, urged upon him the importance of proper treatment before it was too late, but finding all their efforts at persuasion fruitless, they begged me to come home, saying they would go to Canada and take me with them.

Although I lived in constant fear of my life and was nearly wild with longing to go home, yet I could not find courage to take the first step, and I felt unable to bear the scene I knew would follow. I felt, too, that the lives of some of my friends might be sacrificed. From remarks I had heard Mr. Roderick make in past years, I knew if I left I must give up my children, and my imagination, vivid as it ever is in the blind, pictured them being torn from my arms by a frantic madman, and I could hear their pitiful cries of distress. The picture was too terrible, I could not bear it, and I spent hours in laying plans to escape him and avoid these heartrending results.

Outside of my immediate family, I was without one friend in the town of Shelby, at least Mr. Roderick had lead me to believe so ; my sad and unsocial ways having driven away all acquaintances.

Although their friends paid them frequent visits Mr. Roderick led me to believe my people were very unpopular in Shelby and had many enemies. This helped to prevent me from making my trouble known. In later years I learned that the opposite was the true state, and instead they possessed many true and loyal friends and were held in high esteem. I spent many weary and painful hours, and the desire in my heart to see my children, especially the youngest, little Marie, was almost overpowering. All my visitors were given a wrong impression by Rachel's sly and artful tongue, while Mr. Roderick's extreme kindness to me in their presence, and plausible manners, led them to think I was receiving every attention. So, believing it useless, I made no complaints. Once I ventured to ask Mr. Roderick to let me go home and stay only a little while, but he refused in no gentle manner.

My disease had now taken an alarming turn, light having become magnified to such an extent that the faintest ray looked like the burning sun. Although my room was so dark that others could not see their hands before them I had to wear heavy leather bandages, as my room seemed to be flooded with blazing light. Noises were continually sounding in my head like loud claps of thunder, roaring of cannon and pistol shots, varied by ringing of bells, singing, hissing and buzzing sounds. Brilliant lights of all colors were constantly flashing before my vision, beautiful vivid pictures of every description, some of them being of ancient castles and landscapes, such as I had read of but never seen ; also open books, printed bills

and newspapers flitted before me rapidly, while I constantly tried to read them. The sentence, " God is good,"
was all I could ever decipher.   These words often passed
before me in large letters, as if sent to keep alive a little
spark of hope and save me from despair.   Balls of fire,
snakes, pitchforks and sharp sticks seemed to rise before
me, enter my eyes and pass through my head, followed
by terrible crashing noises and excruciating pains.   A
crawling, twitching and tingling sensation was felt through
my whole body, caused by the highly excited state of my
nervous system.   I had violent jerkings of my limbs,
heart, head, eyes and eyeballs.   My eyeballs seemed to
be violently drawn backwards, and I suffered with a
sinking sensation, as if riding or sailing through space.
I had been in this wretched condition about two months,
when on New Year's eve Mr. Roderick, acting on the
suggestion of some acquaintance, proposed that I should
have my spinal column briskly rubbed to relieve the pain
in my eyes.   I found he would be angry if I resisted and
reluctantly consented, my despair being so great I could
not resist.   He and his sister, taking turns, began the
vigorous and painful process of rubbing my spine with
coarse towels and the palms of their hands.   This lasted
about one hour, when both of them, complaining of their
arms aching, and being very tired, ceased.   The skin was
now rubbed from the joints, and they followed this rubbing by a cold bath, while my spine seemed on fire.   One
hour later I was seized with severe pains and a peculiar
light sensation in my head, which sprang about on the
pillow as if on wire.   This was accompanied with extreme heat in my spinal column, and nausea.   On attempting to move my infant I found myself powerless to lift

her. Mr. Roderick and his sister went to sleep and left me to suffer alone. After a night of anguish I discovered that I had partly lost the use of my limbs and body. This was a terrible discovery, added to my blindness and other troubles. Previous to the rubbing I had never felt the slightest symptom of spinal trouble, and now I knew that I was ruined by ignorant treatment.

The next morning I told Mr. Roderick and his sister of the pain I was suffering, and they accused me of hypocrisy and deceit, saying I was putting on, and denied that anything ailed my spine.

Two weeks of great suffering followed, aggravated by these constant assertions. At this time the business of my father and brothers failed. Discouraged and disappointed they would have returned to Canada but disliked to leave me. Brother Edgar, who had taken a deep interest in all of my troubles, and would have beaten Mr. Roderick but for my entreaties, moved to Charlotte, a city near. Hours passed which seemed lengthened into days by suffering, in my lonely, darkened room. The plaintive cries of my infant, in the adjoining room, pierced my heart, and fresh wounds were inflicted while listening to the low tones of Mr. Roderick and his sister, who I felt were planning some new scheme to add to my troubles, and I soon found that I was not wrong.

One day Mr. Roderick told me they were going to take me to his people. Shrinking at the thought of the long, rough journey in my weak condition, I begged them not to do so, telling them I was unable to bear the wrenching and fatigue of traveling over the rocky mountain road. My appeal was in vain, as they only sneered at what they called imagination. The physician, who

5

was entirely influenced by them, and wishing to please and promote his own interests, argued that it would do no harm. Mother called several times hoping to persuade Mr. Roderick to alter his decision, but without avail. I found it useless to contend longer and concluded to make an effort to go, thinking they would return if they found I was unable to travel. My anxiety to see little Stella gave me faint courage, and a hope was awakened that a change in my condition would be effected by the breaking up of our home.

The morning of our departure was very bleak and cold, the ground was frozen hard. I was unable to walk but could sit up a few moments. A bed was prepared in a covered wagon, and Mr. Roderick carried and placed me in it, my mother standing by too much distressed to speak. As we started off she hurried home and informed my father that I was gone; he immediately took a horse and buggy, and came after and soon overtook us. A few days previous to this my family and physician stood by my bedside expecting to see me die, and now I was only slightly better, and was forced to leave my friends and take a wearisome, painful journey. My eyes were still heavily bandaged and very painful, and the seton in the back of my neck was badly swollen and purple from inflammation. Father, finding Mr. Roderick determined to go on, took Rachel and my babe into the buggy with him. Mother had kept little Earnest. I now begged Mr. Roderick to return but he said there was no one to take care of me. I told him mother wanted me to stay with her until I was better. He thought that out of the question and drove rapidly on. Fear of my inability to bear this trip was speedily realized, as a deathly, sickening

SCENE ON SOUTH MOUNTAIN, N. C.

"Oh, no," said Mr. Roderick and Rachel in cold, heartless tones. "You are all right."

sensation crept over me caused from the jarring and wrenching of my spine. I entreated him several times to stop, and begged for water to cool my parched and feverish lips, but kept silent when father was near, fearing he would interfere in my behalf and they would come to blows, when I knew my father would be the sufferer, and I could not sacrifice this beloved parent to save myself. I felt there was no earthly aid for me, and constantly cried to my Father in heaven to have mercy. As the hours passed the intense pain gradually wore away and a feeling of numbness and ease stole over me, although my head rolled uncomfortably from side to side, my neck having become so weak that I could not hold it steady. Paralysis had already set in.

After traveling all day we stopped at Mrs. Bender's, who lived on the road. Attempting to rise I found to my horror that I could not move. I sank back and exclaimed, "My back is broken." "Oh, no," said Mr. Roderick and Rachel in cold, heartless tones. "You are all right." "Yes, it is broken," I replied, "for I cannot move." Then Mr. Roderick lifted my paralyzed form in his strong arms, carried me into the house and laid me on a bed where I lay motionless. Rachel immediately proceeded to Mrs. Bender and told her not to listen to my story, that I was "hypord" as she termed it, and imagined that I had spinal disease and that nothing "ailed me." So the family all avoided me, showing very little sympathy. My father improved every opportunity to urge upon me the necessity of allowing him to interfere in my behalf and stop these terrible proceedings, as, without my consent, he could not lawfully, but would willingly risk his life to save mine if I would grant him the privilege.   But my love for him was too great to admit such a sacrifice and I refused his offer and would not complain or allow him to think that my sufferings were as great as he feared, and passed a long, sleepless night, the silence being broken only by Mr. Roderick's heavy breathing.   The long hours wore slowly on, my body racked with pain.   The unpleasant sensation caused by knowing that a man had been murdered in the room I occupied and that his blood still stained the floor before my bed increased my fear for father's safety should he interfere.   I listened anxiously for his voice and footsteps, fearing for his life.

All my prayers as yet seemed fruitless, and I still struggled hopelessly, finding no rest for my burdened soul. For the sake of my children though I must not yield to despair.   I kept thinking of my friends and my cruel treatment, and how different my fate would be were I among them.   How I longed for the presence of some of them to help my father in preventing the abuse I was being subjected to.   By the next morning I had determined not to be moved any farther and felt relieved on hearing the sound of falling rain, which I knew would prevent our traveling and delay a scene consequent upon my refusing to be moved.   The next night was spent in silence and pain, though my heart ever breathed a prayer. I had not had an opportunity of speaking with my father in private, as Mr. Roderick was constantly in the room. The following morning Mr. Roderick informed me that we must continue our journey.   I told him it was impossible as it would endanger my life or make me a hopeless cripple.   I knew that life was indeed at stake, and I must for my children's sake make an effort to save myself.

Rachel was very angry, and coming to the bed made an effort to dress me, but I refused to let her, telling her that if they persisted in their purposes I would die and they would be my murderers. She immediately went to Mrs. Bender's room and on her return said we must go, that Mrs. Bender would not keep us any longer. Father entered at that moment and I asked him to see Mrs. Bender himself, and ask her to let me stay until I was able to be moved. All hope was destroyed when he returned and said she had refused us shelter. I well understood that Rachel was at the bottom of all this. "Cruel, cruel Rachel!" I thought, "would you have acted thus if your own daughter had been in my helpless condition?" No sound as yet had escaped my lips, showing the inward torture I was enduring; but when again on our way, and I felt the terrible wrenching of the injured portion of my spine I could not suppress moans of pain from the intense suffering except in father's presence. After traveling six miles father persuaded Mr. Roderick to stop at a Mr. Anderson's. Rachel attempted to influence Mrs. Anderson as she had Mrs. Bender but failed, Mrs. Anderson being an educated, Christian lady. I was treated with much kindness at this place by every member of the family, but Mrs. Anderson was in very delicate health, and realizing that our presence would be an intrusion, and being too weak to resist longer I was again placed in the jersey after having rested two nights. Father still accompanied us, sorrowful and depressed, but his presence was my only comfort.

Miles as yet separated us from Stella and I longed to meet her. On we went over rocks and mountains, and vivid pictures of my surroundings passed before my blinded eyes and I could see the high snowclad mountains, the long, winding, rocky road, the covered vehicle in which I was lying, the tired, jaded horse urged forward by Mr. Roderick, who sat with grim determination written in every line of his face, his lips tightly drawn over his teeth as I had seen him in the days gone by. In the distance a picture of little flaxen haired Stella, surrounded by the tall, gaunt people, who had her in charge. Little Earnest left with my weeping mother, my father's sorrowful face, sitting beside Rachel, who with cold, cruel eyes watched the little babe, whose piercing wails rent the air and my heart as we traveled. My mental and physical agony was too great and I moaned inwardly in anguish of spirit. The question, shall I sacrifice my father to save myself ? kept rising in my mind. No, no, this must never be, and I cast away this one earthly hope. A despairing cry to God to have mercy upon me continually arose to my lips, as the agony of death came upon me. The moans that had escaped my lips hushed, the cry of my infant sounded faintly in the distance. My sins magnified the terror of death. In this unforgiven state death became appalling. All earthly hopes destroyed. Oh, my God! Pity me. My father seeing that my suffering was greater than I could bear plead with Mr. Roderick to leave me, even by the road side, but I, fearing for his life, entreated him not to interfere. Mr. Roderick whipped the tired beast and drove rapidly on. On, on, we went, and I lay paralyzed and passive through the long hours that followed, my suffering increasing until it seemed impossible that I could live to reach the end of my journey; while the distressing cry of my poor babe agonized me beyond endurance. Nearing the house of Mr. Roderick's father I heard Stella's voice, which aroused me from the death-like stupor into which I had fallen. Now, at last, they would let me rest I thought, as Mr. Roderick carried me to a bed.

Soon another thing happened to give pain. Stella who was chatting near by uttered such coarse, rough words as had never fallen from her lips while with me. No, I must not die and leave her to grow up thus. Father in heaven, spare me for my children. Two weeks later found me in a worse condition than I had been before, for I had fallen into the hands of people who showed neither mercy, kindness nor sympathy. The inflammation in my eyes and spine had been aggravated by the journey, and all the muscles in my body seemed weakened. I was now as helpless as an infant, being unable to even chew and swallow my food without great difficulty, and still suffering intense pain, and was unable to turn my head or move my body. Some members of Mr. Roderick's family sneered at my suffering, my helplessness and the bandage over my eyes, calling me "a fool, hypocrite," etc., and insisted that Mr. Roderick should beat me and make me get up and go to work, and said that I was trying to play the lady, and that I was as well and able to work as they were. Mr. Roderick was providing them with money and provisions, yet they were unwilling to wait upon his wife, and left me alone with their aged mother, who was an invalid herself, and reminded one always of the witches I had read of, with her small eyes and strange ways; and as she now seemed one of my bitterest enemies, her presence filled me with dread.

Mr. Roderick's family had given false impressions to the neighborhood of my sickness, and the few who dropped in eyed me with suspicion and curiosity. Two of Mr. Roderick's sisters were constantly begging food in my name, telling the people that "Edney ate like a hog." They had made my father think that they were going to treat me well, and he had returned home promising to send mother. So I was looking forward to her coming with an anxious heart. That somewhat lightened my burden. I knew that she would have a physician called in when she came. But I was now having faint, sinking spells, and was fearful that my life would not be spared until she came. One day one of the family came in saying she was coming, but I must not complain to her, as she was in great trouble. They knew that would silence any word of complaint of them. Fearful apprehensions seized me as I exclaimed, "What has happened? Tell me quickly." They replied, "Your brother Harry has accidentally shot himself on the way here and your mother is bringing him in the buggy with her." Then I heard their voices at the door. What new and awful trouble was this added to my others? Harry, my kind young brother, perhaps a mangled corpse. Oh how terrible! But my mind was soon relieved by learning that he was not fatally injured, the ball having entered the fleshy part of his thigh and lodged near the main artery. There was no surgeon near to extract the ball, and after two weeks he was carried home.

Mother, on learning that I was without a physician, insisted upon having one called in. After much violent opposition on the part of my persecutors one was summoned. Before he entered my room Rachel had a long consultation with him, which, however, did not seem to have much weight, for after a careful examination he pronounced my case a serious and critical one, and was doubtful of my recovery. He said it was a great pity I could not have gone North for treatment, but promised he would do the best he could. His opinion brought forth many sneers and unkind remarks after his departure. A few weeks later my life seemed hanging by a thread. I lay so cold and motionless that my unhappy mother often feared I was dead. She seldom left my room, though we were never left alone, as Mr. Roderick's mother was always present and kept a close watch on every movement and word. Often at the keyhole and crevices in the wall they would listen to us—eavesdropping—and we would hear their stealthy footsteps slipping away. This knowledge of being watched was very annoying, as I wanted to talk to my mother and lay some plans for escape for myself and children. I could not go without them, and it was doing them no good to stay there. They took a very great dislike to little Earnest, whom mother had brought with her, and he was very unhappy unless in her arms, or lying by my side. His pleading voice seemed ever calling me back from the dark river, whose moaning waters were waiting for their prey. How could I die and leave my boy ! I was blind and helpless though ! O God, pity me in my despair ! Blind and helpless ! The words rang in my ears like the knell of doom. At last a new light broke over my soul. The burden of sin that had lain so heavily upon me rolled away, leaving in its stead peace, love and heavenly hope. Death lost its terrors, and long hours when I lay cold and still I seemed to be looking into heaven, beholding its wonders, and listening to the songs of angels. I saw my brother who had gone before and he seemed hovering near me amid angelic hosts. Blind to all around me, yet happy in my new hope, during the days that followed I lay so quiet that mother wondered what kept me so silent, patient and even cheerful.

> "O, Edenland, thou land of bloom,
> Beyond the shadows of the tomb,
> Beyond the pain of grief and strife
> That dim and mar our mortal life.
> O, Edenland, thou land of the blest
> Where we alone find peace and rest."

were the lines that continually floated through my mind, like a sweet strain from a far-off shore. One night mother, who had fallen asleep beside me, suddenly awoke and exclaimed she had just dreamed a very singular dream. I remarked, " So have I," having just awakened myself. We were both very much surprised to find that the two were the same. The visions appearing to both were as follows: We thought that after many years of sickness I had returned to my father's home. The house seemed new and strange, but the furniture was the same. My mother sitting in an easy chair in an old accustomed way, the windows, pictures and all had a sweet old familiarity about them. I stood before the mirror arranging my hair, mother saying, " Your hair looks natural, daughter, though not the same as long ago; but the new suit grown out since your long illness is soft and sheeny as of old——." We were not believers in dreams, but the singularity of our dreaming exactly the same thing, at the same time, and both awaking together, impressed us as a strange and perhaps a good omen. A few weeks after mother came a slight change for the better was perceptible in my sickness, which partially relieved mother's anxiety, although the unfeeling remarks, and strange behavior of the family caused her such deep sorrow that she was nearly ill. She had been with me five weeks when she received a letter from her home requesting her to come immediately, as Brother Bradley, always delicate, had lost the use of his eyes, and was quite sick. He had been closely employed keeping books, studying music, etc., and had even been careless of physical strength. The letter informed her that he was going North for treatment. I readily consented for her to leave me, to prepare him for the journey. But my heart was torn with the thought of this loved brother's blighted hopes, and the anguish of mind he would have to endure under the terrible affliction —blindness. O God, could the sight of but one be restored, were it not for my children, I would ask thee to let it be him whom thou wouldst bless! When mother bade me good-bye she promised that my father should come, and bring Tonie, a young sister of Brother Edgar's wife, who would stay until she returned. Some days after, their arrival was welcomed by me, and I felt relieved when they told me that Bradley had gone to Philadelphia and would be kindly cared for by Mr. Wills and family. They said that mother would soon return. Tonie was a bright and interesting girl of fifteen, and proved a great comfort. Through her I learned that some of Mr. Roderick's family were ransacking my trunks and wearing some of my choice clothes, and were also greedily eating the food my parents had brought hoping to tempt my appetite, which was very delicate—as

I often did not eat a spoonful of food. I now understood that Rachel's reason for wanting me removed from Shelby to their care was to get money and provision from Mr. Roderick and my father for taking care of myself and children, as they were in destitute circumstances. I will relate one little incident to show how these people were practicing deception to make the neighbors believe that I was not ill, but feigning sickness. One day in the presence of a visitor, Harriet, who was a tall, angular spinster of forty years, with sly, inquisitive black eyes, and a mischievous, garrulous tongue, brought my dinner upon two large plates. Passing my hand over them I found they were loaded with food. "Harriet," I said pleasantly, "I cannot eat all of this." She replied in a soft voice. "It will do you good." At the same time she left the room calling out the visitor. In about a half hour she returned and taking the plates emptied the contents, of which I had only tasted, into the cupboard. I afterwards learned that the visitor, having a curiosity to know if I really did eat as much as they reported, seeing Harriet return with the empty plates, asked her if I had eaten all of the food in them. "Why, yes," she cried, "every bite of it. She eats like a hog."

Father's business at Shelby had failed, through the dishonesty of one of the members of the firm, and becoming alarmed at the failing health of his family and almost in despair exchanged his property there for some in the mountains across the Blue Ridge in Mitchell county. During the business transaction he passed several times and always called. I had decided to have him take me away, but could never find an opportunity of speaking to him alone, some member of the family always being present listening to every word; but my health was improving under the treatment of Dr. Nichols ; so, fearful of the results, should I again be moved over the rough roads, I concluded to wait as patiently as possible until able to travel without injury. Mr. Roderick's people had not yet been able to persuade him to force me to get up, take the bandages from my eyes and go to work. They repeatedly said that they had to work when they were sick and that I was no better than they. Mr. Roderick had accomplished his object and gotten me away from my people and all prospects of friends, so was now serenely kind and gracious, seeming calm and interested over our ruined prospects. When he was kind I could not help clinging to him in my weakness hoping against hope, though all affection for him had been crushed out of my heart during that fearful journey. My friends at this time were forbidden to remain longer. Tonie was compelled to go home, and I was left alone. Harriet wrote my parents a letter as follows :

" *Mr. and Mrs. Gray:*

" it panes me to write you our condition, as for uther pearson or feamley cummin in here to wait on Edny we will object. This is my residence and I cant take in borders and wold not umer Edny in enything that did not do her eny good. I have always been good to sick folks and allways knew when a pearson done a faver, but thinks it a honar for me to wat on her, but I will show her if she cuts up there is more rulers than Edny and I think my brother is smart anuf to manage his own family. When a man takes a wife, if she is a sensible woman she will go and stay with her husban. she acts like a fool, and all of my nabors ses that tha don't know how he puts up with the way you all don and I will not put up with it. What the D—— is all of your secrets ?

I want them reviled and think I will find out. Mrs. Gray, it seems to me than when you, mr. or mrs. Gray comes up here that there is too much secrets agoin on like you think that Edny is too good to live with her husbans folks. I will not make myself a slave for any sich woman that I believe could help herself, if she would. She can't make a fool of me, if she does the rest. this is written by Harriet Roderick by the consent of my mother."

The above is an exact copy as it was written. This letter was uncalled for, as father amply provided for the members of his family who stayed with me. When father called again he told me he would bring mother and get her boarded near until I was able to be moved. Left alone with my enemies, I was greatly annoyed by the loud, fierce quarrels in which the family frequently indulged and by their rude, coarse jests—stories of husbands whipping their wives to make them behave—were repeated for my special benefit. Often hours were passed alone with Mr. Roderick's mother. The death-like stillness and the thought that she might be standing by my bed looking at me with those strange eyes, sent chills of terror from my lips. The knowledge that Earnest was being neglected and harshly treated brought the first tears that I had been able to shed since my blindness. Many times I was the object of their wrath and vituperation, yet I never returned words or made complaints, feeling utterly crushed by the accumulation of great sorrows I was called upon to endure, and, as I had never engaged in low quarreling, I could not begin now. I had been with them five months when Mr. Roderick heard Harriet whipping Earnest. This resulted in a loud and fierce quarrel, and ended in his coming in and saying he would not stay with such people longer. Other members of the family joined in the controversy and a perfect babel of voices ensued. I lay in my darkened corner trembling and silent, listening to their screams of rage, well knowing that I was the object of their hatred and malice. When Harriet and Rachel entered my room, they came to my bed and poured forth a torrent of vile, abusive language. I was unable to speak and still remained silent. I never heard such language before fall from a woman's lips. Mr. Roderick now said he would take his family immediately away to his farm and began making preparations. I remonstrated against being moved again but it was useless. In spite of all my efforts to get well, I must be dragged forth and the work of months undone. My courage again failed and I gave up the struggle in despair, wondering if God had forsaken me, not a friend near. Must I die? I was no longer afraid to die, but was striving to live for the sake of my children. Stella was the only child Mr. Roderick would take with us, as he said he would not take care of Earnest and the babe. His next oldest sister, Caroline, who unlike the rest was gentle and kind and had ever been pleasant, was left in charge of babe Marie, and while I felt that she would be kindly cared for, my heart ached for poor little Earnest left in Harriet's and Rachel's cruel hands, although Mr. Roderick assured me that he would return for him very soon. Of all my great burdens this was the heaviest and hardest to bear. The dear little boy who ever clung to me and was never happy from my side was to be left alone with these people who hated him. Should I die on the way what would become of him? Father in heaven, spare me! Spare me!! My

6

darlings were brought to my bed and I kissed them
sadly. Hot tears fell from my closed, painful eyes
as I felt my wasted form being lifted in Mr. Roderick's
strong arms, who again placed me in the jersey. We
left Ernest crying mournfully. The horses sprang forward, and a deathly, sickening sensation passed over me
as I heard the lonely, piteous cries of dear little Ernest
sounding in the distance; while I felt that "the burdens laid upon me were greater than I could bear."

"I've seen the colors fading from all that I could prize,
Like day's departing glories from out the sunset skies;
And full roughly I have ridden the stormy tide of life,
Long years I've spent in struggling. in bitterness and strife."

CHAPTER V.

UNDER THE ROD.

Blind and helpless alone I wait,
The way seems dark and prayers too late.
My anguished soul sends forth the cry,
Father, save me ere I die;
Save me for my children small,
Leave them not to sin and fall,
Sending forth the saddened call,
Mother, come back, mother."

Blind and helpless, days wear by,
Sick and friendless, left to die;
The darkness deepens as I grope,
Afraid to live, afraid to hope;
They tell me of a better land;
Lord, I cannot see Thy hand,
Around me steals an icy band,
Save me, or I perish.

IT would be difficult indeed to describe my emotion, when, after a toilsome, painful ride, we drove to our old home. I had wished upon leaving it that I might never see the place again, little thinking in what sense my wish would be fulfilled. That I would be brought back blind and helpless, to the house that had once filled my soul with dread! Oh, why should an all-merciful Providence appoint this to my lot? It seemed singular that my desire should be carried out in so strange and terrible a manner.

The tenants who occupied the house and some of the neighbors stood at the gate watching Mr. Roderick curiously, I felt, as he carried me to the house.

Being informed by Mrs. Burney (the tenant's wife) where a servant could be found, Mr. Roderick immediately sent for her. The news had traveled before us that I imagined my illness, and I felt that those around were not in sympathy with my sufferings. The pain in my spine and eyes had increased to an alarming degree, due to the tiresome trip. In a few days I was lying at the gates of death, and mother had not yet arrived, she being engaged in making preparations for their removal from Shelby, and not aware of what had taken place. Mr. Roderick was furiously angry when he found that the journey had aggravated my disease and loudly upbraided me for not getting well, called me harsh names, and again accused me of hypocrisy and deceit. Two weeks later I was a hopeless wreck, with bloated, livid face, protruding eyes and shrunken limbs. My sufferings mentally and physically were beyond description, my neck was so weak that I could not move my head, and my shoulders fell forward unless held up. It seemed, indeed, that a cruel power was laid heavily upon me. Though it was summer my feet were icy cold, and my eyes at times pained me so that I longed to feel the oculist's knife, and even tried to tear them from the sockets, not quite having lost the use of my hands, and yet I was too weak to raise a cup of water to my parched lips. Medicines and liquids now had to be taken through a tube, I grew steadily worse, and the pain had grown so terrible that it seemed beyond endurance.

The servant neglected her duties, spending most of

her time laughing and chatting gaily with Mrs. Burney, my bandaged eyes being one of the subjects of their mirth.

The physician called once, then refused to call again, saying, "It will be useless; she is going to die."

I felt that Mr. Roderick's relatives had influenced him to abandon the case on account of the expense entailed on their brother.

Stella, was now a mischievous child of four years, and having no one to look after her except Mr. Roderick, ran into all kinds of danger, while Earnest's pale face and plaintive cry were ever haunting me. Would mother never come? Already my breath came in quick, short gasps. Would she come in time to receive my dying charges? Still the hours dragged on.

At last she came, and found that the servant had been discharged while Mr. Roderick acted as nurse. Glancing at my wasted form and face, she left the room and went where I could not hear her violent weeping. My father and brothers came with mother, all of them leaving in a few days for their mountain home, but mother remained some weeks. Revelling in the bright sunshine of hope for an instant, as it were, the horizon had again become darkened with clouds of despair, for I tortured myself with the thought that I had committed an unpardonable sin in allowing myself to be moved when I knew what the result would be. Mother reproved me for this by saying, "How could a poor helpless creature like you resist the wills of brutal people?" Her words failed to comfort me. A dark shadow rested upon my soul as I thought of my Heavenly Father's displeasure.

Lying at the door of death, I seemed to be looking

into eternity, beholding the horror of millions of lost and ruined souls mourning in endless woe, while fiendish forms danced in triumph over their helpless victims. I groaned inwardly at the thought of many gay and reckless beings sinking at last into the bottomless pit, and was unable to understand the Savior's great love and mercy; so I felt afraid to die. Could all realize as I did the horrors of an unprepared deathbed, what cries for forgiveness would hourly ascend to the throne of grace; what piety and devotion would exist; what zeal and labor; what patience, love and charity would inspire hearts. The unconverted state of my relatives weighed heavily upon me, and I shuddered at their frightful fate, should they die unforgiven. The only comfort my burdened soul found was the sweet passages from the Bible read by Mr. Roderick and mother, and the soft, beautiful hymns sung occasionally by Mr. and Mrs. Burney in the adjoining room, whose hearts were slightly touched by my silent suffering, for tears had not come to my relief. Often I was coaxed to sleep under these soothing influences, for the nights were spent in great pain and prayer.

Letters were received from Mr. Wills stating that my brother's case was considered a serious and perhaps hopeless one. Poor brother. What a sad life his would be should he never regain his sight. How earnestly I prayed that God would not condemn him to such a fate, and I am glad to say my prayers were answered, for early in September he returned and came to see me on his way home, giving me a joyful surprise by his restored sight. Mother remained with me five weeks, when she was compelled to return home. She left in great sorrow, feeling that she might never see my face again, but she said she would pray for me daily, and believed that our united prayers would be answered. Words fail when I attempt to write of the painful summer that followed. Left after my mother's departure, entirely at the mercy of Mr. Roderick, without a friend to speak a consoling word, my heart nearly broke over the multiplied afflictions. He was unkind and even brutal at times; often quarrelling and upbraiding me until midnight. I endured the tortures of thirst in silence during the long night; I could not bear to ask him for water, though burning with fever, or to raise my head that I might breathe more easily. The threats he would make against the lives of my family, added to the horrors of the situation, whilst his constant assertion that the people in his part of the country hated them, made me anxious for their safety. My slumbers were disturbed by terrible visions. I would picture them surrounded by dangers of the most frightful nature and see their murdered forms and hear their dying groans until cries of terror rang from my lips, destroying the visions and recalling me to a sense of my helplessness.

Blind and sick, friendless and in despair! Oh, my God, why hast thou forsaken me?

Spiders that had gathered in the curtains around my bed crawled over my face, and my life was tortured. Many times I heard of Earnest getting lost in the woods; as I thought of this little one trying to find his way through the woods which held no terror for his brave little heart, trying to reach the safety and love of the mother's sheltering arms, my soul was wrung with anguish.

Mr. Roderick had refused to allow my parents to take any of the children home with them, making me drink from the cup of sorrow so full and bitter even to its dregs.

Mr. Burney having an altercation with Mr. Roderick, they confined themselves exclusively to their rooms and early in the autumn moved away. It was in September that my sufferings abated slightly, though I still lay motionless and exhausted. About this time father brought Tonie to stay awhile (she had been left in my mother's care by her brother).

Mr. Roderick now became pleasant for a while, making life a little happier. An inward struggle had been going on in my heart, since that fearful journey, as to whether I could forgive Rachel, who was the chief cause of my trouble. At last through the grace of God I succeeded in overcoming all bitterness I had cherished toward her. realizing that I was unfitted for heaven with an unforgiving spirit. The cloud which had rested over me like a pall was now removed, my Savior seemed so near that I felt that I could speak to him forgetful of all around. Lifted above earth, absorbed in the wondrous visions that enraptured my soul with supreme joy and delight, I seemed surrounded with angelic throngs whose faces shone with love and holiness. Could I have died then my face would have been wreathed in smiles, and shouts of triumph would have been on my lips, but it was not to be. The voices of my children called me back from these beautiful reveries to a knowledge of their desolation, bidding me struggle for their sakes to live, though life looked dark and despairing.

> Help me, Lord, to bear with patience,
>   Give me strength, until the end;
> Save me, Father, for my children;
>   Freely of thy spirit lend.

When mother returned she found that Mr. Roderick had ceased to make any effort for my recovery, and had even inquired where I wished to be buried. She tremblingly followed him from the room to ask if he thought my case was hopeless. "Yes," he replied, "she is too 'hypoed' to get well, but she could if she would."

Through mother's efforts a physician was procured, and in a few weeks my condition was somewhat improved.

Mr. Roderick's niece persuaded an orphan girl, who was cruelly treated by the people she lived with, to run away and come to us. Though a poor, ignorant creature, she proved a faithful servant, her kind and tender care giving me a little courage. About this time I was deeply impressed by the cure of Miss Carrie Judd. Her case was similar to mine; she had been confined to her bed for two years, and had been suddenly restored through prayers offered in faith. I almost doubted this wonderful cure, as I could not understand the faith that can heal physical infirmities. Five months later, in June, the month of roses, another little girl came to add to my care and sorrow. Mother offered to take the babe home with her. Mr. Roderick did not object, so when it was a month old she left with it going about thirty-six miles across the Blue Ridge.

Mr. Roderick became very kind now. He let Earnest come home, and when the dear little head was pillowed

upon my breast, we were both made supremely happy
by Mr. Roderick granting my prayer, that he should not
be taken from me again.   I was comforted by the fact
that Marie was kindly treated by the very people who
had used Earnest and myself cruelly, and Stella was
placed under the care of a young Christian lady, who
had recently opened a school in our district.   I found
Miss Holmes, her teacher, a pleasant and sympathizing
friend, ever ready to comfort and cheer me, spending a
portion of her time at my bedside, reading to me Tal-
madge's and Spurgeon's eloquent sermons.

The pain I had suffered had been partly alleviated by
the careful attention of Dr. Green, and I hoped sometime to be able to walk and see.   One of my greatest
desires had been to look upon the face of little Marie,
and one sunny day in September Caroline brought her to
see me, and while she sat at my side a great cry arose
in my heart to God, that he would permit me to look once
more upon her face.   Immediately I raised the bandage
from my eyes.   What did I look upon?   Was the fair
etherial face before me one of the beautiful illusions I
was accustomed to see?   This sweet face lifted to my
gaze with wistful eyes looking earnestly into mine—could
it be a picture created by a diseased eye? Replacing the
bandage the face was hid from my excited vision.
Oh, the rapture that was mine at this moment!   I knew
that I had looked upon the countenance of my own darling.   Again I looked long and eagerly at the face before me.   My delighted cry, "I can see Marie," brought
Stella to the bed, when my eyes closed, leaving only a
faint picture of her eager face.   Days of great anxiety
and suspense followed, in which I tried in vain to open

my eyes. Once only I saw the faces of Stella and Earnest, then followed days of darkness and despair; my hopes fading like some lovely dream. Late in the autumn Mr. Roderick began to treat Maggie (the orphan girl) in a cruel and brutal manner, and one dark night he drove her from the house, throwing a large stick at her retreating form; at the same time he gave vent to horrible threats and screams of rage. Violent tremors shook my feeble frame, as I lay behind the curtains around the bed, listening to the wild din, and sadly thinking of the unfortunate, desolate orphan driven into the lonely night, who I knew would shrink from making any complaint, feeling, as I did, that her story would not be credited. She was not intelligent but had a kind and faithful heart and was willing to obey. Should she never return, I would be again left alone and friendless. Earnest would be sent back to the people he feared so much. As I was thinking this I heard sobs from the next room. Maggie not knowing where to go, and not wishing to leave me, had crept back and, unable to control her grief, had burst into tears. Mr. Roderick discovering her had ordered her harshly to perform her nightly duties. She obeyed and sat down and wept as if her heart would break, for she knew that she would eventually have to leave. I could now find relief in the cries of sorrow rising from an overcharged heart, and I began to weep violently. Mr. Roderick had become quiet, but was again aroused by this outbreak. He loudly censured me, and fiercely upbraided Maggie for being the cause of my distress, his threats becoming so abusive that we were both silenced. In the long cold winter following I suffered much from exciting events, and also from the cold which was intense. Mr. Roderick continually cross, sulky and quarrelsome ; Maggie though faithful, was a poor cook and house-keeper, and my food was coarse, unclean and poorly prepared. The newly acquired strength failed me, and my heart grew sick at the loss of new born hopes. One of my brothers was at home ill, so this kept my mother from coming to my relief, and my only visitors were father and two younger brothers, and at times a little ray of sunshine that stole through a crack in the roof, shining directly in my face at noon.

Light was not so painful now, and I gladly hailed this bright gleam as a heavenly messenger. I felt that Christ was with me helping me to bear all this sorrow, and I knew his loving hands were leading and guiding me through the dark paths I was traveling. Spiritually I was helped and strengthened, but from some unknown cause to me, earthly burdens were not lightened. When lightly sleeping, strange visions appeared before me of the judgment day: I seemed to hear the rushing of mighty winds, the sounding of trumpets, while the sky would become dark and angry; strange sounds, pale horses and riders filled the air and surrounded, me the cries of woe! woe! woe! going up from many voices. My first thought on these occasions was of my parents and brothers, whom I knew were unprepared for the judgment; and in my anguish I would scream aloud, bringing Maggie and little Stella to my bed to know what was the matter. At other times I would see Christ coming in great glory, surrounded with shining angels, and I could feel myself caught up in the clouds to meet him. My soul was filled with joy and rapture, such as I had never known before. Oh, that all the world could know their danger! I would sigh upon awakening, my soul filled with an unutterable longing for the redemption of souls traveling into eternity.

Early the next spring Caroline brought Marie to see me, planting another wound deep in my heart, for I was embittered by the knowledge that she loved the people who had so cruelly wronged her mother and were the cause of her present sufferings; all her sweet infantile smiles and caresses were lavished on another, while her own mother pined for them.

Mr. Roderick's bachelor brother, who had been one of my greatest tormentors, and had said many bitter things of me in the settlement, sneering at my illness and my bandaged eyes and lady-like ways, now took delight in tormenting me afresh by showing his success in gaining Marie's affection, but I would smile and bear it, hiding all signs of the canker-worm gnawing at my heart, for I had learned to control my feelings.

Mr. Roderick now indulged frequently in loud fits of temper, thus straining my mind to the utmost to prevent Stella and Earnest annoying him, and I had to study my own words more than ever before, that they might pacify and not excite his anger. He forbade my father and brothers visiting us, threatening to kill them if they did. I was no longer able to bear in silence the great pain I endured in mind and body, and constantly for two years appealingly raised my hands heavenward and called aloud for mercy. Poor mother, a witness of my extreme mental agony, would often beg me to tell her all, saying, "Edna, my child, tell me what it is that distresses you so? Tell me all." "Mother, I cannot, it is too dreadful to mention; my sorrows are too great, I cannot talk of them." And I would not. I had not the strength and heart to relate my griefs. Was it any wonder that my mother's heart was broken? Often she would leave my room and wander into the gloomy forest weeping for the ruined prospects of her only daughter. Now I am to lose this comfort also, the association of my dear parents, for they were forbidden the house; but for their safety I must give them up, and I could not rest until I exacted the promise from my father that he would not come again.

During those wretched spring months Maggie was driven from the house, as Mr. Roderick became so violent, he kicked and beat her so, she was compelled to fly for her safety. Poor Maggie, her burden had been heavy, and I only prayed that she had found a resting place at last with some good person. She left an old brass ring in my trunk, which I still keep as a memento of her faithfulness. Mr. Roderick made no effort to find any one to fill her place, thinking the story of her hardships had become known. He was, therefore, compelled to wait on me, cook our meals and do the farm work.

Stella was attending school, so I was left entirely alone a large part of the time. The only sound that broke the silence was the singing of the locusts and Earnest's little voice when he came from the field and would say, "Mother, do you want anything?" He was not sent away, as I feared, and Mr. Roderick again became more pleasant. A letter was received from home stating that mother wanted to come to see me soon. Mr. Roderick relenting, sent word for her to come. The lonely hours were spent in listening for her carriage wheels and craving to hear mother's voice and the prattle of little Bertha, whom I had never seen. How I longed for some friendly voice to break the weary monotony of lying, day after day, exhausted from loss of sleep and protracted suffering, heart and brain racked with the struggle to keep Mr. Roderick in a pleasant mood when at the house.

About this time I received the news of the death of my beloved Aunt Mary, the friend and comfort of my childhood. The news caused me no pain as she seemed nearer in heaven than on earth. At times I felt her presence with other angels around the bed, then smiles (that were strangers to me) would flit over my face, causing little Stella to ask what I was thinking about.

One day, now being most of the time alone, I fancied that I heard sighing over the bed, and then I could distinguish strange noises outside as of something being beaten and violently thrown about, also groaning cries. I remembered hearing some one say a few days previous that an insane man was running at large in the settlement. The terrible thought instantly flashed over me that it was he who had sighed over the bed, and that he was now raging in the yard. I feared lest he should return and kill me as I was helpless. Terror took possession of me, and my imagination peopled the place with horrors which were intensified by being unseen. I tore the bandage from my eyes and strained every nerve to raise the closed lids; at the same time I tried to move my paralyzed body, but it was all in vain. In this intense agony every second seemed ages to my tortured brain.

I expected to be seized by some screaming maniac and all the fearful tales I had heard in my childhood rushed

through my excited brain and could my hair have turned
through fear it would now be as white as snow. Many
moments passed as I lay there, straining every nerve to
catch the sound of some voice. Would Mr. Roderick
and Earnest never come? When they came they found
me nearly senseless, although the noises had ceased
sometime before. Mr. Roderick found an out-house torn
down and said some wild hogs did the mischief, but I had
doubts about it, and always after that felt afraid to be left
alone.

About the middle of May mother came, bringing little
Bertha with her. She was now about ten months old.
They placed her in my bed beside me and I passed my
hand gently over the baby face, which mother said
looked like a doll. The little creature was afraid of
strangers, but some instinct seemed to draw her to me
and she placed her sweet little face close to my haggard
one, then cooed softly, and tried to displace the bandages
from my eyes. This was my own babe and I had never
seen her and, perhaps, never would. The last thought,
so bitter, was ever ready to rise and cause me sorrow.
Mother was fifty-five years old, and was weary and nearly
ill from hardships, but finding the house in great dis-
order was compelled to work beyond her strength; but
Mr. Roderick was very kind to her. The baby grew
fond of me and passed much time at my bedside. She
was an affectionate little creature, whose tears were
ever ready to flow at an unkind word, and she would
come to me for sympathy, keeping the pillow stained
with her tears and the marks of her little fingers.
Realizing that mother's health could not bear the
strain, I was very anxious that Mr. Roderick should pro-

cure help. This he promised to do, but he did not
keep his word, yet he helped mother in many ways.
She found the time to read two or three chapters from
the Bible each day, and how those sweet and comforting
passages cheered me no one can ever know. Several
times as she opened the book these words met her eyes,
"And the blind shall see and the lame walk." "There,
my dear," she once said, " you may cheer up. God says
you will walk and see." I could only answer, "Yes, but
it will not be until I reach that peaceful shore where there
is no suffering nor sorrow."

Mr. Roderick having failed to procure anything to
make a light or fire at night, we suffered great inconvenience, and mother was very anxious on account of my
health. One night some hunters passed and she begged
some of their pine, or commonly called " torchlight
wood." This night—the 30th of September—Celeste, my
fifth and last child, was born. The night of her birth
no physician, nor even a nurse, was provided and a great
change was apparent in Mr. Roderick's conduct and he,
more than ever, showed the evil spirit that possessed
him. He even kicked little Bertha over and acted so
strangely that mother, who was entirely overcome as
she thought I was in a dying condition, fainted and sank
to the floor. Mr. Roderick passed by her and, with coarse
words, refused to assist her to her feet.

One week after this my infant lay at the point of
death. It had never been well and cried incessantly.
The weather suddenly changed from warm to cold and
I had become so weak and my form was so wasted that
I could not keep warm. Mr. Roderick persisted in
throwing the cover from around me, and leaving the

7

doors wide open so that the icy wind would blow on my bed. When I was lifted from the bed he would not allow mother to put any cover around me or hose on my feet. For days I lay at the gates of death longing to join the celestial throngs beyond the river. Only my dear mother's tender care and my strong desire to get well for my children prevented my crossing to the other side. Mother's health failed fast. She grew weaker every day, but was compelled to keep up, and for their sakes I forced the few mouthfuls of food I ate to retain the little spark of life and not die. Mr. Roderick, seeing that it was impossible for mother to take care of little Bertha, hired his sister Rachel to take her home, although it was very much against his will and he was very angry about it. They came to take her home and she was torn from my arms with only a farewell kiss.

About this time I received kind messages and presents from our Old Fort friends and from Mrs. Maynard, a Scottish lady, of whom I had been very fond in my girlhood. What joy it kindled in my heart to know that I was not entirely forgotten by those whom I loved so dearly, to know that my memory was still in the hearts of my old friends, even though I was blind and a helpless wreck.

Soon after this father came to see us and when he discovered our condition he immediately went in search of help. He was not successful and, being taken sick with pneumonia, was compelled to return to his home. The following weeks were filled with the most terrible suffering and despair, the heart-rending cries of my little babe and the cruel threats of its father filled my soul with dread. We had neither wood nor lights and many nights my poor mother would sit shivering by a fire made from bark she had gathered in the woods. In her arms lay the wailing infant whom we expected hourly would breathe its last.

One night mother was too exhausted to procure any bark or wood to make a fire or light, and the sick babe cried dismally in the darkness. I asked mother if anything could be done to relieve it. "I cannot tell," she said, "but if I only had a light I would try to do what I could." Mr. Roderick, rising in the bed, stormed at us with an oath. "If you women want a light you can make it. I shall not wait upon you, and if the d—l of a babe wants to die, let it! I don't care!" He continued in this strain, cursing, throwing his arms wildly and screaming in his wrath. Mother lay so quiet for some time that I became alarmed at her unusual silence. Finally she crept from her bed and went out into the dark night. Groping her way to the woods she found some bark and returned, made a fire, over which she hovered with the sick, fretting infant until dawn. Next morning mother told me that during this wild scene with Mr. Roderick she had peculiar sensations as if a great black wave passed over her, and she was unable to move. She now said that for the first time she comprehended why I lived in such mortal fear of this man, and said that some immediate steps must be taken. She would arouse the whole community. My father at home was in ignorance of all this, but we determined to send him word the first opportunity. Opening the Bible, for strength in our trial, her eyes again fell upon the words, "The blind shall see and the lame shall walk," and also, "Daughter, be of good comfort, thy faith hath made thee whole." Coming to my bed, she said: "Daughter, do not despair. Some day you will see and walk and have the love of all your children and have them with you." She said also: "Mr. Roderick will receive his punishment, too. In his old age he will be left lonely and desolate." Her words fell as by inspiration and filled me with hope and confidence in the future. But for this courage I would not have endured the severe trials that followed. Were her words prophetic? Could I, blind and bedridden, ever hope to see and walk and have the happiness of my loved ones with me again in peace and comfort? God is good and his ways past understanding. How will it all end? The result only time can tell. Mother told me, "God tempers the wind to the shorn lamb. You possess a sweet blessing in the five dear children so lovely in disposition and entirely unlike their father." "For this I have constanly prayed," I replied. "I could not bear that they should be like him now, and God has answered my prayer."

Another night, when mother was overcome with sleep and sick from mental and physical suffering, she fell into a heavy stupor, and I could not arouse her, I lay listening to the fitful moans of the baby and I could not arouse Mr. Roderick to get up and do something to relieve it. He would do nothing, calling the poor little sufferer terrible names and saying, if it wanted to die let it, he did not care. From 10 o'clock at night until daylight the poor little infant wailed in almost death's agony, the emaciated form completely exhausted by intense suffering, and Mr. Roderick would not arouse and care for it, and I myself was unable to move. I lay in mortal agony, tearing my hair and groaning in anguish of spirit. My chest and neck were blue, my hands clinched

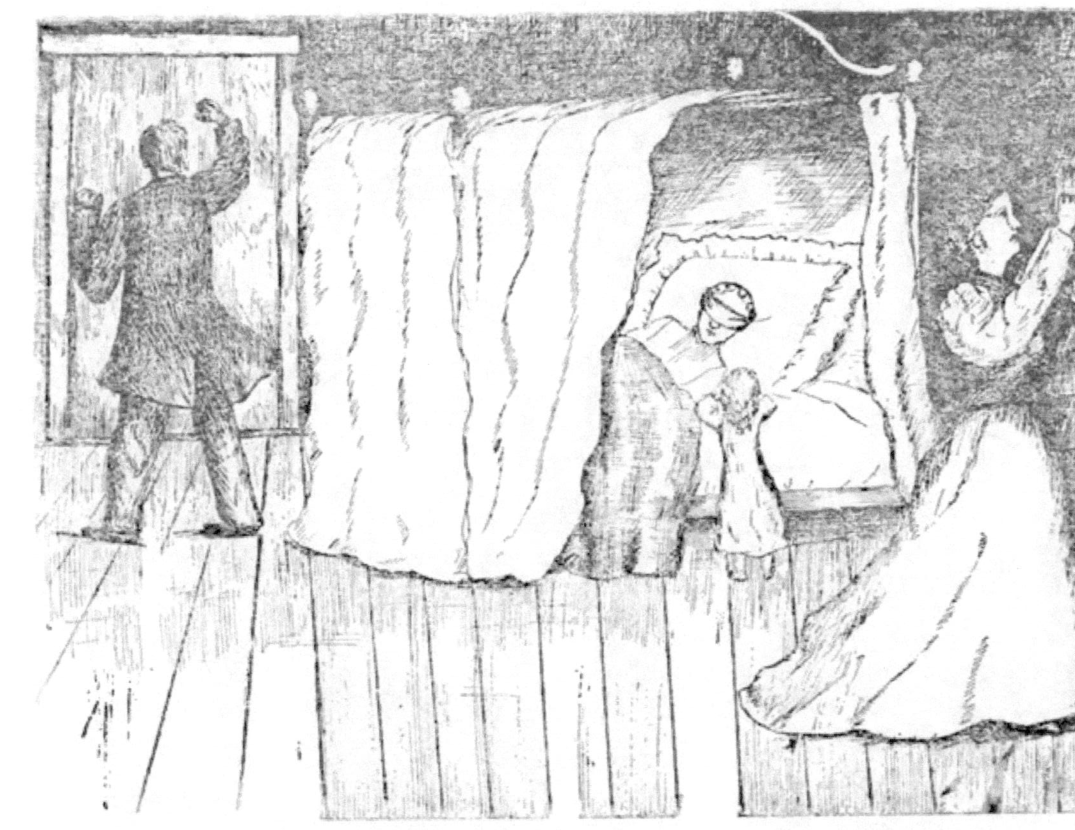

"What have I done? what have I done, to consign my only daughter to such a fate?"

until the nails buried into them through that long, awful night. I can never forget it. As daylight dawned mother aroused from her death-like stupor and soon silenced the sick babe for a little while. It was so thin and ill it had to be carried on a pillow.

Mother had now become completely prostrated from so much care. Her nerves had been shattered by the brutal treatment she had received from the man in whose power we were. She had become so afraid of Mr. Roderick that she would nearly faint when he came into the room. She said she never realized how much I suffered all alone. At times she would wring her hands and cry aloud, "What have I done to consign my only daughter to such a fate!"

One night the terrible truth was forced upon me that my mother's nerves and brain were shattered. How can I attempt to express what my feelings were at this new and unexpected trouble. Father and Bradley came and took her away, and would have taken me, but I was too ill to be moved and would not consent to leave my children. Mr. Roderick had his sister Rachel take the babe. When I kissed it I thought it would be the last time, and I prayed to God if it was his will, to take her to himself, that she might escape the terrible fate that seemed to await her. Better death than left to their hands.

When mother left she said she would return as soon as she recovered, and that she would arouse the whole country and have me taken away. She little thought that years would elapse and many strange things would happen before we met again. Before leaving she knelt at my bedside and offered a fervent prayer to God that we should meet again. One farewell embrace, a parting kiss and mother had left me. My patient, self-sacrificing mother! How her love helped me to bear the heavy burden which had been laid upon me.

Mr. Roderick then procured the services of a young, ignorant country girl, but when the spring came she left. I did not care, for she was very untidy and impudent. The care of the children and house work had always received my attention and was a great strain upon me, but I did it all very faithfully. Letters from home brought the sad news that mother was still failing, and had been carried to the nearest town in order that she might receive the best medical aid.

About this time a strange woman came to the house and Mr. Roderick procured her services. She was, however, half crazy and destitute of all womanly virtues, and I was very thankful when she left. Mr. Roderick made no effort to fill her place. So I was left alone for days at a time when he was on business. I had grown a little stronger during the winter and my little babe had improved also. She and Marie were brought to see me, and I implored them to bring Bertha, but for some reason they would not.

Brother Harry came to see me in June, but I would not tell him my true condition, knowing it would add to the sorrow at home. He said that brother Charley was very ill with typhoid pneumonia, away from home and among strangers. Father could not leave mother to go to him and the doctor could not allow her to be told about it. For the first time in many years father wept over the sad condition of his family.

Mr. Roderick became wild and savage as summer came

on and I would pass sleepless nights in the most intense
fear of him. Imagine my suffering as I lay listening to
the unearthly moans of this being beside me, who tossed
restlessly in his slumber. As I thought of my poor little
children (worse than orphans) I groaned inwardly.
Their mother was a wreck and there was no one to save
them from the anger of their inhuman father. Their
mirth in the day would jar upon me and aggravate my
painful headache. They waded in the creek, would make
bran-cakes and would strew the house with wild flowers;
often they would cover my bed with these. Sometimes
I would tell them Bible stories that I had learned in my
girlhood, and dear little Stella, sitting on my bed, would
tenderly stroke my hand. How little she dreamed, that,
though one of my greatest comforts, she was one of the
greatest causes of my anxiety, for by her thoughtless and
fearless manner she might at any time arouse the unreasonable anger of her father. I kept them close by
me, knowing he might in his passion do them an injury,
and I do not believe that I could have borne my hard lot
without them.

With the intense heat of summer my suffering grew
worse. Oh, why had I been left so desolate?

Mr. Hodges's family had been the nearest neighbors to
us; they were kind but had gone now, and I was deprived of all sympathy, save that given by Mrs. Williams,
a poor old woman who was at death's door and in very
destitute circumstances.

My heart ached for father, whose letters were so brief
and despondent. Although he tried to disguise mother's
true state of health, I felt intuitively that she was nearing
the end. He had employed the best physicians the

country afforded, but all to no avail. Mother became weak in mind and body. Her hair turned white and her form grew emaciated.

Through the long hours of the night I thought of my dying mother, with no one to care for her but strangers, and my father. Again I tried to break the cruel fetters that bound me to the bed. She would die and I would not be with her. She, my most faithful friend and the only one who understood my miserable situation. Drops of cold perspiration stood on my brow and I wrung my hands in despair. Without her care I would have died in the past winter, and now she was leaving me desolate. The violent fits of weeping, which I was unable to suppress, were fast undermining my strength. I could eat and sleep but very little, but the thought that my children would be left alone if I were to die, helped me to restrain my grief, and through God's help I succeeded, and I begged Mr. Roderick to keep all news of mother from me, unless it was good news.

One long dreary night the following lines formed themselves in my mind :

THE SOLITARY LAMENT.

The terrors of night have fallen on me,
The shadows of forms no longer I see,
Eyes that have lingered on objects of light
Are now ever closed by day and by night.
As time passes on I shed bitter tears,
Wearily waiting these many long years,
Oftentimes waking from dreaming to find
Nothing but gloom, I am helpless and blind.

Of all earthly joys I am nearly bereft,
No pleasure of friends, alone I am left,

Kind hearts there are some, though many alas!
Send a curious gaze towards me, as they pass;
One visitor daily—a small ray of sun,
Just crossing my face it gladly doth run,
Bringing me news of the weather and time,
And memories sweet, of my own sunny clime.

Five children of whom three were taken from home
For care; to them mother love is unknown,
Their smiles and caresses to strangers are given;
Alone in despair my fond heart is riven.
Oh, tell me kind angels, shall I ever recover,
To care for my children and heart-broken mother?
While sadly I'm thinking of joys that have past,
For days like my childhood, in mercy I ask.

How strange seems the quiet, how foreign to one
Who reveled in beauty, in pleasure and fun,
As healthy and happy and merry as May,
School-books in hand I would hasten away.
But listen! What noises are those that I hear?
In the silence strange fancies awaken my fear,
And terrible phantoms of lunatics try
To glare o'er my couch and stifle my cry.

Welcome, Oh death, do not leave me alone,
The future's unkind and hopes are all flown.
In pain and in anguish my sorrows untold;
Just twenty and six, yet in trouble grown old.
But God in his mercy one bright hope has given,
A Savior to love and rest in dear Heaven,
There beautiful music and many things fair,
While voices of loved ones with songs fill the air.

This long fearful summer Mr. Roderick's actions were beyond precedent. At times he furiously raved like some wild beast, screaming, shouting, weeping and swearing, and then praying almost in the same breath. Beating upon the table he would utter the most direful threats against the children. He whipped Stella several times unmercifully until I cried out with terror. I momentarily expected to be dragged from the bed, and to be beaten or stamped to death as he raved past the head of my bed. During one of these paroxysms the appalling truth flashed upon me, that I had been living with a maniac, a plausible, polite, cunning maniac ; so cunning that he could deceive the world, while he crushed the life out of his victims.

The unearthly moans, the fits of weeping, the peculiar manner of throwing the head backwards I recalled ; his restless, roving eyes, his voracious appetite, and his unnatural desire for sleep; and I shuddered as I thought of them.

His touch now became loathsome to me, and when I would feel his cold, clammy hands on my face it was only with difficulty that I could refrain from shuddering. He discovered the aversion I had for him, and jealously upbraided me for it. I determined to tell the first person who entered the house my fearful secret, for I realized the great danger should I die and leave my children to his mercy.

I had prayed all summer that my mother would be spared; I had prayed for four long years for friends and patience, for sight and strength to walk, but prayers now died on my lips and I lay waiting for what might come next, and for God to answer them if they were in accordance with his divine will. I believed they were.

While I listened night after night to the sad notes of the nightingale and the lonely cries of the whip-poor-will, my thoughts would wander back through the four years I had lain helpless and blind, then back to the years when

I was a child, a maiden, a bride, calling to mind all the joys and sorrows I had passed through and bringing back every face and incident as if it had been yesterday.

The past arose before me, a panorama of the fitful scenes so strange and sad; all the mistakes which had brought about their fearful result and the weakness that had permitted my subjection to Mr. Roderick's will, the bright prospects of my early girlhood that had so lightly passed away. The courage and will power I possessed had lain dormant all these years and not until now was it about to assert itself. Though still afraid of Mr. Roderick, I now determined with God's help (for the sake of my children) that I would exercise my own judgment and act for myself regardless of the advice or influence of any one. The child-wife died, and from her grave arose a woman with a will, and a purpose, to live to overcome, and save her children. Lying there alone night after night, unable to sleep, in an unclean bed and soiled clothing, tortured by insects, I would wring my hands in agony, sighing for the past and despairing for the future, dreading any sound that should arouse the unnatural sleeper at my side. So terrible were my sufferings that it seemed I could sweat drops of blood. The days were spent in nearly as great misery. The flies and hornets stung me and mud wasps would annoy me with dropping their spiders and mud upon my face and bed. While my anxiety for my children was torture—maddening torture—I could but contrast my present condition with the happy days when in my parents' home, and would almost go wild with grief and disappointment. I wonder now I did not go mad!

The great mistakes of my life torturing me with regrets and with thoughts of what "might have been," the faces of my parents, of my brothers and of my children arose before my mental vision as vivid as on that memorable night when I closed my eyes. The four years I had lain blind seemed like a horrible nightmare from which I could never awaken. I was weary of the world, its coldness and vanity; weary of its friendlessness and deception, and I longed to reach that shore where all was peace and love, where there would be no more pain and sickness and sorrow.

FOR I LONG TO BE THERE.

Dear Father in heaven, to Thee I would raise
A petition and speak to thy bountiful praise,
At Thy footstool of grace, I would offer my prayer,
Take me unto Thyself for I long to be there.

II

Dear Savior I plead, Thou art tender and kind
O'erflowing with love, and for me thou canst find
A safe resting place, that is free from all care.
Draw me close to Thy heart, for I long to be there.

III

Fair angels of light, who with melodies sweet,
Make that beautiful home a celestial retreat,
In your happiness pure, a full part I would share;
Let me come to your home, for I long to be there.

IV

While our pleasures are few and hopes but a name
And while worldliness reigns o'er all things the same,
Our joys are in dreams of a bright Eden fair,
Take me into thy rest, for I long to be there.

V

I am weary of life, weary of its decay.
On the echoless shore full of peace I would stray,
Forgetting all sorrows, for Christ will them bear.
Oh, take me to Jesus for I long to be there.

CHAPTER VI.

THE TRIAL OF FAITH.

"Flow on, mysterious river,
Flow on to eternity's sea.
By faith and a holy endeavor,
The future hath bliss for me."

OTHER, perhaps dying, and I alone, blind and bed-ridden, with two small children, in the power of one who seemed a raving lunatic; would God heed my long anguished prayers and send relief? While so far from friends, my heart grew sick with the sad, dreary days of waiting that followed, and which were filled with unspeakable horrors and dread for the safety of my unconscious children. My hair, which was now long and heavy, almost dripped with perspiration, caused by mortal agony. Can my readers imagine a more distressing situation?

'I was even deprived of the visits of my poor friend, Mrs. Williams, who was too feeble to come. I remembered now what one of Mr. Roderick's sisters, whom I have not mentioned, said to mother shortly before she was carried home. She had strongly urged upon her the necessity of going home, saying her brother would ruin her if she stayed with him, as he had Edna, and pointing to the bed, said, "See what he has done to her, no woman can live with him. He came very near wreaking his vengeance on me on more than one occasion, but I would not give him the opportunity to remain in my house." I also remembered that his two eldest sisters, Rachel and Caroline, had often thought that he would be a lunatic some time. I knew that all the family were afraid to cross him. They told that he had once chased his brother William with an axe, and that he was compelled to climb a tree to save himself.

I had prayed for friends, and resolved to make my case known to the first one that entered the house. Almost ten years I had kept this fearful secret and now for my children's sake it must be done. For myself, I wanted to die. One day, as if in answer to this prayer, a young lady, formerly from Massachusetts, called at our house. Grasping at the last straw, I told her my story, and begged her to write a letter for me to my brothers, which she immediately did, sitting by my bed, and writing at my dictation. She carried the letter to Marion, the nearest town, and dropped it into the post-office. The letter was addressed to brother Bradley, and it so happened that he was on his way to see me and chanced to be in Marion before the letter left the office. It was handed him, and, unable to read it on account of his impaired sight, he took it to a Mrs. Simpson, whom he knew had professed great sympathy for me. She read it to him, and promised not to reveal its contents.

The day the letter was mailed I was overjoyed by his unexpected arrival. I tried to tell him my suspicions in regard to Mr. Roderick's insanity; he said he would go to Marion, consult a lawyer, and see what could be done. After he left, Mr. Roderick went to the mill and returned extremely agitated. Some one had told him the contents of that letter. I trembled violently, knowing well what a storm was to follow. Heavenly Father, how long will this constant struggle last, this weary, weary strife? How could any one be so cruel as to inform him of the letter I had written?

I waited in utter desolation, carried away by intensity of feeling. Mr. Roderick asked was it possible that I thought of leaving him. He insisted upon my giving him my reasons, and his voice sounded hoarse and strange. I scarcely knew what excuse to make, and simply said I was unhappy. "Do you love me?" he cried. I did not answer him, but when he insisted I replied that I did not, that he had treated me so unkindly I could not love him. He walked the house groaning and talking wildly, his voice sounding more like the wail of a lost soul than anything human. Finally he promised that if I would not leave him he would move to Marion and treat me kindly, but said that if I left him I should not have any of the children. When brother returned, he told me that unless Mr. Roderick was willing, I could not take the children, and asked if I was willing to leave them. "No," I replied decidedly, "my anxiety is not for myself, but solely on their account. I will accept Mr. Roderick's proposal, as he has offered to take me to Marion, and promised to treat me with more consideration." My brother remained with us a few days and then returned home, as mother was dangerously ill. Mr. Roderick's mood changed, and he became excessively kind, but I still shrank from him in fear and dread. His terms of endearment had become so repulsive, I shuddered at his touch as from some reptile.

He could get no one to assist him, and had to make

all the necessary preparations himself for our move to Marion. Our clothing was badly soiled and worn, and I felt reluctant to go without suitable preparation, but feeling it impossible to exist much longer in the manner we were living, and longing to be near sympathizing friends, who, perhaps, could aid me, should anything happen, and also feeling that the influence of the Church and Christian people would serve as a shield against further outbreaks, I decided to go. God had heard our prayers, and our prospects now took a more favorable turn.

Letters from home brought the glad news that, contrary to the expectations of every one, mother's health was now improving.

Brothers Edgar and Charlie came to see us and spent a few days. The neighbors dropped in, seeming very kind and sympathetic. Mrs. Williams also informed me that Marion people sympathized with me, and among them I would find friends. I counted the hours that would intervene before I would leave my sad and lonely home, filled with so many bitter recollections.

My health improved daily under the bright rays of a new-born hope and kind treatment. Mr. Roderick's sister Harriet came to see us and loudly upraided her brother for humoring a wife that did not love him and who could help herself if she would. Turning to me she said, "Now Edna, if you want to know the truth, I am the one to tell it. It is the opinion of all the people in the country that you can help yourself if you will." "Harriet," I replied, "intelligent people do not think so, and I care not for the opinion of those that are not. Your unkind talk has caused me many tears, but in the future it will

Blind and helpless rang through my head, keeping time with the ringing of the distant church-bells.

have no effect. I have determined from this time forward to act upon my own judgment, regardless of the opinions of others." She was so astonished at my daring to speak so boldly that she made no answer, and did not speak again until Mr. Roderick entered the house, when they engaged in a loud and fierce quarrel about our moving to Marion, which ended by her leaving the house with threats, and in tears.

True to his word, Mr. Roderick proceeded with his preparations, and in a few weeks said he was ready. Yielding to my earnest request, that I should not be carried in any vehicle, I was placed on a stretcher and conveyed by several of the neighboring men to the railroad, a distance of two miles. The stretcher was placed on a hand-car and rolled to Marion, some four or five miles. Marion is a small town, and the county site of McDowell. It is situated on the Western North Carolina road, near the Blue Ridge mountains, its chief beauty being the mountains on either side and its wild forest scenery. Many worthy people have settled there in the last few years and its business prospect which is chiefly merchandising, has become more flourishing.

I was moved on the Sabbath, as those who had charge of the hand-car would not allow it to be moved in the week, fearing accidents. I lay motionless on the dark, green-curtained stretcher borne by eight men, the tramp, tramp of their steady gait and the new and strange sounds mingled with their voices, borne in vague and solemn tones upon my ears.

Finally my couch was placed upon the hand-car and it slowly rolled down the railroad, while the words " In the world, but not of the world," "Blind and helpless, blind

and helpless," rang through my head, keeping time with
the ringing of the distant church bells.

Sad at leaving my three little children behind, little
ones mine eyes had never beheld! Would I ever see
them? Oh! how I longed for that sight. Totally blind,
too weak to even turn myself or move my limbs, and
racked with pain at every jolt in moving me. What had
the future in store for me and mine! Would God hear
my many long prayers? One earnest prayer had been
answered—that my children were not deformed nor diseased in mind or body—and this had encouraged me to
pray more truly and lovingly. God knows best, and my
faith was strengthened to trust him implicitly for the
future. He had blessed me in my children, had spared
me the heavy cross that might have been laid there. My
thoughts were very, very sad as I entered the town where
I had spent so many happy days during my girlhood.
The church bells were ringing, the chimes of which
were sweet and mournful, carrying me back to the days
when I had mingled with the church throng and lifted my
voice with theirs in anthems of praise. Stella and Earnest,
and Eliza, our new cook, and some of the neighbors were
waiting to receive us, and I felt strangely happy in the
knowlege of the fact that I would not be left alone any
more and that I would be near sympathetic friends. The
neighbors who called wondered how one who was blind
and helpless could smile and appear so happy. Oh! they
little knew what scenes I had passed through and what
reasons I now had to be almost happy, even though I
could not see nor walk.

" And people say that I am bliud
And pity me, although I find
A world of beauty in my mind,
A never ceasing store.

" Of the dear Savior, meek and kind,
And how he healed the lame and blind,
Am I not healed? for in my mind
His blessed form I see.

"The beauty of all outward sight,
The wondrous shows of day and night,
All love, all faith, all pure delight,
Are strong in heart and mind."

My heart was now full of gratitude and praise. My
visitors, both old and new, were pleasant, congenial and
sympathetic. Mr. Roderick was cheerful and more
natural, and I carefully guarded every word that I spoke,
lest I should reveal his past cruelty, being aware that
Madam Rumor had, ere this, painted my unhappy life to
the citizens of Marion. Stella and Earnest attended Sabbath-school and also day school, taught by Prof. Chriton
and wife, who soon became interested friends of mine.
All the clergymen of the town called often, and prayed
by my bedside. Prayers were offered in the churches
that I might be restored to health and sight. Many delicacies were sent to me by the ladies of the neighborhood. Although I was a great sufferer, I almost felt as
if I were in heaven when comparing the present with the
past, and at times during my lonely hours, my room
seemed filled with angels. I still heard favorable reports
from home. Brother Charlie and some of our old Fort
friends made us visits. Among my acquaintances I
found a few true and faithful friends, one of whom (the
wife of Col. Yonge) was one of those rare characters of

whom we read, but seldom meet. She was a gentle, dignified, true Christian woman, mild, yet firm, and always calm and cheerful. Her kind words strengthened me in my weakness, her conversation being chiefly of heaven and heavenly desires and hopes. A feeling of joy filled every fiber of my heart when I heard her soft musical voice at my door. Her three daughters and many others called, bringing kind messages and choice dishes to tempt my appetite, but the knowledge that I was not friendless and entirely forsaken, as I had before imagined myself, gave me more real satisfaction than the dainties they brought. Another prayer answered, that for friends, and has been continually since that time, for God has blessed me with friends wherever I went. I also found friends in Mrs. Chriton and Miss Lina Cleveland (one who could thoroughly sympathize with the afflicted, having herself been an invalid for many years). Mrs. Chriton was an earnest, energetic lady, with a warm, generous heart, possessing cultivated tastes; and the hours she passed by my bedside, reading extracts from different authors, or conversing with her sweet, rich voice, caused the time to pass pleasantly. She afterward proved a zealous, sacrificing friend. The society of those dear ones, and the visits of the faithful clergymen caused my countenance to be no longer devoid of smiles. The hours flew by on "gilded wings" seeming almost a foretaste of heaven. Eliza, our servant, took very good care of me, but proved to be very high-tempered and quarrelsome, often slamming the doors and loudly scolding; but Mr. Roderick was now so mild and gentle that I tried to forget that he had ever been otherwise, and those who came in saw nothing amiss in our daily intercourse. At this time I heard many accounts of wonderful "faith cures" in other States, and I now prayed earnestly for more faith, feeling sure that if God would heal others he would not forget me. One day I was delighted to hear that a clergyman was in town who strongly advocated "faith cures." I sent for him immediately, and my friend Mrs. Yonge greatly urged me to trust my physical infirmities to God's care. She herself was an invalid, having suffered fifteen years with dyspepsia, and having had to live all that time on plain wheaten bread and tea. We were both anointed, and prayers of faith were offered for us by Mr. Barnum. This was a new doctrine in the neighborhood, and Mrs. Yonge, Mr. Barnum and myself were subjected to many criticisms. Mr. Barnum left to work in other fields. The prayers I had offered for many years for sight and strength now became more fervent. I was able to bear the light of the room with only a thin covering over my eyes which were still closed, and I could move my head and turn myself in bed, but still suffered severe pain in my eyes and spine, with my drawn, aching limbs, and long confinement, while the noise in my head and dancing lights had never ceased. My emaciated limbs and thin colorless hands and face often elicited remarks of pity. After a long night spent in prayer for some sign to be given by which I might know that my prayers were to be answered, my friend, Miss Lina Cleveland, called, bringing a beautiful poem headed with this text: "And I will bring the blind by a way that they knew not, I will lead them in paths they have not known, I will make darkness light before them and crooked things straight. These things will I do unto them and not forsake them," Isaiah 42:16.

These words gave me fresh courage and hope, for I took them to be a direct answer to the prayer the previous night. One day I remarked to Rev. Edward Pell, a kind Methodist clergyman now of much prominence, that some of my prayers were being answered, save that one I most earnestly desired, which was to see and walk. He said:

"It would seem then, that it is not His will; you ought to be reconciled."

"I cannot," I replied, "my children are suffering for my care and I am so tired of lying here for days, months and years, in pain and distress, and being a burden to my friends."

"Perhaps that is your mission," he replied, "your patient suffering being an example to the restless, stirring world."

But I could not feel that God intended me to always lead such a life and now believed that some time He would enable me to see and walk. Mr. Pell spent many hours with me, and his conversation and prayers were a source of great comfort. Mr. Roderick and I had our letters removed from the church to which we had belonged and became members of a church at Marion, but the peace and rest that I had enjoyed for three months were doomed to be destroyed.

Our cook became so quarrelsome and abusive to the children that Mr. Roderick discharged her. An ignorant, untidy, though kind girl, was employed in her place. Mr. Roderick again became disagreeable and tyrannical and later in the spring grew so unmanageable and violent that all the old feelings of horror and despair that I had endured so long were once more aroused.

One morning, after a scene, in which he raved fearfully, I became completely exhausted and lost my self-possession and screamed in despair and fell into convulsions. After regaining my worn strength I sent the frightened children after Mrs. Yonge. Feeling that she was a true "child of God," I determined to take her into my confidence and ask her advice. I did not know what course to pursue. Mr. Roderick had broken his promise, my strength was rapidly leaving me, and I felt unable to longer bear those frightful scenes, and I also realized that my physician had spoken the truth when he told mother, sometime before, that I would never regain my health while I lived with Mr. Roderick. "Something heavier than the stroke of the fist—unkind words"—was robbing me of life and health. I believed him at times insane, but knew that others could not penetrate the mask he wore. Should I leave him he would not allow me the children, without great trouble, and while there lasted the faintest hope of life, to leave them seemed indeed heartrending. My parents and brothers, owing to so much sickness, trouble and misfortune, were unable to assist me much and I was too feeble to be carried over the long mountain road to their home.

When Mrs. Yonge came my extreme agitation prevented me from telling her my true condition, save in broken accents. She was greatly surprised, as well as grieved, to learn that Mr. Roderick was not all that he professed to be. She advised me to trust my children to God and leave him, saying that I could never recover under such unhappy circumstances, and that in my present condition I could never be any benefit to my children. I could not make up my mind to this and I got Mrs. Chriton to write letters home, stating the true condition of affairs and telling them to assist me in some way immediately or I would die.

Brother Edgar, who lived in Charlotte, replied that if I would leave Mr. Roderick he would take care of me. Father could not come to see me but said that brother Bradley would come as soon as possible.

I almost censured my friends and thought them cruel to believe that I could leave my children with a man I knew to be insane. My nerves were now so shattered that I could bear no excitement and I lay almost unconscious and nearly lifeless, and as the days passed I felt that I was sinking rapidly, and knew that if compelled to endure that kind of life much longer I would certainly die soon and my children be left motherless. Days and nights were spent in prayer, asking God to show me the right way. For myself alone my condition would have remained unchanged. I could have yielded to death without a struggle, but for my children's sake I felt the necessity of sacrificing my own feelings in making a strong effort to live. I now asked myself, "would it not be better to leave them temporarily than for eternity?" In the one case there was a probability of my being restored to them, in the other I was leaving them to the uncertain fate of an unkind father and his sister, with few, if any friends to sympathize with them or understand their wants. All hopes of having my three little girls brought home were entirely destroyed; they were not even brought to see me. My heart grew sick when I thought of those helpless little ones being subjected to coarse, rough treatment and teaching, perhaps cruelty, and I groaned in anguish of soul at the cruel fetters that prevented me from shielding them.

One morning, after another of those fearful scenes I have described, I was again thrown into violent convulsions from another of Mr. Roderick's raving fits. He entered my room in a storm of passion, seized my wasted body in his arms and threw me to the other side of the bed. Grinding his teeth and moaning he dropped upon the children's couch, and swore and raved in his wild rage. Rising he slammed the doors and hissed curses through his clenched teeth. The thought that we were in the power of a raving maniac threw me into violent convulsions. The pitiful, frightened cries of the children added to my horror, and I screamed in frantic woe.

The neighbors heard the screams but did not venture in until after Mr. Roderick had left the house. My body was almost paralyzed, with blue places around my mouth and eyes, and I was scarcely able to speak. The convulsions left me so weak and exhausted that I felt that if I would save my life I must leave that very day. I now understood that all the threats he had made against my people, to take their lives, etc., were vain. The heavy veil was lifted from my eyes and I saw the truth as it really was. I lost my fear of all his threats against them, still I knew that my own life was always in danger.

Again I sent for Mrs. Yonge and Mrs. Chriton and told them I would surely die if left in Mr. Roderick's power any longer. Stella and Earnest were strong and robust and might escape their father's wrath until I could return, and then by the aid of law and health I could take them and the three little ones from him.

While Mrs. Yonge and Mrs. Chriton were sitting by my bedside, discussing the best plan to pursue, brother Bradley entered. A kind old lady afterward said that she knew God was on my side by my brother coming in just at that time.

He was extremely distressed at the turn affairs had taken. Not being strong he was greatly fatigued by his tiresome journey. On consulting some lawyers he found that no person could take me into their home without the protection of the law, so I entered a suit for divorce. Bradley made all the necessary preparations, and I was carried on a stretcher to a hotel during Mr. Roderick's absence.

It would be impossible to describe my distress in leaving Stella and Earnest, thinking that doubtless I would never meet them again. It was a thought that awakened many sad and bitter reflections, which only my strong faith in God, that he would bless my efforts, enabled me to endure. The public was highly excited over the affair, and I was both pained and mortified by the unkind remarks which came to my ears, for, as I had anticipated, many upheld Mr. Roderick, and many said they believed I could see and walk, while my friends were very indignant, and many said that hanging was too good for him, and in some States he would be hung. I could not convince them that he was insane, and I was not willing that he should be hung. Others wondered how I could appear so cheerful if Mr. Roderick had treated me so unkindly. Some re-echoed the sentiment of his people, and said that I had some one else in view whom I loved better than my husband. Many believed Mr. Roderick's pitiful story, "that he had never spoken a cross word to me and now much he had loved (?) and sacrificed for me." He called to see me once and appeared wild and excited, while his language was incoherent and disconnected. My brother, Mrs. Yonge and Mrs. Chriton, who were in the room, said after his departure that he certainly acted like an insane man, and were inclined to believe, with me, that he was.

Some who had visited me discontinued their visits, and I was left alone in my room much of my time. Bradley went to Asheville to attend to some important business, and I could not leave for Charlotte until his return. Mrs. Yonge and Mrs. Chriton, and a few other faithful friends, "angels of mercy," sent by God to help me bear my sorrows, did all in their power to alleviate my distress; but the one thought that Stella and Earnest were left alone, and in the hands of a mad man, destroyed my sleep and rest. They were running at large in the street by day, with no one to look after them. Mr. Roderick did not prevent them from coming to see me as I feared he would, but the landlord of the hotel did not like to have them running up and down the stairs so much, so I was often compelled to have them sent into the street before they were taken away by Rachel, who came for them. I improved the opportunity and gave them my farewell charges in regard to their future life and the welfare of their little sisters, implored them to be kind to them, teach them their prayers, and take my place as much as possible. Rachel was present when they bade me good-bye, and I successfully hid from her all outward signs of my intense emotions, even smiling as I felt the little faces pressed against my cold cheek. She was so cruel that I could not endure to have her scoff at my suffering.

My old friend, Ada, who was married and living at Old Fort, came, bringing the comfort of her presence and many messages from sympathizing friends. I could not but draw a sad comparison between us, starting in life with such different prospects. Married about the same time, I, to what every one thought an exemplary Christian, but in truth a hypocrite; she to a man "of the world," but who was at heart, honest and sincere, now she comes to me so happy and youthful looking, with her lovely children, enjoying every comfort of life, while I lie, a perfect wreck of my former happy, healthy state. The thought, why should I have been chosen for such a fate, kept wailing through my heart in tortuous perplexity. Oh, what mystery! I could not fathom it! Yet I knew without the sustaining hand of God, I could not have passed through these fiery trials. Some *truth*, some great *power* must surely be proven to the world, by my life of strange suffering and woe. I felt very sad at the thought that I must leave without seeing my father and mother. Mother's illness had been much more serious than I had ever known, they had kept the knowledge partially hid. Her mind had been nearly wrecked, and my father had never left her. Dr. Gaylor, one of Marion's kindest and best physicians, pronounced my illness serious, and advised me to go to some Northern hospital, where I might be much benefited; but he gave very little encouragement of a permanent cure. However, I was not discouraged, and I felt that all things were possible with God. I had been at the hotel four weeks when my brother returned to take me to Charlotte. The day of our departure, I was carried to the depot and placed in a baggage car, as there was no room for my stretcher in the other cars, the train having no sleeping car attached. A green cloth was placed over the stretcher to protect my eyes from the light, and I almost felt as if I was being carried in a coffin, shut out of the world. "In the world, but not of the world," were again my thoughts. My kind friends accompanied me to the depot, also their husbands and my physician, who arranged everything in their power for my comfort, and with floral offerings and kindest wishes, bade me adieu.

The hearse-like procession was witnessed by but few of my lady friends. All had retreated to their homes too sad to watch what they thought my last journey in this world. None thought I could live to arrive at my destination, and did not like to see the sad sight, the darkened couch, with one thin hand out from the cover, clasping some flowers some one had given me, a perfect wreck and shadow of my former self.

The bells rang, the engine whistled, and with a jarring, jerking sensation, I felt myself being carried through space, leaving friends and children behind, whose faces I had never seen. 1 suffered very much from heat, light and smoke, and the jarring of the injured portion of my spine and inflamed eyes. Bradley seldom left my side until we reached Salisbury, about dusk, when he left me a few minutes to order refreshments. We were both very lonely and sad, feeling weary and desolate in the cheerless room in which we waited for the coming train. Some ladies and gentlemen, entering later, expressed regret at my helplessness. The ladies gently pressed my hand and smoothed my hair, lifting the long plaits that fell over the stretcher, speaking admiringly of its

9

length and beauty. Surely God was with me everywhere, His angels hovering near.

The cars came rushing in and I was placed in one. We arrived in Charlotte about midnight, and I felt the warm hearty kiss of Brother Edgar on my cheek, who had been notified by telegram of our coming. Several men were with him, who carried me through the dark and silent streets at midnight to his home. I listened to the slow tramp of men and horses and wondered dreamily what would happen next in my eventful life. I kept repeating, "In the world, but not of the world." Why was I born to such a fate! O, God, pity me. I was aroused by the voice of dear Alice, which sounded strangely low and subdued. Was she sorry I had come? I asked myself. Why did she appear so quiet and strange? I learned afterwards that she was so agitated at the sight of my stretcher, looking so much like a coffin entering her door at midnight, that she could scarcely speak. After two weeks of rest, I was informed that Mr. Roderick had left the country and taken the children, and that no one knew where they were. It was reported that he had taken them to Texas. At the same time I heard that the physician who had been employed by Brother Edgar to treat my case, had pronounced it a hopeless one, saying that I would never walk, as he thought the portions of vertebræ which had been injured by the rubbing and the long rough journey over the mountains, had been dislocated. Two fearful blows at one stroke! It would be impossible to describe the horror and despair that I now endured.

Thus all my recent hopes were suddenly destroyed. The livid, distorted face of Mr. Roderick, as I had seen

it in bygone years, arose before my mental vision so
magnified that I could not repress cries of terror.   I slept
but little, my dreams being filled with horrible pictures.
I imagined my children enduring all kinds of suffering,
until heart and brain reeled at the maddening thoughts.
I continually saw these frightened little creatures, trying
vainly to escape their cruel, frantic father.   While in this
state I composed these lines:

MIDNIGHT THOUGHTS.

In silent hours of midnight, while earth is wrapped in dreams,
I ponder o'er my present life, how desolate it seems.
Scan each page so wakefully penned in despair and grief,
Then turn to my fond childhood's home for comfort and relief.

A cottage white was standing there upon a grand old hill,
Among some spreading shady trees, and everything was still.
In that dear home my parents lived, five brothers large and small,
And uncles, aunts and cousins near, and I the pet of all.

But now my children call for me, I hear their plaintive cries,
Away from mother and their home, tears in their sweet blue eyes.
They call for mother, call for me, while slumbers o'er them steal,
But mother is too far from them to hear their sad appeal.

O take us to our mother, a stranger's love we are told,
Is nothing like a mother's that never can grow cold;
She praises us when we do right and gently strokes our hair,
And kisses us when we lie down, then breathes a silent prayer.

Poor little ones! their pleadings fall as if on hearts of stone,
Four helpless girls, and one small boy, are left to weep alone.
No mother there to kiss their brows, nor soothe their childish fears,
Nor teach them what is right or wrong, nor smile away their tears.

When last they came to visit me I could but calmly smile,
For cruel eyes were watching o'er my darlings all the while;
I feigned a cold indifference to hide my deep despair,
I kissed their sweet and dimpled cheeks and softly stroked their hair.

Wide seas may roll between us, and my gold brown hair may seem
A snow drift, and my present life be only as a dream;
My darlings will return to me and all life's dangers brave,
Perchance be folded in my arms or weep around my grave.

During the following month I came very near losing my faith in God. He seemed so deaf to my frenzied prayer. I had trusted him and he had not answered me. I felt as if engulfed by waves, dark, deep, and merciless. But for the kindness of Sister Alice and her sister I could not have borne my terrible lot. An unfortunate scoffer, who lived near, frequently said, why did not God, whom I believed in, restore me to sight and strength. He insisted on reading to me from Ingersoll's noted works until doubts arose in my mind. At last, feeling that if I lost faith in God, I would surely go mad, I determined that though he might slay me, I would love and trust him, and prayed all night till the morning light, as Jacob wrestled with the angel, for I could not "go" without a blessing. I *must* be heard. The prayer of faith would avail and I cried for mercy and help—that he would hear and bless me yet. I begged he would send one of his faithful ones right away who would encourage and strengthen my faith and prove to me that I was not forsaken as it seemed, but that my prayers were heard and remembered.

That very day, in direct answer to this prayer, Dr. Miller, an elderly divine, called and spoke such words of comfort and peace, that my doubts were at once removed and my soul was at rest. I now received letters from mother, which were hope-inspiring and full of comfort. Edgar's business had been prosperous, but he was in poor health, and was greatly troubled over the future for his family as he felt his life must be short, as he frequently said, and what he did he must do quickly. He was fully impressed with the idea that his children would soon be left father-less. He ate and slept but little, and often walked the house in anguish of spirit, saying, "What will become of my family if I die?" Poor, dear Edgar! He felt that his life was fast ebbing away, but did not think how soon his fears were to be realized, and he be laid in a pre-mature grave. I had always loved sister Alice, but during those dark days I clung to her as a child clings to its mother, and ever found her faithful and patient, gentle and kind, ever willing and ready to leave her work or bed at night, to encourage and comfort me in my hours of passionate grief, which were so frequent that I could not gain my strength. Her children, Herbert and Laura, strove in their childish manner to alleviate my sorrow and my pain, by running to wait on me or sitting on my bed. Little Laura, who was just the age of my Bertha, often said, "Don't weep, Aunt Edna. I will bring your children to see you some day." Those little forms were ever flitting about my room, and their sweet chattering voices whiled away many weary hours. I became deeply attached to them, as I also did to the baby girl, who came that summer. Late in the autumn Edgar's business called him to Clio, South Carolina. He had been working on an invention, which proved a success. Time only was needed to make him a wealthy man.

This business called him away, and he wanted to take his family with him. He said I could accompany them if I desired, but he had given up all hope of my going North, or of getting well, believing what my physicians said, that I would never walk again. Though discouraged, my faith and trust that God would answer my prayers sustained me. When Mrs. Ivanston, an old schoolmate who was living in Charlotte, learned that I was there and called to see me, I felt that He was directing my way. She begged me not to give up trying to recover, but to remain and go to a hospital in the city, where she believed I could be benefited. I thought seriously of this and prayed over it; at last I concluded to take her advice and make one more effort. Arrangements were speedily made, and a few days before Christmas, I was carried on a stretcher to the hospital. The last thing I heard was dear little Laura's voice calling, "Mamma, Mamma, I want to go with Aunt Edna!" This she did repeatedly until the echoes but faintly reached my ears. My thoughts wandered back to my own children. I wondered how long it would be ere I met them again. Ah, those dear childish tones! I heard the voices of my own poor little ones, and I cried out from the depths of my heart, "Once more, my darlings, mother will make an effort for your dear sakes! You are my life, my purpose to live. I must not die and leave you!" So, with this one hope, and trust in God that he would in time restore me to strength and sight, that I may see *your* smiles and innocent eyes again, mother will struggle on, I will endure yet a while longer, and surely God will hear my cry. God help me! God pity me and give me faith by which to see and walk! My little ones, I press onward! I turn my heart from the dark and horrible past, my hopes and my trust are before me, and the thought of them suggested the following lines:

WHY I LOVE THEM.

I would tell thee of Stella, how she made glad the hours,
So oft calling Mother with strewn wreaths and flowers;
Blue eyes brightly glancing, till they sparkle and dance,
While singing so sweetly, gaily skipping perchance.

Then comes my son Earnest, an affectionate boy,
So true and so thoughtful, never aught but a joy,
E'er steady and happy, eyes earnest and clear,
His dear voice so merry, methinks I still hear.

I would say of Marie that she is very fair,
With ways of a lady, and golden waved hair.
She scolds and laughs sweetly, ever chattering they tell,
With curls and long lashes; she'll yet be a belle.

Three-year-old Bertha, whose housewifely care
And womanly habits call forth praises rare;
Sweet little maiden, whose large, tender heart
To blame makes thee timid and thy tears swift to start.

Tall, slender Celeste, whose spirited fair face
And excelling talents could a palace well grace.
Five faces so pretty, eyes brighter than gems
And hearts kind and loving, is why I love them.

CHAPTER VII.

LIGHT IN DARKNESS.

HOMELESS.

Once more I breathe the city air,
Hear many speak of objects rare,
And hear the din of crowds that throng
The thoroughfare the whole day long.

Again I see the human form,
The clouds that gather and the storm,
Yet there's naught to make me glad;
My heart is heavy, sore and sad.

Another cross I have to take,
Beneath its weight I shrink and shake;
The dregs of sorrow still must drain;
The bitter draught is full of pain.

For those I love I cannot see,
The childish faces full of glee,
No little hands hold mine and press
A kiss to lips that long to bless.

No little forms stand by my bed,
No more I hear the words that fed
My soul with love. O God! I cry,
I'm far from home, alone I sigh.

Y brother and family soon left the city and I accepted Mrs. Ivanston's kind invitation to remain with her during Christmas holidays. She was a pleasant, cheerful lady, and deeply interested in my recovery, consequently my visit was as pleasant as could have been expected under the peculiar circumstances in which I was placed. I had regained my lost faith and again felt the presence of angels in my room, which brought smiles of joy and peace to my pallid face. I longed to return with them to their "Heavenly Home," where there was neither pain nor sorrow—there to reign with my blessed Saviour for time and eternity!

THE LAND OF LOVE.

We are told of the beautiful land of love,
Of bright jeweled mansions in blue skies above;
Of mansions that glitter with diamonds and gold,
While airs of sweet odors their fair walls enfold;
Of heavenly music, soft, thrilling, divine,
Fountains that sparkle, and bright suns that shine;
Birds of gay plumage with song fill the air,
Flowers all lovely and crowns with gems rare.

All this we are told and many things more,
Of Heaven's fair Jordan, an evergreen shore,
Its golden gates ever are standing ajar,
Where fall huge burdens we have carried so far;
Shining robed angels there welcome us home,
Joyously lead us through fair fields to roam;
Heaven alive with sweet praises shall ring,
We bow at the throne of our Saviour and King.

Blessings there are bestowed just suited to all,
No more vain regrets, no more tears to fall,
No hearts there to ache, no sins to repent,
No leaving of friends, nor wrongs to resent;
No asking of bread to be given a stone,
No needle-worn fingers that ache to the bone;
From this fair land all life's cares have flown,
Queen happiness reigns and love is her crown.

My afflictions, perhaps, were blessings in disguise, since they had brought me so near my heavenly Father, and revealed to me so many hidden mysteries. The comforting words of St. Paul, "For our light affliction which is but for a moment, worketh for us a far more exceeding and eternal weight of glory, while we look not at the things which are seen, but the things which are not seen, for the things which are seen are temporal, but the things which are not seen are eternal," were ever in my mind.

The following Sabbath, while the family were at dinner in a distant room, I was alarmed by the smell of something burning. Several moments passed ere I could make my weak voice heard, when some one came in screaming "Fire!" and then left me alone. The flames proceeded from a closet in my room and were already bursting through the roof. For a few seconds I thought myself forgotten and made a few frantic efforts to crawl from my bed, unwilling to taste death in a "fiery furnace." The excited family ran hither and thither, but at last, when I thought myself forsaken and left to perish in the wild flames, I heard voices and felt Mr. Ivanston's strong arms lifting my trembling form, which he carried into the yard and laid upon some bed clothing. I was soon picked up by some women, who carried me into Mr. Burden's house. The city was alarmed and the flames of the building soon extinguished.

Although my friends lost valuable clothing and furniture, yet every article belonging to me was mysteriously saved. I believed this was providential. Strange as it may appear the excitement of the fire caused my eyes to open and I dimly saw the faces around me. During the next two days faint visions met my gaze when, alas! my eyes again closed.

Mrs. Burden was a noble Christian lady and in her house I passed the happiest Christmas I had known in five years ! Each member of the family endeavored to make me forget that I was a helpless stranger ; even the cook, a kind-hearted creature, seemed to anticipate every wish. After remaining with them two days, not wishing to intrude longer, I insisted upon being removed to the hospital, and was accompanied there by Mr. and Mrs. Burden, who left many charges with the nurse, that I should be especially cared for. They departed, with the promise to return soon, and left me alone in a large, strange room, listening to the moans of an old lady in the room above. I felt strangely, lonely and desolate. I had been informed that "St. Peter's Hospital," of which I was now an inmate, was under the management of nine Episcopalian ladies, and that it stood in the outskirts of the city, in a cool and pleasant place. The matron had died recently and no one had been found to fill the position, so a Mrs. King was acting as nurse to the patients, and now took charge of me, while Mr. Grundy, a gruff old Englishman, did the errands and chores. Before the lapse of twelve hours, I was very homesick, and regretted my hasty decision. Edgar had been opposed to my leaving him, but had kindly offered to bear my expenses in making what he termed a "useless effort," as he considered my case hopeless.

The day after my arrival, I was visited by an Episcopal clergyman, Mr. Cheshire (now bishop of North Carolina), who became my warm friend, also by Mrs. Fanen, president of the hospital, and Mrs. Wilkinson, secretary and treasurer. Very soon a deep interest was manifested by the managers and visitors in my behalf while many who had never visited the hospital before, hearing of my singular case, called to see me, and my table was kept loaded with flowers and delicacies of every description. I soon gained many warm and devoted friends, who strove in every possible way to divert my mind from my many sorrows, but my mental strength had entirely failed, and I wept unceasingly, through the long, lonely hours of night, being haunted by thoughts of my motherless children, and the face of their father, whose eyes seemed burning into my soul like coals of fire, while the thin, cruel lips were ever parted with some taunt or fearful threat. I had been an inmate of the hospital two or three months, and my physical condition was somewhat improved under the careful treatment of the kind and proficient physician, Dr. Brevard, when I met with a great loss. A telegram was received, bearing the sad intelligence that brother Edgar was no more. He had died suddenly in a strange place, leaving to the cold mercy of the world, a delicate young wife and three small children. I remembered his words, when he last visited me. Walking up and down the room, suddenly he stopped before my bed, saying, "Edna, you will live years after I am dead and buried." "Why," said I, "you have changed your opinion. You did think it useless to try to regain my health." "Yes, I think differently now. You will yet live to see and walk."

His words were prophetic. Presently passing from my room, he said he would return and say good-bye, but business prevented and he never saw me again. Shortly thereafter came the news of his death. His last words, "You will see and walk," filled me with strange, sad longing. Could it be ! Would I yet see my darling children ! Were he and my mother led of God to speak thus? I believed they were, and that I would yet see and walk as they had predicted.

I could have borne his death better, could I have been with him, but oh! it was so hard to have him die a "stranger in a strange land—unhonored and unblest!" Had I even been able to have rendered him some small service, or to have spoken a comforting word to his desolate, crushed wife, this fact, in itself, would have been consoling. He being the only member of my family able to assist me, my grief was even more poignant.

A notice in a Charlotte paper spoke in great praise of his energy and brilliant prospects, stating time alone was necessary to make him *a prosperous and wealthy man.*

> Eyes that are closed to earthly sight
> Can never wake to weep,
> Nor pain, nor woe, nor grief, nor blight,
> Can move that slumber deep."
>
> His sleep is sweet, without a care,
> Feels not the cold, nor heeds the storm,
> Near his Saviour, without a fear,
> He waits the resurection morn.

But, as mother had once repeated to me, during one of my hours of despondency, "With all your sorrow, you have one comfort: your children are clever and pretty; you must remember, Edna, 'God tempers the wind to the shorn lamb.'" So the winds were now tempered to me. My friends read, sang and talked to me. In Mrs. Wilkinson, I found a second Mrs. Yonge. She spent many hours by my bed, and I learned to depend upon her very soon. She was a noble woman and her efforts in my behalf seemed untiring; her strong energetic spirit and the deep love she awakened in my heart for her often caused my sensitive, weak frame to tremble with pleasure. Mrs. Fanen likewise was a kind and good woman, being an active worker in the "Master's Vineyard," and did much to contribute to my happiness and comfort. I will not attempt to describe the many other dear friends, who took such an interest in my welfare (they were so numerous, over one hundred and fifty, it would take a volume to do them justice). However, I will say they were among the noblest and best. Three dear ones especially were my spiritual comforters. One, a sweet woman, I accidentally discovered, had been one of the merry party who had laughed at me in Asheville, years before; but I loved her now, and she failed to recognize in the unhappy creature before her, the healthy young girl whose draggled appearance had excited her mirth in "days of yore." I had prayed for friends, and my prayers were answered; but for this I would have died. I now received comforting letters from all my old friends, and one from mother containing the following lines :

"TO MY DAUGHTER."

My child, the cold dews of evening are around thee,
    Bereft of thy sight,
And dark lines of sorrow and trials surround thee,
    By day and by night.

To-day I am sitting so dreary and lonely,
    Heartsick and in pain,
And wishing 'twere Heaven's will I could only
    Once see thee again.

If so, I could bear all the pain and the sorrow
    Of life and its cares,
And not fill the hours of the coming to-morrow
    With sighs and with tears.

Like you, many hopes of the future I cherished
    When free from life's care;
Just so, all my brightest fond visions have perished
    Like mists in the air.

I still hope that God, in his merciful kindness,
    Thy sight will restore,
And permit thee, when perfectly healed of thy blindness,
    To see us once more.

But restore thee or not, one hope I will cherish,
    At home and abroad,
That I may submit to my fate, though I perish,
    And trust in my God.

I shed many tears o'er the ruined prospect of my father's family. The property he had fairly purchased in Mitchell county, and honorably owned, was now under a heavy lawsuit, the former owners pretending there was a flaw in the deed. He, together with my youngest brother, was now publishing a paper called the "Mountain Voice."

Financial pressure was added to our other troubles. I had been in the hospital about six months, when my physicians said they had done all they could for me. They advised me to go North, saying there was a possibility of recovery under treatment of physicians more skilled than they. I was deeply grieved at the thought of leaving the dear friends and the hospital where I had received such untiring kind treatment, to whom I had become so much attached, to go among cold, disinterested strangers. I was so weary and exhausted from continual grief for my children, not knowing where they were nor what was being done for them, which even the great kindness of my friends had failed to overcome, that I did not have sufficient courage to make another struggle.

The inflamed cartilages, which connected the vertebrae in my spine, were now strong enough to admit of my sitting up a few moments, but I was fearful that if I should again be moved, I would receive fresh injury. My eyes were beginning to open, and I could dimly discern the outline of objects within the range of my vision, but I was too overwhelmed by grief about my children to rejoice at this unexpected good fortune. Yet I smiled in the presence of visitors, partially hiding from them my mental suffering. When alone I would sing low to myself the dear old songs of childhood to relieve my full soul and keep up courage for another change. After many prayers, I was given courage and faith to take the dreaded journey, trusting in God's promises. At this time, I received visits from my mother and Mrs. Chriton, who strongly encouraged me to act upon my physician's advice. It had been between two and three years since I had met my mother ; during these years we both had passed through scenes of fearful suffering. She was still weak and nervous, but was determined to come to see me. Father was prevented from joining her on account of business perplexities. His business no longer prospered as it had in former years. I must not forget to mention that about fifty sweet little children were numbered among my regular visitors. They came often, bringing flowers, fruits, cakes, etc. When all the necessary arrangements were made, principally by Mrs. Wilkinson, for my comfort, and I again was placed on my stretcher, many of these children, with my mother, Mrs. Wilkinson and other friends, accompanied me to the train, and with tears, kisses and best wishes, bade me "Godspeed !" I was put in care of a Mrs. Thurmond, who was returning to Washington, and placed in a comfortable sleeper. Feeling that God was with me, I gently dropped to sleep. Arriving in Washington the next morning about nine o'clock, I was taken in an ambulance to the Columbia Hospital, and was left in charge of Dr. Murphy. He was a very intelligent and learned Irish gentleman, and underneath his gruff and surly manner, beat a warm and generous heart.

Unfortunately, I learned that my diseases did not come under his line of treatment, but he promised to do all he could for me. In the meantime he told me that my friends would better make arrangements to have me admitted into some other good hospital. My parents, being unable to bear my expenses, I was placed in the free ward, which was filled with the lower class of Germans, Irish and Americans, and was compelled to pass the long, weary days in the society of these coarse, uncongenial companions. Only the strong desire to return to my suffering children enabled me to endure the thought of receiving charity. In addition to my other sorrows my cheeks now burned with mortification and humiliation, but I felt that God was helping me and not the people, although they were instruments in his hands. I had never asked help from any one but Him.

Mother, in her great distress, had appealed to a few of her wealthy relatives living in distant States, for help, they, in former days having expressed interest and affection for her. One of them advised her to trust in God, another politely and coldly refused, saying he must look to the interest of his own family, while two did not reply. She did not make another attempt in that line. Mrs. Terwald, the matron of the hospital, was very kind,

but was making preparations to visit Montana, and I saw
but little of her. In Miss Sewell, a lovely lady who
took charge in her absence, I found another sympathizing friend and a good Christian. The marked attention
that she and ladies in other rooms paid me, subjected
me to the jealous criticisms of a few ill-natured patients
in my room, and I was made to feel very uncomfortable.
Through the influence of Mrs. Wilkinson, my Charlotte
friend, I was visited by many nice people, among them
the daughters of Admiral Wilkes, Mrs. Judge Stockerd
and Mr. Curtis, an Episcopal clergyman. For the first
time in nearly six years I slept soundly as a tired child the
entire night through, only free from physical pain, but
the inmates of the hospital were often aroused by my
thrilling, piercing screams, caused by horrible visions of
my suffering children—frightful nightmares in my dreams
of trying to secure 'my children. Often I thought I
would start with them through a dark wood, would
nearly reach the station where we would take the train,
when Mr. Roderick, his brother and sisters, Harriet and
Rachel, would suddenly dash down upon us, and my wild,
agonized screams would arouse many in the hospital,
even those upon the third floor, so heartrending and despairing were my cries. This sleep, though disturbed by
frightful dreams, gave me new strength, and I soon became
strong enough to sit up several hours through the day.
My eyes also grew stronger, the pain having partially
abated; and now, oh, joy! I could see across my room,
and see the faces of my visitors. At first they only remained open a minute or so at a time, and often they
would close at intervals of several days, causing great

anxiety as to whether they would ever open again. I had been blind about six years, and it would be useless to attempt to describe my feelings upon finding that I was not hopelessly so.

A deep interest was now manifested in my behalf by Mrs. Terwald, who had returned, and also by the nurses and patients—the unkind feeling was gone. Eliza Reeves, an orphan girl, became very much attached to me, and often sat by my bed, reading in a sweet, pathetic voice, passages from the Bible and other religious books. I had already found friends among those I had looked upon as cold strangers, and know that they had been provided by my Heavenly Friend.

I had been in this hospital ten weeks, when Mrs. Thurmond informed me that she had made arrangements to have me admitted into a fine hospital in Baltimore. I had been left in her charge by my mother and Mrs. Wilkinson. She was a stranger, but had volunteered her services, and had been very kind. I felt like one in a dream when I was seated in a carriage, by her side, and found that I was once more able to see the beautiful sky, and streets lined with magnificent shade trees and fine palace-like residences. It seemed like some wonderful vision, too unreal to be true. I had lain so long in darkness, my fingers doing the work of eyes, that I felt deeply impressed with everything I saw, as it all seemed so strange and new.

When we reached the depot, I was too weary to sit up longer, and was again placed on a stretcher and carried to Baltimore. As Mrs. Thurmond did not feel well enough to go with me, I was accompanied by Mr. Thurmond, her husband. Arriving in Baltimore, I was sur-

prised to learn that there had been no arrangements made
for my admission into any hospital.   Mr. Thurmond took
me to one hospital and begged them to let me remain
until he could make arrangements elsewhere.   I was carried upstairs and left in a large, well lighted room.   Looking around I observed three other patients.   The first
was an uncouth Irish girl, who had her head bound in a
handkerchief ; the second was a small, red-headed girl of
twelve years, who was afflicted with St. Vitus' dance ;
the third, a strange-looking German girl.   The nurse,
who entered soon, questioned me sharply as to where I
had come from and the nature of my disease.   She was
a spinster of about forty summers, with keen, cold, black
eyes, and her name was Sally Johnson.   I anxiously
awaited Mr. Thurmond's return as the gloomy atmosphere of the room threw a chill over my spirits.   At length
he came and said it was impossible for him to remove me
that day as he was compelled to return immediately to
Washington, but said that he had made arrangements
with a friend to take me to another hospital the next day,
as the one I was in at that time did not admit free patients out of the city.   Just before dark a number of students came around and asked me many questions.   I was
indeed drinking the bitter cup of humiliation, being subjected to a pauper's treatment and classed with them. My
soul was filled with fear and dread of the place, and I
longed for the night to pass that I might leave its gloomy
portals.   All the next day I listened anxiously for the
welcome voice of Mr. Thurmond's friend.   Would he
never come!? Night sat in drearily, for I knew I had
been cruelly deceived and left alone and friendless in a
large, strange city.   Nurse Sally questioned me sus-

piciously regarding my friend's strange desertion, and in a few days my despair and misery bordered on to madness. Sally, finding that I was friendless and forsaken, shook and dragged me about mercilessly. My pride, will, and independent spirit, were entirely crushed, and I begged her in tears not to add to the pain I already suffered. My tears and entreaties had no effect on her hard, cruel nature. She was determined that I should walk and continued to shake and drag me about until I could with difficulty breathe from pain and weakness. She refused to give me water and would not allow the patients to do it, saying that if I wanted it to get it myself. I was able to sit up, but could not bear any weight on my weak and almost paralyzed limbs, consequently was compelled to live without water, and also was neglected in many other distressing ways.

The pain and inflammation in my spine from this severe treatment became almost unbearable. She taunted me with my friendlessness and being separated from my husband, said she guessed they sent me off to get rid of a troublesome burden. The patients were afraid to interfere, and sat coldly by without speaking. When the physicians made their daily rounds, accompanied by a large number of students, I ventured to tell them how Sally treated me. This only added to my distress as she inflicted fresh tortures when she learned that I had been making complaints. Dr. Trimble, the physician to whom I appealed, was as cold and heartless as she, agreeing with her that I could walk if I would. Other patients had been brought in, and two of them were placed on either side of my bed. One a large, coarse, filthy Irish woman, with a broken limb; the other a more decent person, yet ignorant and common. On the opposite side of the room were patients, victims of typhoid fever and like diseases. One of these poor creatures and the one with the broken limb were subjected to most unkind and cruel treatment. I was greatly distressed by being an eye-witness to their sufferings. Their friends were not allowed to visit them. The sufferer from typhoid fever vainly tried to leap from a window in a frantic endeavor to escape, and when a large club, which was brandished over her head, failed to subdue her, she was held under water until nearly suffocated. Mr. and Mrs. Thurmond had taken what money I had, so I could not pay my fare back to Washington and had no one to write to my parents, who were not yet aware that I had been moved. The past eleven years of my life arose before me like some ghastly, mocking phantom, pointing to my mistakes and wrecked life, tearing open old wounds. My suffering had only been lessened for a time that I might gain strength for this new affliction. I feared I would go mad as I could no longer eat, sleep, pray nor weep, only one cry arose to my lips: "My God! my God! why hast thou forsaken me?" My faith was shaken. Why did God permit such abuses? Why had he brought me through so much and then at last left me to die homeless, helpless, friendless and alone in a great city, surrounded with horrors and suffering?

A sudden impulse seized me. I reached a postal card which was lying on my table, and scrawled, almost illegibly, the words agreed upon previously as a signal of distress by brother Bradley and myself, "Then you'll remember me." I handed the card to the patient who occupied the bed next to mine and begged her to mail it when she left the hospital, which she did in a few days. My nurse grew more merciless every day and I longingly watched the door, hoping to see some familiar face, though I knew this was useless as my friends were hundreds of miles away. I also watched the busy throng surging through the streets, and the large, imposing residences on the opposite side, wondering could I make my distress known to the inmates would they pass me coldly by. Even the dreaded face of Mr. Roderick would then have been a welcome sight. My limbs and a large portion of my body were covered with painful, purple bruises received at the cruel hands of my nurse. My physical pain was greatly increased. Tears, food, sleep and even prayer forsook me for days and I lay in such terrible mental anguish that my brain seemed on fire—my memory a blank. Madness seemed inevitable, and I was not the only sufferer at the hands of those cruel rulers of that hospital. Poor, sick, suffering humanity! The Homes purporting to care for and bless you are sometimes a curse and a torture. "Things are not always what they seem." And while many of them are indeed a blessing to our land, some few are more than a curse and fraud. My eyes were now wide open, though they were very weak, yet I could see quite distinctly.

My parents received my card and money was sent to me to return to Washington. They also wrote to the Masons to visit me, my father being a Master Mason in high standing. I did not wait, but got the hospital physician, Dr. West, to send me to the depot in an ambulance, and returned to Washington in a breakfast cap, wrapper and slippers, which, with my short, straggling hair (it having been cut off in the hospital), and large colored glasses, caused looks of wonder from those whom I met. The man who drove the ambulance tenderly lifted me into the car, purchased my ticket, checked my trunk, then left me in the care of the conductor, who kindly assisted me from the car, and engaged a cab to take me to " Providence Hospital," where I was admitted, through the influence of Miss Jennie Wilkinson. May God forever bless the kind-hearted men who drove the ambulance and cab, and the pleasant conductors! They had spoken almost the only kind words I had heard in the last four fearful weeks of misery. How thankful I felt when I found that I was once more safe from the reach of cruel, hard-hearted people, and outside of the tall, massive building which had seemed to me like some awful, gloomy dungeon, in which the unfortunate, miserable prisoners pine for life-giving words and affection. Kind words cost nothing, but often heal a broken heart; and yet so many forget to speak them! " Providence Hospital " was under the management of the "Sisters of Charity." One glance into their pure, good faces was sufficient to satisfy me that I would be kindly treated while with them. I was taken to the fourth floor and placed in a spacious, pleasant room, containing nineteen beds. 'Twas my joy to find among the patients Eliza Reeves, the orphan girl of "Columbia Hospital." She was startled by the look of agony in my face, and it was whispered among the patients that I had come there to die. But I was now almost happy, surrounded by kind faces on every side, kind doctors, kind nurses, and kind, holy "Sisters of Charity." At last my wandering feet had found rest. My physicians now pronounced my disease inflammation of the membranous coverings of the spinal cord, and spinal irritation. My trial of faith had been severe and the waiting long, but I was to receive the blessing I had so longed for. The medical treatment given me was simple and effective. God stretched forth his hands and blessed it, and a sudden and miraculous change was apparent in my physical condition. I walked; my first attempts at walking were very painful and ludicrous, as I was compelled to hitch and slide upon the floor to relieve my swollen, aching feet and drawn limbs, unable to set my feet level upon the floor. My tottering steps were guided by the hand of Eliza Reeves, who, as I, was striving to regain lost health. I felt so thankful to God for leading me through the "dark waters." Praises to His holy name! I was once more enabled to see and walk, and to report the glad tidings home to my distressed parents. The letter bearing the news of my recovery found my parents at church with prayer for their afflicted daughter; the answer came, saying I could see and walk. The joyful news was so gratefully received that thanks to God were immediately offered in the church, and the news afterwards published in the papers for the benefit of my friends.

One day I asked for a mirror, and when it was handed me I shrank from the face reflected therein! The face I now saw was dark, haggard and sallow, lined with purple veins and heavy dark circles under the eyes, so little resembling the face I had seen six years ago that I would not have recognized myself. I could not bear the change, and with a deep sigh for the health and happiness of which I had been robbed I laid the glass aside. I soon became deeply attached to the "Sisters." "Sister Beatrice," or "Sister Superior," was a kind, motherly woman, apparently about fifty-five years of age. She allowed me many privileges, which again aroused the jealousy of some of the patients in my ward; for a time I was exposed to their malicious tongues. This feeling, however, soon died away, and I afterwards became quite a favorite even with the rough patients. My room was always full of patients, and I saw suffering in its most distressing forms, some were afflicted with epilepsy, others with asthma, and other distressing diseases. It was a ward especially for the poor, and was filled from the lowest class in Washington, yet I never saw the sweet "Sisters" treat any one with disrespect or unkindness. While here I became acquainted with some nice ladies in private rooms, who took an especial interest in my sad history. They seemed to desire my society, and before I left were my friends. More "angels of mercy" provided by God! How could I ever have doubted Him?

Early in December, 1884, assisted by Miss Nettie McCameron, a fair young lady from North Carolina, to whom my parents had written in my behalf, I made arrangements to return home, although cordially invited by "Sister Beatrice" to remain with them during the Christmas holidays; but I was anxious to see all the loved ones, and weary of being confined to a sick-room. With a heart full of gratitude, I bade the dear "Sisters" and friends farewell, and for the first time in six long, long years I stood upon the ground, and, accompanied by a friend, walked down a beautiful street near the Capitol, no longer helpless and blind, but seeing and walking as other people! I counted the hours that must intervene before I could look on the faces of my children, parents, brothers and friends. After examining the spot where our noble President had fallen, I entered a comfortable coach and received a farewell kiss from my friend Miss Nettie, whose energy and loving care had provided me with everything necessary for my comfort and pleasure. My heart swelled with intense joy and my pulses throbbed with excitement at the thought of the great pleasure awaiting me. Homeward bound! home again! the rattle of the cars seemed to say. My joy was too great for utterance, and prayers and thanks for the blessings God had again bestowed upon me filled my heart. The hours could not pass fast enough, so eager was I to see face to face father, mother, home, children, and the other dear ones.

The many prayers and those which had been made for my recovery by churches and friends were now answered, and I was returning home walking and seeing.

THANKS TO PROVIDENCE HOSPITAL.

In our own native land a hospital stands,
   Its praises I faintly would speak,
To me it seems grand, enclosed in love's bands
   By the sisters of charity meek.

These sisters are lowly and humble and holy,
   All striving their God to obey,
They watch o'er the poorly, while dreaming they surely
   Can all of their sufferings allay.

Heaven's blessings are resting on them as they're testing
   Their freedom from sorrow and sin,
And God will uphold them and angels enfold them
   Till a heavenly crown they shall win.

My happiness lost on the world tempest-tossed,
   Weary and heart-sick with pain,

Providentially I came to Providence by name,
  Where my health I did quickly regain.

In language though weak my thoughts I would speak,
  My gratitude is without bounds.
To my nurses while blind and physicians so kind
  And the owners of Providence grounds.

SCENE ON THE ATLANTIC OCEAN.

The moaning ship and waters seemed to bewail my future.

PART II.

CHAPTER VIII.

"AFTER MANY DAYS."

"Only thy restless heart keep still,
  And wait in cheerful hope; content
To take what'er His gracious will,
  His all discerning love hath sent;
Nor doubt, our inmost wants are known
  To him who choose us for His own."

 LEFT Washington on the night train and sat with my face pressed against the window, peering into the gloom, through which we were flying, and thinking of the many changes that had taken place since first I traveled over this road, a happy young girl with a heart full of sunshine and hope, while now I was a sorrowful world-weary woman, seeming to have grown fifty years older in the past six years of suffering, which had brought me very near my dear Saviour, although they had robbed me of every earthly hope and pleasure. In some mysterious way I had received my sight without the treatment of scientific oculists; by some unseen hand my spine was being healed without the support of braces or artificial means, except such simple remedies as I had

used from the beginning of my illness. Some unseen influence had provided me with friends and means necessary for my comfort and recovery. Even my wardrobe had been replenished at a time when I discovered that I could see and walk, but was coatless, hatless, shoeless and far from friends.

Would God leave his work unfinished? If he had restored me in answer to prayer, would he not give me those I had prayed for six sad sorrowing years to be spared for, my children? Yes, I believed he would. I could not feel it my duty to again live with Mr. Roderick. In fact, I believed it would be a sin under existing circumstances, for though my physical condition was greatly improved, still I was very frail and my mental faculties had become much weaker and I felt unable to endure unkind words, harsh treatment or severe trials and sorrows. It only lacked a few months of being two years since I left my home seemingly a hopeless wreck, and was carried on a stretcher over this road with closed, aching eyes and paralyzed frame, and now I trembled with intensity of feeling at thoughts of soon being permitted to look upon the faces of my children and other loved ones. My own children for whom I had suffered and sacrificed so much, would they recognize me! Had their young hearts been influenced again against their mother! Were they suffering and unhappy? I asked myself. My heart hungered for their love and tender caresses. God speed the moments until I shall meet them.

My parents lived thirty-five miles from the railroad across the Blue Ridge Mountains. They were not expecting me so soon and I felt too weak and weary to think of undertaking the rough fatiguing journey until rested ; and as I did not feel physically and mentally strong enough to meet those in Marion who were unkindly disposed toward me, I concluded to pass through and continue my way to Old Fort, where I felt sure I would receive a warm welcome. After traveling two nights I arrived there just before day. My friends were not aware of my coming, and I was compelled to call upon a stranger to show me the way to Mrs. Tremont's house, Mrs. Tremont being no other than my old friend Ada.

Once more I was walking through the place where I had spent my childhood days, and had become a trusting bride. Oh! that home, the connecting link of my joyous early life—my bright girlhood so soon blighted in that fatal mistake! Was it a wonder I loved to return to its dear walls to dwell upon that happy, dead past, to somewhat feel I was once that happy being and call up from memory's store all the dear old associations! I trembled at the recollections and the knowledge that I would soon look upon the dear faces of old familiar friends, yet saddened by the thoughts that one of the loved members had gone to her last resting place. Dear Mrs. McCoy had departed this life while I was in Charlotte, and Old Fort seemed desolate without her. My friends were not up and I waited several moments at the door before being admitted. In the lady who greeted me, surrounded by small, pretty children, I recognized the mirthful girl I had gayly laughed and chatted with years before. During the week following I was called upon by all my Old Fort friends and cordially welcomed and invited to remain with them.

The weather set in cold and stormy, preventing a speedy return to Marion, where I hoped to meet my children.   A card being dispatched to Mr. Roderick, informed him of my coming and my inability to travel over rocky roads in the cold, and expressing my desire that our children be allowed to meet me in Marion.   But I was destined to be cruelly disappointed and my heart grew faint and sick when I received his cold refusal, saying that if I wanted to see his children I would have to come home.   I had waited so long, how could I bear to return to my parents without looking upon my darlings' faces ?   It seemed too cruel to be deprived of a happiness that could have been so easily granted.

Having received a kind invitation from Mrs. Yonge to pay her a visit I determined to accept it, and with feeling of timidity and dread I entered the town that had been the scene of my humiliation.   Leaving the depot I walked slowly up the familiar streets, failing to recognize the faces of old acquaintances whom I passed. I entered the hotel to rest (where I had found shelter on leaving Mr. Roderick, and had the pleasure of looking for the first time upon Mrs. Yonge's face, who had come to meet me, which was as I fancied it, sweet and pure.

My return to Marion walking and seeing was a theme of wonder and excitement and many incredulous people would not believe until they saw with their own eyes that I could really see and walk.   My strange illness and decided step I had taken in leaving Mr. Roderick had brought me unconsciously into public notice and I knew that I was watched and criticised, which was a sore trial to my nature, especially when old acquaintances avoided me who had been friendly previous to my leaving Mr. Roderick. I felt and knew that I was right in trying to save my life for my children's sake, but my nerves were so shaken by the unkind remarks that were continually floating through the community that I gave up the thought of visiting my children, as I could not brave the fury of Mr. Roderick and his unfeeling sisters, whom I was sure to meet.

In answer to my numerous inquiries I was told that my children were well and happy, and were well cared for and were attending school. I wondered if all this could be true; but hearing the same story from almost every one, I was only too willing to believe it. It was such a relief to know that my fears were groundless, even though an evil motive prompted the good deed.

In the suit that had been entered upon my leaving Mr. Roderick two years ago, the judge gave me the custody of two of my eldest daughters for some months, and an alimony until the final trial for all my children could be decided. When Mr. Roderick knew the decision of the court he took the two children given me and left the country, giving out the report that he had taken them to Texas, but in reality crossed the mountains to Tennessee. Into a covered wagon he thrust them together with a large box into which he would hide them if any one approached. Arriving in a small town in Tennessee, he stopped, still reserving the box into which he would store the children if he thought any danger of discovery. Fearing to remain in town he took them into the country, boarding at a farm in a lonely, secluded spot. With the story of their heartless mother forsaking them, he won the sympathy of the people and made his way easy.

After the term expired he returned with the two children and again placed them under the selfish care of his sisters, where they were at this time.

I had struggled so long for health and was afraid my nerves would receive some severe shock, and I also thought the extra sixteen miles through the mud and cold in addition to the tedious journey across the mountains would again lay me upon a sick bed, so I decided to wait until I had strength; listening to the voice of reason rather than the promptings of my heart, which continually cried out for little voices so long hushed to me, for little forms flitting before eyes less loving than a mother's, for little hands on others bestowing caresses.

A familiar face was at the door, a face more haggard and careworn than when I saw it last, more than six years ago, the beard whiter, longer, but the kind, tender look unchanged. My dear father! with mingled feelings of sorrow and happiness I greeted him; forcing back the tears wrung from me by my great disappointment at not seeing my children, I prepared to return with him.

Crossing the mountain in winter is anything but pleasant. It was now the middle of January and the muddy roads almost impassable. Only ten miles were gained the first day; the second day, which was extremely cold, muddy and blowing snow, we reached the top of the Blue Ridge, all the fine scenery through which we passed was entirely hid from my view by a shawl that enveloped head and face for protection against the bitter wind and flying snow. Finding it impossible for us to proceed, father left me in care of hospitable Mrs. McDuff, a friend of my childhood who was living on the top of the mountain, while he continued his way to Bakersville, promising to send for me as soon as the weather moderated and I became rested.

While here, my loved brother Harry, who was married and lived near, came to see me. In the tall, fine looking young man, with a small, pretty woman clinging to his arm, I failed to recognize my young brother, and we both gazed curiously at each other after meeting, wondering at the great change that had taken place in the past. A few days later Mrs. McDuff said a young gentleman wanted to see me. Bidding her ask him come in, I glanced carelessly toward him as he entered the room, then eagerly, then anxiously. Was this Charley? this young man the little boy I had spent so many hours searching for, and at length find engaged in some boyish mischief? Yes, it was he; and in a moment I was kissing him with delighted surprise. It was hard to realize that during my six years of blindness the two boys had become men. Charley had come for me; and after bidding Mrs. McDuff (who had become deeply interested in my affairs) and her family good-bye, we started home, over rocks and hills, through mud-holes and rivers; and just as night with its gloomy shadows was throwing its sombre mantle over mother earth, as if ashamed of the wickedness it beheld, and with a frown of displeasure was attempting to shield her from the wrath to come, we drove into Bakersville, a town lying at the foot of Roan mountain, surrounded by hills, and the county site of Mitchell.

Not waiting for assistance, I climbed from the hack,

which had stopped before father's door, and hastened toward the house, where I met a white-faced, white-haired woman—my mother. Was it possible! I was shocked at the change wrought by great sorrow, which I knew had been suffered on my account. Poor mother! Like myself, she had endured untold anguish, and was a wreck of her former self. Mr. Roderick had once said that Dr. G., my Shelby physician, had advised him to take me away from her, because she believed that I was suffering, and sympathized with me. This was his pitiful excuse for removing me from Shelby when nigh unto death. Cruel people, they would have deprived me of the one friend and the loving sympathy that sustained me through shadows dark and heavy that compassed me upon every side. Oh God! how could such injustice have been permitted? Truly man's ways are past finding out, and yet I know that Thy hand has led me and Thy strength sustaineth me.

I had come home to stay, and my parents' hearts and steps grew lighter and their strength increased with new hope and courage. All the tender chords of my heart were touched at sight of the delight expressed on their care-worn faces over my return and at the tender solicitude for my comfort, while I felt I owed them a life's care for the trouble I had unwillingly caused them. That night I had the pleasure of meeting my dear brother Bradley and his pretty brown-eyed wife. His health had improved, and he had recently married and had started in business for himself. Many friends called soon, expressing pleasure at my wonderful recovery, as well as numbers from county and town, reading in the papers of my return and restoration. Prayers had been offered in the churches in my behalf, and they now gave thanks for my safe return. When rested sufficiently to walk out, I found that Bakersville was situated on the banks of Cane Creek, that flowed between hills and lofty mountains, breaking the silence with its soft lullabys. It was a queer looking place, with houses built upon the hill-sides and the banks of the creek, as if planted there by the force of some cyclone.

The many prayers I had offered in regard to the conversion of my people had been answered. One by one they had been brought into the fold, and my brothers, were now members of the church of God, while my parents had become interested workers in the Master's vineyard. Churches were near our home, so I was enabled to attend regularly, and was soon given a class of little girls in the Sabbath-school, which I joined upon the return of warm weather. One day my mother was sitting in her room, I standing before the mirror arranging my hair. Mother remarked upon it, when the remembrance of our dreams flashed upon us—the strange room, but our old furniture, mother in the easy chair, and her remark was all just as in our dreams, and we both realized it. We felt God was encouraging us to trust. He was with us always and would care for his own. I now heard that Mr. Roderick had changed his style of dress, playing the part of a gentleman, and was again seemingly a devoted Christian, taking an active part in the country church near where he was located.

He had left our children with his sisters and had bought some property near my father's old mill in Mitchell county; and had sworn that before he would allow me to have any of his children he would spill every drop of blood in his veins.   He was tall, powerful, with muscles that stood out like knotted cords, and a sinewy body denoting extraordinary physical strength.   He had been more than double my age when I married him, though I had not known it, and possessed an unconquerable will. Our children were in his possession.   He had political friends, many relatives and some means at his command. It seemed almost impossible for me ever to regain my darlings, but I felt that God was more mighty than many such powers, and could help me in the battle for right. False reports were circulated, damaging my cause. My children were being taught that I had wantonly forsaken them.   But I had well learned the lesson of patience.   One by one they had been torn from my arms. Sorrow had been followed by sorrow, more bitter despair by deeper despair, I could not afford to yield now even though the *world* was against me.   I remembered that I had felt sad and depressed before my marriage, and now wondered what strange influence Mr. Roderick had exercised on myself and all the members of my family, especially mother, who was very sensitive and susceptible to outside influences; but then I had often heard him laugh and boastingly say he could make any person think and act just as he wished them to, his power for deceiving was so great, and I had heard him talk bitterly of the people who now believe him a saint, so that I need not think strange of the uncanny influence he had thrown around me or wonder that I feared him.

With the exception of strange, wild looks at times, no person had observed any symptoms of insanity in his appearance, but I could not believe that I had been mistaken, and consulted several physicians, some of whom agreed with me in thinking his strange conduct due to insanity, while others said an evil, wicked spirit possessed him. As I recovered from the cold, severe journey across the mountain, that had materially increased my physical suffering, I could no longer curb my restless longing to see my children. So, one warm, bright day in May, feeling that I could not bear the unutterable wretchedness that constantly forced from me bitter tears, accompanied by my father I started to see them. An interest had been manifested in my trouble by many of the kind hearts in Bakersville, giving me courage and strength to bear the meeting, the thought of which caused me to shake as with an ague. I had no thoughts for the grand mountain scenery, no thoughts for dangers, but only for those I expected soon to meet. My heart ached with anxiety and long suspense, for "hope deferred maketh the heart sick," and I was sick with long waiting.

A wild, tumultuous tempest was raging within which no calm could soothe, no tears relieve. The first day we stopped at Mr. Cox's at the foot of the mountain. Mrs. Cox informed me that night that Mr. Roderick and his little boy had remained with them over night some time before, and had occupied the same room I was in. I wept sorely over the spot where Earnest's little feet had trod, looking long at the things hallowed by his touch, and questioned her anxiously as to his appearance and whether he had spoken of his mother.

How slowly the hours passed through the long, long night! But all things have an end some time. So morning came at last, which would bring the day with it, and, oh! happy thought, I would see my loved ones before another night.

The day was dark and dreary, and long before the midday hour the rain commenced falling. Shivering from the damp air, I drew my cloak more closely about me and shrunk into the corner of our covered buggy. As we passed through Marion father showed me the house Mr. Roderick and I had occupied during my blindness. The sight of the room that had been the scene of my suffering filled my soul with sad and bitter reflections. It was here I had passed through the fiery ordeal of leaving home and children; it was here I had lain hours, days, weeks, months in utter blindness: it was here Stella or Earnest had sat by my bedside holding my hand or stroking my hair; here Mr. Roderick had uttered those last cruel, bitter words that had driven me in despair from him forever; here I had been comforted with sympathizing words from my friends, and here I had lain for hours sadly listening to the church bells, but unable to enter the church portals.

Now I was walking and seeing and on my way to see Stella, Earnest and Marie, whose faces I had not looked upon for nearly seven years ; on my way to see little Bertha and Celeste, whose faces I had never seen, and I would also see the place where I had suffered for five wretched months ; see the cruel people who had tortured me until heart and flesh quivered in mortal agony, and they were still rendering my heart strings with anxiety for my precious little ones.

I was determined to be brave and not let my enemies see the pain they inflicted; to hide my tears and appear indifferent in their presence. This required unnatural mental strain, so while praying for strength to bear the pain and the pleasure in store we drove rapidly on.

By 12 o'clock the rain was falling in torrents and in spite of all father's efforts to protect me a portion of my body became drenched. Stopping at a farm house by the way-side I was helped from the buggy, as my limbs were so cold and cramped I could not stand alone. Warming by a large fire the good-natured farmer hastened to build upon our entrance, after a comfortable meal and getting our garments and wraps dried, we prepared to start upon the last eight miles of our journey.

Noticing that the railroad ran in sight I asked the farmer's wife if we were near the place where a blind and helpless woman had been carried nearly three years ago.

"Yes," she cried. "That spot," pointing with her finger to a point on the railroad, "is the very place where a large crowd of men brought her from her home and placed her on a hand-car to be rolled to Marion. I saw it all from my door."

"I am that woman," I said quietly. She looked at me in astonishment.

"Is it possible!" But I was lost to her other exclamations, my thoughts wandering back to the sad scene that had taken place long ago, where I, the chief actor, yet a silent, powerless one, was carried upon a stretcher under dark curtains, hoping against hope that this last effort might be crowned with success and I be permitted to remain with my dear little children, for whom I would so willingly have died.

Very soon we were driving by the Nebo Camp Ground, which had for me many pleasant and painful recollections. I had first visited this place a merry, light-hearted girl, surrounded by gay and pleasant friends of both sexes. On my second visit I had been a wife not quite a year. I remembered that I had then been sad and melancholy without fully realizing the cause. On my third visit I was the unhappy, sad-faced mother of a poor little girl scarcely three months old. The fourth visit had been made when Stella was over a year old and shortly before we moved to Shelby. I had basked that day in the sunshine of my Old Fort friends, whom I dearly loved, forgetting in their presence a part of my sorrow, and in consequence of this thoughtless act had been kept awake until nearly midnight listening to the moans and complaints of Mr. Roderick, who loudly bewailed the fate that had given him a wife who could enjoy herself in other society than her husband's. Thus a dark cloud had been thrown upon my momentary pleasure. Once more I was on the spot under very different circumstances: the mother of five children, not one of whom I would recognize should I meet them and whom I knew would not know their own mother. In a few days I would be twenty-nine years old; part of these years seemed a blank. I felt as one in a dream, from which I vainly tried to awaken, for I could not realize that I was over twenty-two, the age I was when I lost my sight, and yet I felt old; old in care and anxiety, old in pain, old in sorrow, old in disappointment and bitter experiences.

It was all very strange, yet a sad reality. But where are we? Father looked puzzled, I anxious. By this time we should have been passing through familiar places, but all is strange on this road. Yes, we both concluded we had taken the wrong road. My spirit sank, I was so tired and cold. Making some inquiries of a farmer we learned that we had traveled two miles in the wrong direction and would be compelled to go back to Nebo and take a fresh start, which would make four miles of useless traveling in the mud and rain, and delay the time I had calculated upon meeting my children. Father becoming alarmed at my being so long in the rain urged forward the tired horse and soon we were back at Nebo when we took another road, which proved to be the right one.

In spite of my discomfort I could not help but admire the beautiful green trees, intermingled with wild flowers and plants that lined the road we were traveling. I had loved the woods from my childhood and found pleasure wandering beneath the sheltering branches of lofty trees or sitting within their huge arms absorbed in books and pleasant reveries while hid from passers by. But I must not digress, as perhaps my readers feel something of the anxiety that filled my soul to meet my children. We were now passing Mr. Sims' house, where I had once been a welcome visitor, but now they were my enemies, because I had left Mr. Roderick.

Mrs. Sims was standing in the door. I wondered if she knew me, but I concluded as she did not speak she did not recognize us or did not want to speak. I would like to have asked her if my children were still with Mr. Roderick's people, and if they were well, but as I wished to surprise them I concluded it was best not to make ourselves known to enemies who might send word before us of our coming.

Another mile brought us within half a mile of Mr. Roderick's farm, where I had spent those six years of horror and despair. I felt a strong desire to see the place, but could not take time now. Stopping at Mr. Kelton's house, one of our old neighbors, father borrowed some wraps, as mine were wet through, and we still had four miles of rough road. I was informed here that my children were still with Mr. Roderick's sisters. Relieved of the uneasiness I had suffered in regard to these questions, I prepared to endure as patiently as possible the rest of the tedious journey. Persons who have never traveled over the country roads of Western North Carolina will have but a faint idea of the slow, wearisome lurching and wrenching to which a traveler is exposed, therefore they could not sympathize with my weariness. The excitement caused by the happy thought that it could not be long before I would be with my dear ones set my heart wildly throbbing, sending a feverish current through my veins and prevented my suffering with the damp and cold as I had done all day. Two miles were traveled over and now there were but two more, which lay through the woods.

Here two or three roads confronted us, but finally we decided the anxious question as best we could and continued our way for a mile or more, when again we were puzzled by the strangeness of surrounding objects, so we concluded we must have taken the wrong road. My spirit fell to zero. Surrounded by woods, night not far away and the rain still falling, it almost seemed as if fate was against my ever seeing my children again. I could not repress tears and moans forced from me by agonizing suspense and the pain I suffered in my cramped and aching body.

Father tried to comfort me by saying that he believed that we were right, but there had been some changes since we were here. "See," he said, "there is a little hut in the woods, you take the reins while I make some inquiries.

"Don't weep, Edner," he said upon returning, " we are right and very near your children."

I was weak to allow my feelings to master me just as my long, passionate yearnings were about to be gratified. It will never do, O my God! help me to bear whatever may be in store. Turning into the lane which led to the house we found it was crowded with limbs and bushes, which rendered it almost impassable, but we were determined to get through some way and we succeeded, although the wet limbs scratched our buggy top and shook showers of water in our laps and faces. I was wild with anticipation, and strained my nerves to catch some sound from the house, now within sight, but all was still as death ; not even the dogs, which had ever announced the approach of a stranger, gave a warning bark. No one saw us enter the gate leading to the house, all was silent.

That my readers may better understand my impressions upon seeing my children I will give a brief description of the place where they now lived. Mr. Roderick's father had once been a well-to-do farmer. Came of good family who claimed to be descendants of a signer of the Declaration of Independence and were of good blood. His people were of great prominence in the State at one time. But misfortune and varied circumstances had brought them to a low plane of life. His father did not forget his early training and had naturally a kind heart. Once he had come to my bed, looking kindly down upon me, said "Edna, I am sorry to see you suffer so, God

knows I would have things different here if I could."
Poor old man ! Now he rests in his grave.

They now owned a large tract of poor ridge land
which is too barren to produce sufficent bread for the
family, consequently they are in a state of semi-starvation. All the members of the family are tall and gaunt
and generally hungry except when they visit some of
their neighbors and stow away an astonishing supply of
food, which gives them courage to take another trip and
loosens their vigorous tongues for a fresh bit of scandal.
Three or four hounds lie about their doors, so poor that
a sight of their skeleton frames would cause a shudder to
pass over the observer. Their buildings consist of a
large log house erected many years ago, only two of
its rooms, sufficient for the family to sleep in, ever having been finished. The windows, being planked up made
them dark, damp and gloomy. A small log hut daubed
with red clay stood near this building which the family
used to cook, eat and sleep in. This hut like the other
buildings was cold, filthy, and uncomfortable, it having
two doors opposite each other that were kept open summer and winter to admit light.

The family cooked their corn dodgers and greaseless
salads by open fire place and used their cooking utensils
for many other purposes. The female members of the
family worked hard with their hands as well as their
tongues, picked berries, dug roots, gathered herbs to sell
and carried grain upon their backs to mill a distance of
two and one half miles and did all kinds of rough outdoor labor which prevented their taking proper care of
their persons or house and rendered them unfit to have
the care of delicate children.

As father helped me from the buggy I saw Harriet's tall form, clad in a ragged cotton frock standing before the door of the hut. "Thar's your mother," I heard her say to some one within. I did not wait for an invitation to enter, but walked boldly and calmly through the open door, my will now having all my feelings under subjection.

"Good evening," I said quietly, at the same time glancing around the cheerless room, when my eyes rested upon a tall, thin child of about ten summers, the face which was pale, even livid, was turned to me, the flaxen hair, forehead and blue eyes giving it a slightly familiar look while the bare limbs and feet were poorly hidden by a soiled cotton frock.

"Is this Stella?" I asked, approaching the child.

"Yes that's Steller," Harriet replied.

Clasping the little ragged form in my arms I kissed the pale, thin cheeks repeatedly, saying "my poor little girl, are you glad to see your mother?" "Yes'm," she answered hesitatively, looking shy and half smiling while I turned to look for some of my other children, and after giving a careless glance at a small, ragged, dirty boy with a straw hat pulled far down upon his ears, while beneath the brim and through holes in the crown straggling locks of hair were visible. I asked for Earnest.

"Thar he is," said Harriet, pointing to the dirty boy in the chimney corner.

That Earnest! I said in surprise, striving to force back the lump in my throat, which choked me at sight of Stella, my dear eldest born, and this forlorn little object who they said was my boy. I kissed him over and over,

12

stifling the pain in my heart as best I could, for these people should not have the satisfaction of knowing how they trampled upon my breaking heart, and I knew that the only hope to gain my children lay in my seeming independence and courage. I must be externally bold and resolute, even though my heart fainted within.

These people had had everything their own way, but they should never again control my actions, I was decided upon that point. Here's Marie, said Harriet, calling my attention from Earnest to a little figure that had just risen from a nap in a rude cradle she had slept in, in her infancy. She was now watching me with looks of wonder and disappointment; but I was prepared for cold looks, and kissed her cheeks, while I softly smoothed her golden curls, clustered in tangled masses about her round face. Like Stella she was clad in a soiled cotton frock without shoes or stockings. No word of welcome had yet greeted my coming, my kisses and caresses had been received passively, but had not been returned.

Not even by Stella who was old enough when I left her to have remembered me, and who was always so anxious for my recovery, saying that if I could only get well she would be so glad. "So glad I would jump right over the top of the house," she often said. No childish eager voice announced its joy over the restored mother. All remained quiet, looking very solemn and a little sullen I thought. From what I had heard, I had expected to be received coldly, still I was deeply wounded and all my heart arose in insurrection against those, who, not satisfied with their past work, were robbing me of the one solace left, my children's love.

It seemed more than I could bear and I groaned inwardly, while I talked pleasantly to Harriet of the weather and other trifling matters, at the same time relieving myself of my wet wraps and bonnet and glancing occasionally at the solemn faced children still watching me curiously. Harriet and her younger sister Jane who was a simple minded, harmless creature, became very communicative, talking incessantly of how well and happy the children had been since I left them, how well they had been taken care of, how much they thought of them and so forth.

"Their looks belie your words" I thought, but I said pleasantly, "Indeed I am glad, but I must go to Rachel's and see Bertha and Celeste before night."

"Celeste is not at home," said Harriet, "Rachel's daughter Sarah who is married and lives two miles from here has her at present, and Rachel will be over with Bertha soon, so you need not go."

"Children, would you like to see what I have brought for you?" I said turning to them and trying to hide the keen disappointment I felt over my baby's absence. "Yes mar'm." Then come with me to the other house, where I see they have carried my things. They followed in silence until we were safe from the sound of Harriet's voice, when Stella opened the conversation by saying, "I did not know what fine tall lady that was getting out of the buggy, until aunt Harriet said it was my mother." The ice was broken and Stella and Marie chatted freely while I helped father open the large box friends had filled with presents for my children.

"Mother," suddenly said Marie, "Bertha says she ain't goin' to love you."

"Why, my dear?"

"Because you went away and stayed so long."

" I went away, dear, to keep from being put in the cold ground. Would Bertha not rather have a live mother than a cold dead one?"

"You talk mighty funny," said the little lady looking puzzled.

"Do I? Then I won't say any more about things you cannot understand. Look at these pretty books, toys and cards your little friends at Marion, Old Fort and Charlotte have sent you." The children were delighted, even Earnest, who had only spoken in monosyllables became talkative and looked happy. Poor children I had perhaps mistaken their shyness and reserve for coldness, I was their mother, but almost a stranger to them ; even Stella could only remember me as blind and bedridden and very unlike the woman in a long cloak she had mistaken for a fine lady, and besides they had been taught that I had wantonly forsaken them and doubtless they thought me cruel and heartless, and I dared not say anything in self defence, knowing they would be compelled to repeat all that passed my lips after my departure, and I had yet no lawful authority to take them away should Mr. Roderick forbid it. So I must remain silent, and only by my manners teach them I loved them and was not heartless. Night set in dark and dreary, making it impossible for me to see Bertha that night. When supper was announced all repaired to the table, but I scarcely tasted the food set before me. The excitement of meeting my children had destroyed my appetite, and the black, bitter coffee without cream or sugar with the scanty, poorly prepared food not being inviting appetizers. The scene I had expected to take place upon my arrival was for some unknown cause postponed. Rachel, Caroline, Mr. Roderick and his brother William were not present, and Harriet doubtless wished for supporters before she attacked me. That night I shared Stella's bed, and before she retired I noticed she took great pains to place her clothing close to mine.

This silent childish act betrayed the affection she felt for me, which either she was too shy or too much afraid of Harriet to express. After thanking my Heavenly Father for his great mercy in permitting me to look upon the faces of my darlings, I fell into a deep sleep, from which I was aroused before day by feeling three little pairs of arms about my neck and hearing three sweet voices calling "mother," mother, wake up! I felt as if I were in fairy land I was so happy.

What did it matter if they were ignorant, dirty and ragged, they were mine, my own and all the world should not come between us! Harriet informed me before breakfast that Rachel had sent for Celeste and would be over soon, but I was too anxious to wait, and asked her, she being still good natured, to let Stella, Marie and Earnest drive over to Rachel's house with us, which request she granted. I helped to prepare them for the ride. Stella and Marie's cotton frocks were replaced by clean calico ones, but Earnest did not have anything to put on, though he allowed me to wash his face and hands, which made him more presentable.

In spite of the rags I felt proud of this patient little fellow, with his beautiful eyes so full of deep feeling, while my heart ached for the neglected state that had given his face a sad and thoughtful expression far beyond his years.

He does not resemble his father, either in features or expression, neither is he like myself or my family.

"Who is he like?" I asked Harriet.

"Nobody but himself," she said, laughing.

"There's Bertha in the yard," pointing to a bright-looking child, about five years old, who had just entered the gate and was talking to Dick, Rachel's boy, a great big, strapping fellow, over six feet in height. So this was the little girl who declared she would not love her mother. I was greatly agitated at sight of the child born during my blindness, the child who had no remembrance of her mother, who was now eyeing me suspiciously with large bright eyes shining from beneath the odd little poke hat upon her white head. Rachel had washed and put a decent calico dress upon the straight little form, making her quite tidy. I walked slowly to her and quietly kissed the pink lips, a pang going straight through my heart when she shrank timidly away. I was her mother, her best friend and yet a stranger, from whom she shrank. Once so loving, now trained to doubt. Appearing not to notice her coldness, I re-entered the house, where she soon followed, saying that Celeste had not come yet.

The buggy was at the door. Bertha, Marie, Earnest and I were helped into it, while Stella walked with Harriet through the woods.

"'There's Celeste, there's Celeste," cried Bertha, pointing to another little figure, in Rachel's open door, the counterpart of her own. Another little girl, born during those terrible years of 'suffering and the one Mr. Roderick called such fearful names, saying that "if it wanted to die, let it die, nobody cared." She was now looking at me with eyes exactly like my own, set in a pale face. She met me just as the others had done, answering to the question who I was: "It's my mother." Overcome by painful emotions, I sank into a chair, praying for strength to subdue the storm of tears I would freely indulge in, but for those cruel eyes watching on every side. It seemed a little singular that I had seen my eldest child first, then the second, then the third and fourth, and last of all my four-year-old baby.

After dinner, of which I partook sparingly, my appetite having entirely failed, Rachel and Harriet were unable to control their wrath any longer, now my father was absent, and assisted by Rachel's daughter, Sarah, they began an open tirade against me for leaving their brother and for bringing false charges against him, whom they said had ever humored me as a baby. They all talked at once, therefore, I remembered but little of their conversation, but heard them say that their brother had left orders that I should not be allowed to take any of *his* children away, and that all the men in Marion and thereabout were their brother's friends, and despised me for daring to walk so boldly through the streets after openly accusing one of their number of such bad things as I had Mr. Roderick.

"I am independent of the opinion of the people," I replied, "and have not done anything to be ashamed of. I will not be influenced by what people say. These children belong to me as well as to Mr. Roderick, and he has no right to keep them from me." Although I talked so independently I was growing weak from excitement and mortal anguish and trembled so that I dared not trust myself to speak again, therefore, I remained quiet during the rest of the degrading conversation, listened to

by all my children, and I thought bitterly of the unfortunate step that had placed me in the power of this despic-
able family, whose highest ambition in life was to get
something good to eat and engage in some low gossip.
The fire burned lower now, only these words ascending
in the blackening smoke:

"Brother Jake talked of sending these children to
school, but we think they'll do mighty well if they get
enough bread to eat.   He ain't able to educate them and
they'll do mighty well without any."

Well did I know if left in their care they would be
denied even the most common education; denied religious instruction, deprived of all Christian influences
and raised to deceive, quarrel and engage in coarse conversation, which would forever shut them out from
refined society and a high and noble life.   How bitter the
thought, and oh! how powerless I was to prevent it.
What shall I do ? What shall I do?   I asked myself.   I
had neither strength nor means sufficient to steal them,
which I would have felt justifiable in doing; and if I
resorted to the law I knew I would not receive justice,
on account of public opinion in Marion, where the suit
would be tried, being in Mr. Roderick's favor.   If I won
the suit I felt the judge might not be willing to entrust
the children to my care while my health was so delicate.
Then I could not bear the humiliation and the exposure
of my life's trials being brought before the public courts.
The judge might give over to me one child or two, but
I could not leave even one, and began revolving in my
mind the best and surest plan to recover them, while
Rachel and Harriet fumed over my seeming indifference
to their threats and unkind charges.   A keen pang pierced

my heart every time I looked at Earnest, for he seemed more neglected than the others, and looked so pitiful. Mr. Roderick was making great professions of love for his children, declaring all through the country that this love was his motive in keeping them from me, but I knew better than this. I knew that his object was to force me back to him, for had I not heard him say many years before that a man could make his wife do anything he wished by keeping her children from her. If he loved them why did he leave them in this wretched condition and stay in the Mitchell mountains, where I learned he was devoting his time to teaching other children. Stella and Earnest had even forgotten the little prayers I had taught them. Why were people so blinded by his hypocritical expressions and sanctimonious looks ? But then myself and family had been deceived and doubtless there were others as trusting as we were, who failed to look beneath the surface.

Compelled to return our horse and buggy we spent but two nights and then were forced to leave. Rachel's and Harriet's efforts to move me, having proven futile they now showed more respect and invited me to visit the children at any time. I had hoped to be able to take some of them home with me, but now saw this was out of the question, for all the family watched my every movement, and tall Dick especally kept a watchful eye upon me. I was too weak from long fasting and repressed suffering to take them forcibly and endure another scene. Again smilingly I kissed my children's pale faces and tried to seem unconcerned at the thoughts of leaving them. But once safe from the range of cold critical eyes I leaned my head against the side of the buggy and wept unrestrainedly. The agony I endured in heart and mind gained complete mastery and I longed to escape into the woods and throw myself on the ground where none but God could witness my grief, and there weep out my misery. There in solitude give vent to the passionate sobs that were shaking every nerve and fibre of my being and loudly cry to God not to forsake me, but give me my little ones. Smothering my grief as best I could, on account of father, who seemed so distressed, we drove into Marion and consulted my lawyer, Col. Clan, as to the proper thing to do. He said I could not take my children until the court gave them to me and then only a part of them he was sure I would get. But I would not be satisfied to leave even one of them with those people. My determination to forsake Mr. Roderick and get my children had become known in Marion and the notoriety and criticisms hurt me deeply for they did not know my side of the story as they did his. He had long talked his views of the matter to them and given anything but the true state of affairs. Many had thought I would return to Mr. Roderick at once and now censured me severely for not doing so.

I shrank from all the publicity of the affair. It was so painful I could scarcely endure it. We called at Mrs. Yonge's house for a few moments. Mrs. Yonge spoke comforting words, telling me to take my trouble to Jesus, that he was both able and willing to bear my burdens, if I would only trust his promise. By night we reached the top of the mountain, where I was kindly cared for by my friend, Mrs. McDuff, and the next day, worn and depressed, we arrived in Bakersville and was received by my mother, who keenly felt all my sorrow and was ever ready to sympathize with me. Truly there were some gleams of sunshine even in my darkened life—my father's and mother's deep love for me. That night mother handed me a letter that had come during my absence, which read as follows:

Mrs. Edna Roderick.

"The church in Marion, where your membership now is, at our last meeting took up your case of refusing to live with your husband. On the scriptural ground there is but one cause for which a husband or wife is justified in putting away the other, the church instructed me to notify you and also to ask you if you were now willing to live with your husband. Please answer by next Saturday.

"By order of the church clerk."

Cold comfort was this from the church that should have been a shield and refuge from persecution. Not even the common terms of respect had been used. I was indignant. Knowing the source from which it sprang and the motive that influenced even the church of God, I sat down immediately and penned the following words:

"Your letter of May 10th received and in answer I will say that I positively refuse to live with Mr. Roderick. I have good and sufficient reasons for the course I am pursuing and feel justified in the sight of God. The church can act in this matter as it thinks best. Close communion with God and great suffering has lifted me above the fear of anything man can do.

"EDNA RODERICK."

Perhaps I wrote too independently, but my heart was sore and their letter touched its tender chords when I

thought even my church would condemn me to a cruel
death. Before retiring for the night I knelt by my bed
and lifted a fervent prayer to God to show me the right
way to gain my children, to show me if it was my duty to
again live with Mr. Roderick, and if not a way might be
provided for their restoration to my care. For long
years I had prayed day and night that they might be
spared until I could see them. This prayer had
been answered and I now prayed that they might be
spared until I could gain power to bring the cause in a
just light before some good Christian judge, able to discern wisely and without prejudice. I also prayed for
the friends who had aided in the recovery of my sight
and strength, and for those who still persisted in adding
to my load of burdens, that had long since become too
heavy.

> "Too many burdens in the load,
> An I too few helpers on the road."

"Father, forgive them, for they know not what they
do," I cried. After tossing restlessly until midnight I
fell asleep, while there whispered a voice, 'twas the voice
of my God, "I love thee, I love thee, pass under the
rod."

CHAPTER IX.

"NOT AS I WILL."

"The way is rough, my Father; many a thorn
Has pierced me! and my weary feet all torn
And bleeding mark the way, yet thy command
Bids me press forward; Father, take my hand,
   And through the gloom
   Lead safely home
      Thy child.

"The throng is great, my Father; many a doubt
And fear and danger compass me about
And foes oppress me sore, I cannot stand
Or go alone, Father, take my hand
   And through the throng
   Lead safe along
      Thy child.

"The cross is heavy, Father, I have borne
It long and still do bear it, let my worn
And fainting spirit rise to that blest land
Where crowns are given, Father, take my hand
   And reaching down
   Lead to the crown
      Thy child!"

DAYS filled with unspeakable anguish followed the visit to my children. In vain I tried to cast off my sorrow by walking to and fro from room to room, or in the open air, where cool breezes fanned my cheek, but failed to extinguish the fire in my heart. The sad, pale faces of my children looked forth from every nook and corner,

the ragged clothing in which I had first seen them adding
to the forlorn picture want, distress, and neglect. My
mind was more disturbed than before meeting them, for
my visit had laid bare the falsehoods told by some people, that they were well cared for; and feeling greatly
dissatisfied, I determined to return to them as soon as
possible. The fifteenth of July found me again on my
way, with some comfortable clothing for presents, and
the following day I trod upon ground made sacred by
my darlings' footsteps. This was the tenth anniversary
of Stella's birth, and I had made great haste in order to
spend the day with her, but found she and Marie absent.
Accompanied by Bertha and Celeste, who had greeted
me shyly, I walked over to the dismal place where Earnest
stayed, and there, to my surprise, I found Mr. Roderick.
In the conversation that followed this unexpected meeting I learned that he wished me to return, but said if I
did not it would be useless for me to make any attempt
to gain possession of HIS children, and vowed to spill
every drop of blood in his veins before he would permit
it. My heart sank at these words. It seemed impossible to gain them in the face of such a powerful opponent,
and yet how could I give them up, or accept the only
alternative, to live with him?

"All in weakness, all in sorrow,
O my God, I come once more,
Lifting up the sad petition
Thou hast often heard before,
In the former days of darkness,
In the time of need of yore!"

The next day Mr. Roderick appered moody and quiet,
sitting apart; from the rest and jealously watching me.

Not gaining a response from me when he remarked that
he must return to his " mountain home," he called his aged
father and sisters and began in a loud voice to tell them of
my misconduct, as he termed my coldness to him.   His
rage, encouraged by their sly remarks, soon became fearful,
his voice being raised to its highest pitch.   When they,
frightened by the storm they had helped to arouse, after
striving to divert his attention from myself, left the room,
while I sat almost paralyzed, terrified at the thought of
being left alone with the demoniacal-looking being before
me.   I arose to follow them, when Mr. Roderick, seeing I
was about to escape him, ran after me, shrieking from the
passion that had for the time dethroned reason.   The
presence of his family prevented personal violence; and
as I left the house and yard I lost all self-control, and
wept hysterically from excitement and the heavy cloud
overshadowing my mind caused by the dreadful scene
through which I had just passed.   Rachel and Harriet
seemed slightly touched at sight of my grief, and strove
to pacify me as best they could.   In a few moments the
wild tempest of sobs was subdued, and I again faced the
future with a sickening sense of inability to cope with
the powers combined against me.   Oh! why did not
God help me in my weakness?   I moaned in despair.
Of all his creatures I felt myself the most forsaken and
miserable.

> "The way is long, my Father, and my soul
> Longs for the rest and quiet of the grave;
> While yet I journey through this weary land
> Keep me from wandering; Father, take my hand
> And in the way to endless day
> Lead safely on,
>   Thy child."

"The way is dark, my Father, cloud upon cloud
Is gathering thickly o'er my head, and loud
The thunders roar above me; yet see, I stand
Like one bewildered; Father, take my hand
    And quick and straight
    Lead to heaven's gate
        Thy child."

"Not now my child, a little more rough tossing,
A little longer on the billow's foam,
A few more journeyings in the desert darkness,
And then the sunshine of thy Father's home."

Mr. Roderick left the morning after this incident, leaving orders that Stella and Marie should not be brought home while I was there; but from some unknown cause his sisters now became very kind, and sent for them to please me. While with them I learned that their and Earnest's food consisted at each meal of a piece of bread and some kind of vegetable cooked with a scant allowance of rusty bacon, of which they were given each a piece about the size of a thimble once in two or three days. Bertha and Celeste fared somewhat better, as they were given a small allowance of milk. Stella and Earnest were compelled to work in the field, carry grain upon their backs to mill, and perform other heavy tasks. Although tortured by a knowledge of these facts, my heart was lightened by the certainty that I was gaining their love, they daily showing tokens of awakening affection; and my heart was filled with gratitude at sight of the many beautiful presents sent them during my illness by my kind and generous friends. After remaining with my children three weeks, I returned to Marion and spent a few days with Mrs. Yonge before going home. While with her I was told that the church had, upon receiving

my letter, taken steps to expel me. I was turned from
God's church and left to wander as best I could, con-
demned, spurned by those who could have made my sorrows so much easier to bear.

Indeed, I could not give up the church, but continued
to attend services, and as soon as in Bakersville again was
admitted to membership in another church. My con-
science acquitted me in what I was doing for my childrens'
sake. I could not let them grow up in ignorance and
sin under such pernicious influences as were now thrown
around them. Even could my health endure (and it could
not, as had been tested several times), it was impossible
to be happy with the knowledge that my children must be
brought up in ignorance and a useless, vain life, and myself a blind, sick burden upon them, unable to teach or
help them as I should. All my nature revolted at the
continuance of my miserable, unhappy life with Mr.
Roderick, as I knew him to be at times insane and my
life in danger in his hands.

My blind, helpless condition would return as before. I
could not again place myself in the power of one possessed
with a demoniac spirit and bring more misery and greater
ruin upon myself and children. Reason and prayer
alone now governed my every decision over and above
every other feeling of my heart. And the right and entire performance of my duty was the effort of my life.

> "'Tis bitter to endure the wrong
> Which evil hands and tongues commit.
> The bold encroachments of the strong,
> The shafts of calumny and wit,
> The scornful bearing of the proud;
> The sneers and laughter of the crowd.

13

"And harder still it is to bear
The censure of the good and wise
Who, ignorant of what you are,
 Or blinded by the slanderer's lies,
Look coldly on, or pass you by
In silence, with averted eye."

"Preserve me, O God! for in Thee do I put my trust. Plead my cause with them that strive with me. Save me, for the waters are coming into my soul. Turn Thou unto me, and have mercy upon me, for I am desolate and afflicted, the troubles of my heart are enlarged. O bring me out of my distresses. My life is spent with grief, and my years with sighing, and Thou only art my refuge in time of trouble."

The remainder of the summer and autumn months were spent in Bakersville. I had promised God, while in Charlotte, that if he would heal me, I would proclaim it to the world, and I now felt that if I expected to be blessed I must not break so sacred a vow, but with strength given me from above, write of the loving care that had brought me thus far safely and trust Him for the future.

At the beginning of winter and about the time that my parents left Bakersville for brother Harry's, accompanied by myself, I began the slow task of writing a biography of my tempestuous life. Our new home, a small house built in the wild forests of Mitchell county, at the top of the Blue Ridge mountain, was lonely in the extreme. Buried amid wild, rugged mountains, denied the privilege of using my eyes but a short time each day, deprived of congenial associates, robbed of my children, mocked by the past and well aware that my parents' useful days were o'er, that our ruined prospects could

never. be retrieved. Sick and feeble, unable to gratify
the tastes I possessed so far above my reach, can my
readers wonder that, upon the receipt of a cruel letter,
written by Rachel, refusing to let me ever visit my
children again, my reason was nearly dethroned? Again
my mind became darkened with the heavy gloom of
despair, and the third time in my life I doubted God's
mercy and cherished an unforgiving spirit towards those
who were robbing me of all that could make life endur-
able. While brooding over my many wrongs, I became
mad enough to study a way, to end my miserable existence. My patience was exhausted and I fretted and
wept in an agony of grief, my prayers coming only from
my lips and not from my heart. It seemed useless to
pray when God was deaf to my entreaties, my agony,
my tears. Of what use had been all my struggles? I
argued. Why had my friends not left me to die when
death would have been so sweet? And then I should
have been spared the trial of seeing my children growing up in ignorance, poverty and sin. Why had I been
spared to suffer alone, without a home I could call my
own, robbed of the one treasure I so eagerly coveted—
my children's love, isolated from kindred, loving spirits,
and denied necessary comforts?

Besides all this were the persecutions and threats of
Mr. Roderick and his followers, and the great dangers to
which my children were exposed; especially Stella. Sight,
strength and reason failed under this continued strain
upon my nervous system and my wearied heart and
frame, and I sat as one crushed, tearless, hopeless, prayer-
less; my heart frozen within me and the horrors of
insanity added to the future of blindness and helpless-

ness. "O, my God, why hast Thou forsaken me !" was again my heart's cry. My work of writing was dropped, as my sight failed.

A sudden change. Love for friends and kindred seemed dying, and I rejoiced over the burial of troublesome affections that had never brought me anything but pain. My heart was hardening under the ceaseless stroke of sorrow's hammer and I laughed in wild delight. My parents pitied me, bore with my impatience, my weaknesses and my unpleasant moods, striving to hide the great fear arising in their hearts for the reason of their child, now laboring under a cross too heavy to bear.

One dark night in a paroxyism of grief I ran into the wild-woods, and throwing myself upon the cold, damp ground gave way to passionate weeping, the lonely woods resounding with my sobs and cries of despair. I know not how long I had lain there with my face buried in the cold leaves, unmindful of the poisonous reptiles and wild animals that infested those lonely mountain haunts, when I heard brother Harry's voice and saw lights flashing through the woods. They were calling me, but I could not answer. My whole being was shaken by the intensity of my grief, and the wild hope that they would not find me, but leave me to die, silenced me. God did not intend this, and soon Harry and his frightened wife were standing by, pleading with me, for our mother's sake, to return with them. Tenderly Harry pressed my cold hand to his cheek, his voice quivering with pain at my distress as he half carried, half led me to my poor mother, who, overcome with fear for my reason and safety, was lying in an almost fainting condition on her bed. "Too many burdens in the load and too few

Father, help me, for my soul is engulfed by waves deep and pitiless.

helpers on the road." Father, help me, for my soul is engulfed by waves deep and pitiless.

Mother, ever ready with sympathy and love, after talking over my trials, opened the Bible at these words: "Fret not thyself because of evil-doers, neither be thou envious against the workers of iniquity. Rest in the Lord and wait patiently for Him ; fret not thyself because of him who prospereth in his way, because of the man who bringeth wicked devices to pass. Commit thy way unto the Lord, trust also in Him and he shall bring it to pass." "Rest in the Lord and wait patiently for Him," etc.

"See," said mother. "Edna, you will yet live to prosper and be blest. God says so, and I believe it more than ever before. And Mr. Roderick will yet receive his reward."

Her words again gave me fresh courage. My prayer was heard, and I was awakened from the sad state into which I had fallen before I became quite a wreck. Tearless and wretched I knelt at the foot of the cross, imploring God's help, imploring Him for mercy, forgiveness, for renewed strength and faith. Once more I became a rational being and began life anew, with a sadder but wiser heart. With one motive, one hope, one love, bidding me press forward—*my children.* Oh! my children! I was unable to converse on any subject without my words and thoughts drifting away to them, forgetful of all else. In company with my parents I attended services held in the small log schoolhouse close by, listening with a sad heart to the gospel words falling from the lips of the country clergyman for the benefit of his small audience of mountaineers.

One night, father being absent, mother and I were alone in the little one-room house that had been erected until they could have time to build. About dark we saw a large, burly man approaching the house, head and chin covered with an immense mass of black hair and beard, coming with a limping gait towards us. He walked, uninvited, right into the room and seated himself, saying he wanted to stay all night. "No, we cannot accommodate you, we have no room. You must try to find other shelter." "That is impossible," he said. "I cannot go on my lame foot any longer. I must and will stay." We could ill conceal our dread and fear of him, but were powerless to force him to go. By this time it was too dark for us to go in search of help. Finding we must make the best of a bad matter, we gave him his supper and prepared him a bed. Seeing some axes were in convenient reach, we sat by the fire reading the Bible, while the tramp snored heavily upon a bed in the far corner of the room. Sometimes he would raise up and watch us closely, then turn to sleep again.

Slowly the hours crept by, one—two—three, until finally dawn dimly lifted the mantle of night and relieved our anxious hearts. Refreshed by his long sleep, he ate his breakfast, thanked us kindly and left us in peace. "Be not forgetful to entertain strangers," we thought, as he took his departure, so grateful that he had not molested us. This incident suggested the following lines:

SOMEBODY'S BOY.

The battle cry is sounding loud, the bugle calls to arm,
The hills and dales are clouded o'er, troops gather in alarm;
With winds are mingled sighing prayers from many a dying
    brave;
A youth, with pale lips lying low, turns, moaning o'er a name.

A soldier boy's dying call is heard amid the roar
Of battle strife; among the slain he sinks, and breathes no more.
Somebody's boy, it matters not if clad in blue or gray,
If fighting for the right or wrong, is hurried to his grave.

Amid the beats of drum and fife, his pillow but a sod,
With folded hands and marble brow, his soul returns to God.
Somebody's boy is resting where the lonely willows weep,
Sweet whispers float upon the breeze, and angels watch him sleep.

* * * * * * * * * * * * *

Now comes along the highway a dusty tramp forlorn,
A tattered coat conceals beneath a bent and aged form;
With wearied, hardened visage, the bell he faintly rings;
The air is rent with pitying notes, an angel softly sings.

Upon this frozen nature no love for years has shown;
His life is made of cruel words, and knows no kindly tone;
And could you see into his past, as a mother clasped her boy,
He then was innocent and fair, her pride, her hope, her joy.

She never dreamed her darling child a weary tramp would be,
For o'er his tasks or youthful sports he laughed in hopeful glee.
Perhaps he sinned, but O! forget, for suffering must repay,
And somebody's boy has now become wretched, old and gray.

* * * * * * * * * * * * *

Within a large and gilded hall a revel wild is held,
The sounds of oath and laughter loud upon the breezes swell;
A man is seen with bloated face come reeling to the streets;
He turns his fierce and lurid eyes as friends he loudly greets.

Somebody's boy has fallen low; we hear the broken sob
Of angels who have watched for years his footsteps turn from
    God.
Somebody's prayers have oft been made o'er him in childhood's
    day
When, rocked in love, he knew no wrong, a smiling infant lay.

Some mother's tears have freely flowed, and lonely vigils kept;
Some mother's heart has often bled while others coldly slept.
Somebody suffers for the wrong, and angels sadly weep,
Whene'er some careless, wayward son has sown what he must
    reap.

* * * * * * * * * * * * *

A scaffold high with spreading arms on yonder height we see,
Waiting to take its victim's life, exulting horribly;
While zephyrs blow, birds hover o'er a soul in dire distress,
With troubled gaze breathes out a prayer. Will God attend and
    bless?

What matter if he's clothed in sin, what matter if he's wild,
Guilty, loathsome? Remember that he is somebody's child.
We cannot tell how hard he strove to shun temptation's snare,
How often on his mother's breast he wept in his despair;

How oft her lips had softly pressed his dimpled infant cheek,
How oft her hand in love caressed the sinless baby feet.
Then, strangers, pause and listen well; so might your own have
    been.
But Christ can freely pardon all, though scarlet be his sin.

Somebody's boy! The sweet refrain is breathed in accents mild.
Somebody's boy! If bent and gray, if pure or all defiled.
Somebody's boy! Soft bells repeat in sad and sweetest chime
Somebody's boy! Some mother sighs; perhaps he may be mine.

Becoming restless from the monotonous life I was leading, I determined to leave my brother's home and seek my fortune in the busy world for the purpose of regaining my children. Feeble and without money, I started forth, trusting to God to bless my efforts and provide a way for their recovery. Unable to procure a conveyance to Bakersville, where I intended stopping for a few weeks, with my brother Bradley, I decided to walk, and set forth, my staff and satchel in hand, in company with my father, who was now quite feeble from a recent illness, my mother journeying along with us for a short distance. A romantic party we presented on that memorable day; my gray-haired parents, each with staff in hand, and myself like some hunted creature (so the wild, hungry look in my eyes suggested, that so often distressed my mother), assisting my faltering steps with my staff, the rugged mountains covered with gorgeous honeysuckles or the more modest ivy, the lonely chirp of some frightened squirrel, or the rustling of some creeping thing moving away at our approach : all combining to fill our hearts with strange, lonely thoughts. Only my faith in God gave me strength and courage for the effort I was putting forth. Only my love for my children imbued my heart with the desire to surmount every difficulty and gain the victory over enemies and ill health. Tenderly my mother kissed me, forcing back the rising tears, bidding me press forward, trust to God, and with his help she felt sure I would succeed, in spite of the difficulties now piled mountain high.

> "O'er my heart in the days that have flown
> No love like mother-love ever has shone,
> No other worship abides and endures,
> Faithful, unselfish and patient like yours.
>
> Backward, flow backward, O tide of years,
> I am so weary of toil and of tears,
> Toil without recompense, tears all in vain,
> Take them and give me my childhood again."

Several days later I entered the little town of Bakersville, weary, dusty and sore from traveling. I had been kindly assisted on my way by the timely loan of a horse, therefore, suffered no serious inconvenience from my adventure. While with brother Bradley, I worked faithfully upon my book, striving to finish it, but found this impossible as my eyes and brain refused to perform their duty consequently my efforts must be turned into some other channel, and the longing to see my children became overpowering. So I decided to visit them in spite of all obstacles, even too, if I should be compelled to walk the forty-five miles that separated them from me. My father and brothers were ignorant of my plan, but some friends interceded and procured for me a comfortable conveyance. With but one dollar in my purse, I again set forth, resolved to make one desperate struggle for independence and my children; with only faith in my one Master, my loving Saviour, to uphold my wavering, uncertain steps, which might lead me again into Mr. Roderick's power. But I must press onward and upward, not allowing my feet to slip into the many pitfalls digged for me by my enemies. Comforting words were spoken by my faithful Bakersville friends, and being assisted by kind hands, I arrived in Marion fully persuaded to return no more to the mountains, but to call upon Masons for protection and assistance, my father having been a Master Mason for many years. Contrary to my expectations, I was very kindly received by them in Marion, where I had so many bitter opponents. My call for protection for my intended visit to my children's home was heartily responded to and an elegant turnout was offered me, also the company of a Mason to protect my rights and help in the search for my children, should they not be at home. Happily I found them all at home, and the circumstances I had related in regard to their condition seemed to have had the desired effect, for I found them much better clothed, a healthier color in their once pale faces, and looking quite happy. A burden was thus lifted from my mind, but fell again with a dreadful weight, for I discovered the fact that their young minds had again been steeled against their mother, they appearing perfectly indifferent as to whether I stayed with them or not, although I was refused that pleasure by their cruel aunts. My heart seemed tearing in twain at this unexpected coldness, and for a few brief moments I allowed the hot tears to flow unrestrainedly, unmindful of cold spectators rejoicing over my grief. Then recalling my presence of mind, I effectually crushed hope and love into silence, leaving my children's presence with a more hopeless wound in my heart than had ever been planted there before. After all my prayers, my sacrifices, my struggles, my agony and my tears, I had come for my reward, my children's love, and had lost. My heart broke and the pain has never since left me. It was more than I could bear. Life lost all its impetus; I had nothing now worth living for. Why could I not die? No one would grieve for me but mother, and even she would be relieved of care and anxiety which was breaking her heart. Children, hope, and love, farewell, farewell.

> "A few more partings here,
> A few more struggles o'er,
> A few more toils, a few more tears,
> And we shall meet no more."

> "Peace, troubled soul, whose plaintive moan
> Hath taught each scene the note of woe,
> Cease thy complaints, suppress thy groans,
> And let thy tears forget to flow.
> Behold the precious balm is found
> To lull thy pain and heal thy wound."

The days I spent with my friends in Marion were passed in grief, confining me to my room and bed a portion of the time; but I must not remain a burden upon my friends. Necessity now required exertion and forced me into activity; I must be up and doing. Unfavorable replies were received to all my letters desiring a situation suited to my health and strength. Many times while with my friends in Old Fort, I would yield in despair and start to return to Mr. Roderick, but was deterred by the resistance of Mrs. Tremont, and letters from my mother begging me not to throw my life away.

A letter from my home stated that Mr. Roderick had fallen senseless in a fit of passion, had frothed at the mouth, gnashed his teeth, presenting a picture frightful to behold. Again I saw the fearful visions of the past, recalling the intense fear and suffering I had endured on these trying occasions.

But my friend Ada, ever true and loyal, kept up my courage and would not let me go back. "No man, having put his hand to the plough, and looking back, is fit for the kingdom of God."

Some of my friends urged divorce and marriage as a relief from my distressing circumstances, and the temptation was indeed great, for I felt the need of a home of love and longed to make and be made happy; but knowing that the Bible says: "Let not the wife depart from her husband, but if she do depart, let her remain unmarried." These were Christ's own words. I would not do anything contrary to Bible teaching—nothing that would endanger my hope of heaven. I had lost all in this life; now heaven was my goal and the great desire that filled my heart. Resolving that rather than disobey one of God's commands, so direct and decided as that, I would die in the poorhouse on a bed of straw, unloved, unknown and uncared for.

The temptation never again entered my life. I put it from me and am happy in my decision.

Receiving a letter from Asheville requesting me to come immediately, as my services were needed at once to superintend a certain part of work in a large establishment at that place, I prepared to go.

When I received the letter I was unable to sit up, but the next day I forced my self from my bed, dressed, and bidding my friends adieu, prepared to enter upon my new life. Strange enough I felt as we whirled along the picturesque winding road crossing the Blue Ridge where I had once experienced such strange adventures, my new existence, that of maintaining myself, opening before me like some hopeless dream formed by an overwrought brain.

Late that night, in company with several married ladies and gentlemen, I reached my destination, and while waiting in the reception room to see mine host, shed hot and bitter tears over the dark past and for the hopeless future. One long hour passed in this manner, when I was aroused by the entrance of my new employer who, upon giving one brief glance at my face, declared me unfit for the place, saying that I was too frail and delicate for the duties he required. I left his presence and once more found myself sick and helpless, among cold strangers, poor and unknown. Poor and unknown! God pity those who are poor and unknown, and God pity those who are proud and scornful, whose glory will shine in this world only, and whose riches must be left behind when they enter into eternity, worse than poor and unknown.

I could no longer accept help from friends. What then was I to do? Die, I could not until God willed; live I must, even though living was dying daily. " God, pity me," my only prayer, trembled upon my lips as I turned to consult a physician regarding my eyes. "Their condition can be improved," he said, "if you can remain in the hospital while they are being treated," which chance I eagerly grasped, also thanking him for his kindness.

Friends from Old Fort now interested themselves in my behalf, using their influence to gain for me other friends, making my sojourn among strangers much more agreeable than I had anticipated. My health improved, glasses were procured enabling me to see much better than before; and, assisted by Masons with pecuniary aid, I concluded to go to Charlotte, the place where I had once been received so pleasantly.

Once more I passed through the streets of Charlotte at the hour of midnight, walking and seeing, but more hopeless than when carried blind and helpless upon a stretcher to my brother's door, I had made the effort and lost.

With a desperate feeling, born of despair, I entered my dead brother's door. I had given my children up, but the effort had been too great. My heart was crushed, the pain in it being so great that at times it seemed that I must fall lifeless.

> "Though sorrowful tears must fall,
> And the heart to its depths be riven
> With the storms and tempests;
> We need them all
> To render us meet for Heaven,"

and doubtless I needed this lesson of patience.

Mrs. Wilkinson and other friends I had once loved, who had interested themselves in my behalf, I now had the pleasure of meeting, if pleasure it could be called, for the sight of each face recalled all the hope and grief, the love and despair, the suffering and waiting, and the joy I had felt in having their loving sympathy and tokens of affection. Often I avoided meeting them, the pain being so intense I could not bear it.

In company with my dear sister Alice, I visited the hospital where I had received such kind care that hope had been awakened in my heart, giving me courage for renewed efforts. A longing to do something for Christ seized me, and to a few of my faithful friends I imparted my desire. My wish was granted and I was given charge of a home, recently organized in Charlotte for my fallen sex, and I began my labors with new zest and energy, feeling the daily presence of God's Spirit, and knowing his blessing attended my footsteps.

Again Charlotte people had opened their arms to me and bidden me "God speed." Faithful and true my friends of that city, my regular attendance upon divine services, and the daily occupations of the home and city mission work, at last at work in "his vineyard," gave me peace and such happiness as I had not known for years, notwithstanding the fact that my dear children were deprived of their mother; but hope bade me toil and wait and it would all come even yet, and I would bless and be blessed with their love, and teach and lead them.

Dr. Miller and Mr. Cheshire, friends of long ago; Dr. Fair, my pastor, and other clergymen, did all in their power to encourage and help me, while my dearly loved friend, Mrs. Wilkinson (of the hospital acquaintances), and many other lovely Christian women, strove in every way possible to cheer and brighten my life, and showed the deepest sympathy and appreciation for me in my work. I can never forget those dear people and always have pleasant memories of the city of Charlotte and my first mission work, so dear to me. "My Father worketh hitherto and I work" brought peace to my soul and in God's mercy saved my tottering mental powers. I was brought back and given the work best suited to my anxious heart, to know I was doing some good by living. This enabled me to bear the burden of the sorrowful life of my dear children, though often when listening to the inspiring words of my pastor or some other minister, I would feel as though I were a "whited sepulcher," the outward peace in my work and friends, and within the torturing thought of my darling children's sufferings and our separation. I could truly say with Paul, "I am crucified with Christ, nevertheless I live, yet not I, but Christ liveth in me, and the life I now live is by faith in the Son of God."

I had suffered too much to recover immediately from the sad effects of the past, which I continually sought to bury, that I might consecrate my life entirely to God's service. Weak nature would assert itself, and in spite of my efforts, my hours of gloom and despondency were many. Powerless to better the condition of my unfortunate children, I tried to wait as patiently as my restless nature would allow for God's own time for answering prayers made in the dark, sad past. Regrets for my mistakes were over, and I thank God I no longer desire to recall the first fatal steps I had taken. God knows best, has ordered all things wisely, and I thank him that he has permitted me to suffer with his Son and am still permitted to bear for his dear sake, who alone is pure, meek and lowly. The future is a sealed book and I thank God I have not the planning of it.

> "What though the record of lost and gone years
> Be bright with our laughter, or dark with our tears,
> We can make of each sorrow or joy of the past
> A step that will help us to heaven at last."

With no tie to bind me to earth, I mark with feelings of sorrow and pity the weak struggles of man for position, wealth and fame. Mark the weak, proud sister as she passes her more unfortunate sex with cold looks of disdain, their hearts being wrapped up in the world's pleasures, glory and approval. With eyes of sorrow I look from my window upon the passing throng, who will soon pass away into eternity, and yet they rush madly along in search of more gain and of the world's applause; but know ye, O man, that the hour will come when lucre, pomp, vain glory, friends, hope and life will fade; where, then, is thy end?

> "Only waiting 'till the angels open wide the mystic gate,
> At whose feet I long have lain; weary, poor and desolate.
> Even now I think I hear them and their voices far away;
> If they call us, are we waiting, waiting, ready to obey?"

God grant that my waiting will not be long and that my faith will grow brighter as I near my journey's end. Father, forgive me for the hours of despondency I have allowed myself to indulge in, and enable me to look up with an eye of faith, bearing my cross patiently to the end, trusting to thy promise, I wait.

"The way is dark, my child, but leads to light,
I would not always have thee walk by sight.
My dealings now, thou canst not understand,
I meant it so, but I will take thy hand,
  And through the night
  Lead up to light,
    My child.

The way is long, my child, but it shall be
Not one step longer than is good for thee,
And thou shalt know at last when thou shalt stand
Safe at the goal, how I did take thy hand,
  And safe and blest,
  Lead up to rest,
    My child.

The path is rough, my child, but Oh how sweet
Will be the rest for weary pilgrims meet,
When thou shalt search the borders of the land
To which I lead thee, as I take thy hand,
  And reaching down,
  Lead to the crown,
    My child."

CHAPTER X.

RESTING ON GOD'S PROMISES.

HE serious and prostrating illness of my dear mother at this time called me home. Leaving the "Home" in charge of a party very desirous of the position, I hastened to my mother's bedside ; again passing by my children without seeing them, Mr. Roderick having forbidden my coming and I dared not face the lion in his den. I found poor mother indeed very ill both in body and mind, the physician thinking recovery impossible, and we watched over what we supposed was her death-bed. But her physical powers rallied ; not so the mental, and oh, how much worse than death this was to me! Not herself! Not my mother! But a sad, pitiful shadow of her former self. Her life of extraordinary suffering and disappointment was too great for human endurance, and the cord of reason broke. Sadly I returned to my work, feeling a natural death would have been comfort compared with this worse than death, this blank existence.

Oh, the wretchedness, the misery one man's sins can

cause the innocent! Bitter, indeed, the suffering, almost
more than human heart can stand!

Mr. Roderick's work was nearing its end. The asylum to receive my precious mother, the bitterest of all
his work. Then my darling children yet in his power!
Oh, how could I endure it! My heart bled within me as
I passed by without being permitted to stop and see
them. Is the author of all this suffering responsible for
his acts? Can he be a sane man and make so many
lives miserable? Yet, if responsible, then God pity him!
Another epileptic fit had attacked him, I learned. These
fits must have affected his mind; yet to the public he
maintained a quiet mien. In my struggle for my children
am I dealing with a maniac or a man of reason?

The "Home" in Charlotte of which I had charge, now
closed for want of funds to maintain it, and I spent several months in the city with friends engaged in other
work, principally that of having my children placed in
good schools. For this purpose I induced Mr. Roderick's friends, members of his own church, to write and
persuade him to let the children be sent to the schools I
had provided for them. Through the kind influence and
help of Mrs. Wilkinson and other friends, arrangements
had been made for them in some of the best schools in
North Carolina, could I gain them either with their
father's consent, or by the help of the law. The latter
I could not do, that is all of them, and that did not satisfy me. So persuasion was the best means I could em-
ploy. Only in moments of great weakness and despondency had I ever entertained the thought of not rescuing
them from the wretched life of ignorance, sin and neglect they were forced to lead; even then it was not my

wish to give them up, but the despair of weakness, no strength for the struggle, the insurmountable barrier that arose before me and overshadowed my soul into deep darkness of night. My strength at this time was overtaxed in every way, both in body and in mind, trying to save money to support myself and assist my children, and the additional disappointment and burden—the refusal to allow them to be placed in the excellent schools I had provided for them. I felt myself again fast sinking into that awful weak state of blindness and helplessness as of old, despair for the moment following fast upon my vanishing health. Groaning in agony of body and mind, I lay upon a sick bed nearly blind again, my only comfort that of pressing to my heart the blessed Bible; though unable to read, I clung to it as the one comfort, the only source from which my help must come. God knows best, and his promises are sure. My one solace was in this faith, this lifting myself out of my sufferings and away from earth, pleading as Job of old for this burden to be lifted, the tearless agony for my children; could it be removed until health be restored, I could then again take up the thread of life and battle to the end. Then for a season it was lifted, and faith, strong faith, upheld my wavering spirits. I felt that God had heard my pleadings and would care for my children and save and protect them from their father, and permit me to make a fresh effort in their behalf. The outpouring of the Holy Spirit filled my soul with unspeakable bliss.

> "Like strains of music, soft and low,
>   That break upon a troubled sleep,
> I hear the promise old and new,
>   God will his faithful children keep
>   'In perfect peace.'

> From out the thoughtless, wreck-strewn past,
>   From unknown years that silent wait,
> Amid earth's wild regret there comes
>   The promise with its precious freight,
>   'In perfect peace.'
>
> Above the clash of party strife,
>   The surge of life's unresting sea,
> Through sobs of pain and songs of mirth,
>   Through hours of toil it floats to me,
>   'In perfect peace.'
>
> It stills the questionings and doubts,
>   The nameless fears that throng the soul,
> It speaks of love unchanging, sure,
>   And evermore its echoes roll;
>   'In perfect peace.'
>
> 'In perfect peace.' O loving Christ!
>   When falls death's twilight gray and cold,
> And flowers of earth shall droop and fade,
>   Keep thou thy children as of old,
>   'In perfect peace.'
>
> And through the glad, eternal years,
>   Beyond the blame and scorn of men,
> The hearts that served Thee here may know
>   The rest that passeth human ken,
>   'Thy perfect peace.' "

were the sweet strains that floated through my mind
night after night when all was still and all outward appearances dark and drear as the night's gloom. The
soft echoes of these lines faintly sounding even in sleep:

> "In perfect peace,
>   God will his faithful children keep."

I now resolved to return to a hospital in the North and
regain my health, but pleading letters from my parents

urging me to come to them, saying they could not bear for me to go so far away and not see them again, induced me to postpone the trip and return home. Listening to their pleading, however, only prolonged my recovery, while reason's voice and my own judgment would have shortened the time, but they did not know and could not bear for me to leave them for strangers, feeling their loving care would be the best, and fearing that again I would be subjected to unkind treatment and suffer away from home and friends.

Passing my children without the gratification of the sight of them, I again crossed over the Blue Ridge mountains—that grand and sublime scene! Words cannot paint its wild, magnificent beauty. The inspiring sublimity of nature's grandeur! Ten miles from Marion, then four miles ascent up the rugged picturesque mountain made beautiful, clothed in the rhythmic dress of the sweet bloom of rhododendron, honeysuckle and laurel, and rugged and picturesque by its crude trees and rough rocks. Sublime with the awful voice of Nature in its immensity of space and mysterious presence of the unknown spirit of Nature's realm. Nearer to God, nearer to the spirit land! The soul soars above and presses its prison bars for flight with the inspirations that fill it. Thus came the soothing comfort of the Great Spirit that strengthened me.

> "Nearer my God to Thee,
> 　Nearer to thee,
> E'en though it be a cross
> 　That raiseth me."

Though rough and precipitous the road, a quiet peace possessed my soul, and its dangers were passed unheeded. Crossing over the summit we traveled on a slight descent on to a ridge for about ten miles, when we arrived at my father's house, nestled among the trees and vines and surrounded by flowers, while the murmur of a distant mountain rill added music to the scene. My mother's condition was somewhat improved since I saw her last. But unfortunately my own helpless suffering state and the additional care necessarily given her soon proved too much for my frail mother, and again she was prostrated and her mind wavering. Often she would say, "Don't, Edna, don't look so! I cannot bear the hunted look in your eyes! My poor, poor child!" Often I would sit by the window viewing the lovely landscape and pour forth my soul in sad song. But mother could not bear my sad voice, and I would wander away to the little mountain rill and watch the pure, clear ripples gurgling over its rocky bed, and alone and unheard my soul sought relief in song. Soon I would be again totally blind, and lonely and helpless. Having contracted malaria in Charlotte, it developed into malarial fever, and now we were both confined to our beds with fevers. Pour heart-broken father watched beside us night and day, tears often blinding him as he strove to alleviate our sufferings. Some of the mountain people were kind and sympathized with me in my efforts to procure my children. My father and brother Harry were held in high esteem by them; they would do anything to help me for their sakes, if not for mine. Brother Harry was their magistrate and deputy sheriff, also president of the Farmers' Alliance. They were very proud of him. They now showed their appreciation and friendship by being willing to go and steal my children for me and help me away with them, proposing to go down with me in a wagon and get them. Oh, I wish I was well and could go for them. Only to save them from their awful life, no matter what way or means employed to accomplish it, it was a charity to do it! But sick and unable to go, I lay there, picturing the covered wagon, myself and the honest-hearted people driving slowly over the rough mountain road, the hiding away in the dark woods near Mr. Roderick's, the wild mountain scenery, the drear moonlight, the chirping of insects adding to the awful loneliness and romantic situation. Alas, alas, the futility of human efforts! Again the trial of patience, of waiting, waiting, longing to know! What would be the end!

> "There are those who go forth to labor,
>   Joining the world's great bands,
> There are those who walk but softly,
>   Or sit with folded hands."

> "And if by the word of the Master,
>   The task must be laid aside,
> And the joy of abundant service
>   By His holy will be denied."

> "Oh, think, as the patient silence
>   Drifts down o'er the quiet hours,
> That the Master's will accepted
>   Is a cross enwreathed with flowers."

> "And if it be thine to labor,
>   Then do it with all thy might,
> But if with thy pale hands folded,
>   He bids thee wait for the night,"

> "Look up, though the swift tears gather,
>   And be glad that thy Lord commands;
> For the sweetest grace of heaven
>   May be shed over folded hands."

Finding the burden too heavy for father, brother Bradley sent for me to be removed to his home in Bakersville. There with good care and physicians, I was soon able to be up again. When strong enough to be out I organized a ladies' prayer-meeting, anxious to be at work in His vineyard and feel that my life was not entirely a blank. As I put my whole soul and energy into the work, the ladies seemed inspired and filled with love of God, and good was accomplished. Together we visited the prisoners and others needing the comfort of God's word. We would read, sing and talk and in this free gift we felt we received even more than we gave, for love was reflected in our own hearts and faith strengthened. As the burden for my children had been lifted off, so now this burden too, of blindness! Ill health and my mother's sickness was removed through prayer and faith, and I felt happier than I had for many a year.

> "My faith looks up to Thee
> Thou Lamb of Calvary,
> Saviour divine."

My physician now determined that a skillful surgical operation was necessary for a perfect restoration to health and advised me to go North for special treatment. He and father's pastor gained me admittance into "Seney Hospital," Brooklyn, N. Y., and with many kind letters from Masons, clergy and friends, I started upon my journey in search of health, to a large, strange city with only sufficient means for my transportation there. Mother's health rallied somewhat, though barely out of danger, when I left. Without any further knowledge of my children, still not being permitted to see them, I went away, not knowing for how long, but love for them

I stood before the barred door of a large, unfinished building, alone in a great city, night near at hand and only a small sum in my purse.

and my parents urged me to make the effort to regain
my health and seek the means whereby I could obtain
my children through theft as no other means seemed
effectual, intending to carry them away beyond their
father's reach. Many, many plans had formed in my
mind to get possession of them, but lack of means and
the necessary strength hindered. These must now be
gained, I would have them, I was determined upon that.
My journey was made pleasant by new friends, who seemed to spring up all along the way, and at last I was set down
in front of an immense building in the city of Brooklyn.
Satchel in hand, I looked for an entrance to this building,
but the front seemed to have an unfinished appearance,
barred with planks. No person responded to my ring.
My heart trembled with anxiety, as I turned away, wondering if some mistake had been made in the directions
and now left me exhausted beyond further efforts, night
near at hand, and only a small sum in my purse, alone
in a great city, hundreds of miles from one familiar face!
Striving to collect my scattered thoughts and decide
what step to take, I noticed another building near, where
I resolved to make inquiries, when to my joy I found it
to be the wing of the hospital, the place where I was expected. After necessary delay and explanations, I was
sent up-stairs on an elevator to a large hall where I
rested upon a couch, watching and waiting further events.
Doctors in their long white operating-coats passed and
repassed ; nurses passed to and fro ; weeping and moaning came from distant rooms; still white forms were carried by upon stretchers; and thus I was introduced into
Seney Hospital. Nurses and patients coming around
me, I heard that private and free patients were for the

time occupying one ward, containing twenty-five beds, as private rooms were not completed. I rejoiced to hear this, as I felt that among the more cultured class I would find those friends I could never expect to find if confined to the ordinary free wards of city hospitals. Among others were clergymen's wives, missionary workers occupying beds close beside my own, and pleasant intercourse sprang up between us. Yet the daily sights and rounds were most distressing, and only those who have had experience in a surgical institution know of its horror and suffering. Patients undergoing all kinds of operations and treatment constantly being rolled in and out on wheeled couches, while distressing sounds daily and nightly harrow on heart and ear. Doctors Pilcher and Bogart showed much interest in my case and story and ordered every attention given me, prescribing plenty of quiet, rest, and light, nutritious diet, principally boiled milk. Many kind hearts beat beneath that roof in spite of the daily scenes of distress that might harden. I soon found myself surrounded with kindness, comfort and friends. Lovely young girls kept the room bright with their cheerful presence and sweet flowers. An operation was necessary, so painful that nurses and physicians advised an anesthetic to alleviate the intense suffering. But knowing my bodily weakness and having perfect faith in God that He would spare me for my children's and parents' sake, I bravely refused the anesthetic and submitted to the operation, trusting to God's mercy to sustain me. For two hours, while I lay dressed in an operating-suit, upon stretchers, in a room adjoining the surgeons, the apartment seemed filled with angels and Jesus was so near I was almost lost to the painful and unpleasant

situation.   In him I found strength and peace that quiet-
ed all tremor, fear, and aversion.

"INTO THY HANDS."

"Into Thy hands, O Father! Now at last,
　　Weary with struggling and long unrest,
Vext by remembrances of conflicts past
　　And by a host of present cares opprest,"

"I come to Thee and cry, Thy will be done!
　　Take thou the burden I have borne too long;
Into Thy hands, O mighty, loving One,
　　My weakness gives it all, for Thou art strong!"

"For life—for death. I cannot see the way;
　　I blindly wander on to meet the night;
The path grows steeper, and the dying day
　　Soon with its shadows will shut out the light."

"Hold Thou my hand, O Father! I am tired,
　　As a young child that wearies of the road;
And the far heights towards which I once aspired
　　Have lost the glory with which erst they glowed."

"Take Thou my life and mold it to Thy will;
　　Into Thy hands commit I all my way;
Fain would I lift each cup that Thou dost fill,
　　Nor from its brim my pale lips ever stay."

"Take Thou my life! I lay it at Thy feet;
　　And in my death my sure support be Thou;
So shall I sink to slumber sound and sweet,
　　And wake at morn before Thy face to bow!"

I at length was wheeled into the room occupied by
many physicians and nurses. They having heard of my
strange request, one they said that never had been made
there before, came to see how such pain could be borne,
and eyed me curiously and with much interest, while my

15

own kind doctors spoke in the highest praise of my bravery, but only the support of the Holy Spirit sustained the courage, and strength came only from Him and upheld me through all the agony that followed, without tears or complaints. Placed in my bed again every attention was bestowed upon me, and though life hung for some weeks as by a thread, the tender care, the loving friends, and skillful physicians, and sympathy and consolation from some of Brooklyn's most celebrated divines at length aroused me to new life and hope.

Later, recovering sufficiently, I paid a visit to relatives in New England, just before the death of my favorite and loved uncle John, and had the pleasure of meeting him once more. Together we visited the church graveyard, where he showed me the spot selected for him. Oh, how soon to that long last earthly home he was laid! I had not left them long ere the news of uncle John's death followed me.

At Boston I had my eyes treated and my general health improved so much that after a year's sojourn in that exhilarating climate, I felt myself quite a new person. During this time I endeavored to raise the means to assist my children through school and gain possession of them in some way—by law or stratagem.

Kneeling at the altar one day I poured forth my soul to God, humbly dwelling in this atmosphere of prayer, long, so long! I started at the low rich tones of the clergyman saying (as if almost in answer to my prayer), " Put your trust in God and He will yet bring it to pass." "Turn ye, turn ye to the stronghold, ye prisoners of hope. Even to-day do I declare that I will render double unto thee." My eyes seemed riveted upon the speaker and eagerly I drank in every word that fell from his lips. Oh, that sermon! Never had my soul been so deeply stirred, and I went home feeling it was good to be there indeed! Several evenings later, calling upon a friend, I was ushered into her presence, while she was chatting pleasantly with some one in the cool, dusky parlor. As he came forward in response to her introduction, I recognized the owner of that rich, deep voice. "Rev. Mr. Thornton," she said, and I glanced up into the penetrating eyes.

The conversation touched lightly upon some cheerful commonplace, then as into deeper thought we plunged, I could not but realize the depth of strength and wisdom so unostentatiously shown. This was the beginning of a very sincere, pure and elevating friendship. As time advanced we saw much of each other and grew to feel the need of the sympathy and spiritual growth we derived in this higher plane, this ideal world of ours, not then realizing the dangerous ground upon which we were wandering. But time revealed it to us erelong and both saw in a moment the heart of the other, and as he was aware my husband still lived and we both knew divorced people should not marry, not a word was spoken. One sad despairing look as soul gazed into soul for one short moment. Oh, an eternity of life! of hopes! of bliss! of truth—something greater than this world contains! One quick clasp of the hands and Mr. Thornton strode away and vanished from my sight and out of my life. Each knew the other's heart and ideas of right and wrong and respected them. Discovering the truth only one course was left—immediate and final departure. Humbly I knelt at the throne of grace, praying God to help me through this temptation also. Save me from myself! Break every barrier down and let me worship Thee only! Long and often I sought strength from this trial, and it at last came and with it peace. Consecrate myself entirely, perfectly to Thee, O God!

I now determined to return to North Carolina and visit my children and make a desperate effort in their behalf. The means I hoped to raise for the purpose was a failure. If there was nothing I could do for them·; if their condition was improved and they did not care for their own mother, then if God did not intend me to have them perhaps He would let me devote my life to Him in missionary work.

Leaving relations in Portland, Maine, where I was visiting, I again turned my face homeward. In order to save means for my children I procured a cheap rate on a small steamer. I was put in care of the captain, who was very kind and gentlemanly. But the voyage was exceedingly rough. Indeed the roughest, the captain said, that he had ever known on those waters. A gale set in and stormed furiously. The boat pitched, groaned and tossed, seeming a premonition of the stormy life yet in store for me. The moaning ship and waters bewailed my future.

> "He who hath set thee in the race
> Will speed thee to the end."

So I trusted and felt no fear, but the seasickness was so awful and I not very strong, that my life was despaired of by my faithful watchers. Praying in my more quiet moments that God would spare me for my children, I offered a vow that if He would mercifully restore me I would again take up the work of my life—that of writing a biography of it, and show to the world the many great works of faith and answers to prayers, that it might prove to others God's great love to mankind and how truly He will hear and answer the prayer of faith and love. I believed that he had restored me thus far and would further my work. I would not doubt and no fear entered my heart. "He leadeth me," and I know in whom my trust is placed. He will yet bring it to pass and my life will yet prove a light and blessing to others.

Next day the captain kindly invited me up to the pilot house, as I happened to be the only lady passenger. He was very entertaining with his stories of his eventful life; of many hair-breadth escapes and thrilling experiences. Grand indeed was the magnificent view spread out about me. Words cannot fitly describe its wonderful sublimity. The vast expanse of water, the immensity of space, bound only by sky and water, inspires one's soul and lifts us above the earth. Arriving in New York at night the brilliantly lighted steamers and white sails made an attractive picture. I spent a month in New York and, Brooklyn amongst friends.

At Dr. Simpson's "Faith Home" I stopped about two weeks—a period of most delightful soul-inspiring growth. This Home was filled with spiritual-minded people. The greatest faith and love to God was evident in all their daily life. This association and strengthening of faith elevated me very much and well prepared me for future trials. Daily services in the building and constant association with Christians of such strong faith gave me a spiritual growth I had not yet known. Many were healed of diseases and all seemed to breathe an atmos-

phere of purity and peace. Their faith was not without
works. Almost a daily round of charity and new fields
continually sought. Truly "My Father worketh hitherto
and I work" seemed their motto.

Mrs. Whittermore was the founder of the "Door of
Hope," another great and good institution. Here was
an example of great faith and great works also. Into
the lowly houses she would go, seeking to save. Dressed
as a working woman would, in cotton dress, apron and
bonnet, she made herself, for the time being, "one of
them," came to them lowly, and in full sympathy and
with prayers, and of course won many souls to Christ.
She showed me the dress she wore and gave me many interesting accounts of her attempts to save souls in the
slums of that great city. Oh, how I longed to give my
life to missionary work. First to save the souls of my
dear children and *then*—"Go ye into all the world." Oh,
indeed I would be happy!

Homeward bound we arrived in Richmond. Here I
met at prayer-meeting my kind pastor, Dr. Fair, who
gave me a hearty greeting and welcome to his church.
The remainder of the journey home was brightened by
pleasant companions, among them General Baringer, a
member of my church in Charlotte, N. C., who very
kindly offered to assist in my efforts to educate my children; also my Brooklyn friends had offered to help me
if I would secure them and bring them North. Doors
seemed opened, ways were made for the success of the
work before me.

> "Yet this one thing I learned to know
> Each day more surely as I go,

> That doors are opened, ways are made,
> Burdens are lifted or are laid
> By some great law unseen and still
> Unfathomed purpose to fulfill
>   Not as I will."

The reports that my children were "doing well" and were being well cared for, were corroborated by the people of Marion. So I was led to believe that my fears were groundless and that they were in kind hands and receiving good Christian training and an education. Often when I heard no ill of Mr. Roderick, my whole life with him seemed a hideous dream, and I would really question myself if it could be true and not an awful creation of an excited imagination. In my heart, oh, how I wished it was only a dream and now forever gone! Although some claimed the children were all right, yet none were willing to accompany me into the presence of Mr. Roderick, even advising me not to go. So alone I must venture once more into that dreaded presence for my children and their benefit. Four long years I had been away from them trying to regain my eyesight and restore my feeble health. Now that God had blessed me with renewed strength and I had given myself to him and entered the work for which I felt my restoration had been granted—my life-work to secure and educate my children and write this book—I would go— go to them, see Mr. Roderick and urge him to let the children be put into schools. Perhaps he had changed and would be influenced for their good. Arriving at Rachel's about dark, I staid all night. Bertha and Celeste were there. But not the loving little children I had left. They did not seem to know me, stood away off and treated me with indifference, did not care anything for me at all. Ten and eleven years respectively were they now, but they had been trained to forget and despise their mother.

Early next morning we three started for Mr. Roderick's home to see the other three children. Mr. Roderick was away, and Stella, Earnest and Marie received me about as indifferently as Bertha and Celeste had done. I was shocked at their appearance and wondered how people could say they were "doing well." Oh! I never saw such a pitiful sight. Dirty, ragged, ignorant little things! Poor Stella, the oldest, I will mention particularly, as her care-worn, wan, sick face shocked me almost beyond endurance. Pale, with hard, deep lines about the mouth and forehead, a strange, hungry look in her large expressive eyes. The sad, set expression of her face shocked me. Glancing over her figure, clad in coarse cotton cloth, and bare feet, though sixteen years of age, hands hardened and rough with work out in the fields. Poor, poor child, could I wonder at her appearance! How could the expression be sweet and bright, with such surroundings, rough treatment and harsh words, and so much care and grief. For naturally proud and spirited, her circumstances chafed and shamed her. Life was full of grief and pain and no bright star gleamed in her future. Taught to believe her mother a fraud, she showed no love nor confidence for the mother whose heart was breaking for her. Poor, miserable, unhappy waifs! And what can I do when you refuse me your love! So distant, I can scarcely speak to you or approach you in any way. What am I to do to make you love me and know I am willing to give my life to save you! Did a mother ever have a more difficult, distressing task?

Later persuading them to walk with me to the spring, I began to talk to them *any way*, and suggested that if they *did not* care for me, did not want me to help them, I would return to mission work in New York and leave them to the life they seemed to prefer. As I talked on I heard sobs from some one behind and saw poor Stella convulsed with grief. When questioned she said she did not want me to leave them. She hated the life she led, and I was her only hope for relief.

"Oh, if you will only stay," she said, "I will do anything, will work harder and take good care of you and not let you get sick again." So will I," and "I," and "I" echoed many voices.

Although they refused telling more, I saw and knew they led very sad and pitiful lives. Afterwards I learned that Stella's motive for not speaking was fear that if I knew all I would go away and never return. I did not make them any promises then, as I felt that I must know my way well and be sure God was leading me. So saying I would consider the matter and do all in my power for them, I promised to see them again soon. They did not have love and confidence in me enough to agree to run away yet. But the thought that they even wanted me with them was joy unspeakable. Mr. Roderick came home in a very pleasant mood, though somewhat stiff and formal, offered his hand, but called me by my maiden name "Miss Gray." To look at him now one would never dream he ever could have been the cruel, inhuman tyrant of former days. Never did he appear so affable and anxious to please me and make my visit a happy one.

Even his sisters were kind and did not utter a single harsh word. I had never seen such a change. Mr. Roderick took me over to see a new house he was having built and repeatedly talked of my coming back, saying he would be so happy if his wife and children were only with him in his little new home. That he was a changed man now, a far better one; had learned to control his temper and would be kind and good to me, if only I would come home and stay. All this was promising and I felt for the children's sake I could almost make the sacrifice, though I knew even then that it meant loss of health and perhaps sight. I could not trust him and refused to give a promise then. Kissing the children goodbye I went to my father's house to think and decide this weighty matter now before me. Go back to Mr. Roderick and my children! Submit to the life he would continue to lead us, and to the cruelty he would eventually fall into! For I knew his nature was not changed and he would continue to have those insane fits thrt would soon destroy my health. I felt all this show was only to get me back into their power. Must I do it? or give myself to missionary work and trust to persuading my children to forsake their present life and come to me? Which way was right! Which must I take! God make my way clear, decide for me, lead me in the path of right and duty.

> "Plan Thou for me, I humbly ask,
> 　Whatever seemeth good to Thee,
> And let me simply rest in faith
> 　As trusting as a child should be."

> "Choose Thou, since Thou dost know it all;
> 　Thy heart is kind, Thy way is best,
> With joy I'll take Thy guiding hand
> 　And trust Thy help to bear the rest."

Not being able to fully decide the question, I began
to make plans to do both. A call for a missionary to
work in Asheville attracted my attention and I responded, believing that God would open the way for me to yet
obtain my children, if that was the right thing to do. Arriving in Asheville, I found the "Home" could not yet
be opened for a year, so that was postponed, they having
changed their plans. The other course now seemed the
only one open for me. Go back to Mr. Koderick and the
children ! My heart sank in despair at the thought. I
would rather have stepped right into my coffin and heard
the lid nailed down than return to him. The awful picture of that horrid face looking menacingly down upon
me, eyes glaring in their frenzied wrath and teeth tightly
set as he hissed curses upon my head, made my blood
run cold : and shuddering, I felt that I *could not* return.
Then the thought of the five dear souls to be saved,
saved from him and from an evil life! I must make the
sacrifice. Five souls are more precious than one life, I
would go !

After that long night of fearful agony and trial I
arose calm and determined in the morning light. God
pity and strengthen me for the dark days in store!

> "Simply trusting every day,
> Trusting him whate'er befall,
> Trusting him whatere befall
> Trusting Jesus, that is all."

CHAPTER XI.

A MOTHER'S SARIFICE.

"As thy faith is so shall it be unto thee.

"Does He lead me beside the still waters,
In pastures so pleasant and green?
Then why do the dark storm-clouds gather
In skies that have been so serene "

HE quiet refuge I found in my brother Bradley's home in Asheville afforded the rest and time for meditation and for making the necessary preparations and plans to begin the sacrifice now seemingly so clearly laid before me. Bradley stood high in the city in business and social circles, his musical talent, affable manners and genteel dress made him a favorite in church and society; and his prompt and skillful management of business gave him much prominence there beside being a Mason of high order. Of course his friends soon became my friends, and I was kindly received and encouraged in business so I soon had some means to provide for my childern and help in their education.

With this means and many presents from brother Bradley I again started on my journey to my children and Mr. Roderick's home. Back, turn backward, to the old life. Humbly as a sheep led to the slanghter, I went to he sacrifice, knowing my physical powers could not en-

I waite l there about two hours, a thinking space before the
awful doom.

dure the strain, but with my life I would purchase my children's freedom and in a measure fit them for eternity. Since I left them in the spring, four months ago, I had only received one short unsatisfactory letter from Stella. And though I had written I would return, I did not state the exact time, consequently no one was looking for me.

Driving up to the house I found it closed and no response came to my knock. I sat down upon my trunk in the yard, the boxes scattered about, waiting for some one to return. Oh, the dreary, dreary, lonesome spot, surrounded by the poor, desolate landscape. A fruitful source of homesickness nourished by the harsh treatment I knew was in store for me. Already rumor said Mr. Roderick's people did not want me to return, and had vowed they would not give up the children and I should not have them. But I knew that with Mr. Roderick lay all the power, and to his mercy I now committed myself. They had no longer a child in their power, but a woman —a woman filled with a purpose determined and true even unto death if need be. I waited there for about two hours—a thinking space before the awful doom. They are coming. I see one of the children—nay, two appear against the horizon, as over the hill they come, Stella and Marie, dear little girls, how tired and sad they look! Poor dears, how glad I am to be able to help you! As they drew near I think I never saw a more beautiful face and form than Marie possessed. Thirteen years old, thirteen to-day, her birthday. I gazed at the slight form clad in an old faded frock which was unable to hide her natural grace and loveliness. A face so lovely and sweet in its piquant beauty, I could not withdraw my gaze of admiration. A decided contrast to her pale, care-worn sister, Stella, the abused, neglected, hard-worked, eldest of the five, now sixteen years of age. Poor child, it makes my heart bleed even now to think of her. I can never bear to recall that haggard, broken-spirited look in her face. I drew her to me and kissed and kissed her as though I would with the power of my love remove the burden from her heart. Could love reach and melt that heart-broken look from her dear face! Oh, my poor girl, how hard a fate was yours. For I afterwards learned she was hated by her aunts and abused and taunted with her resemblance to "your old mother," as they termed me, "that old hussy" in their rough parlance, until the poor child really hated the name of mother. I was represented to them as not caring anything for them and deserting and leaving them to be a "fine lady" away with my friends, throwing them aside, and that I was never blind or sick, it was all "put on" for an excuse to get away ; but for them and their self-sacrificing care they would have been left to die ; sneering and laughing at my ladylike ways and cleanly habits, making sport of all neatness and refined manners and language.

"A stuck-up lady" they termed me. "She's a purty thing to come to boss you young uns. If she attempts to say one word, you get a stick and beat her, beat her away from here. She cares for nothing but her curls and ribbons—even has lace on her petticoats. Stuck up hussy! you bring her down and beat her. Never hoed a hill of corn in her life and does not know how to make a hoecake. She's a purty one. Never do you wear the old toggery she brings you; nobody knows how she come by it, and don't you be seen with it on, I tell ye.

The old heifer, a disgrace to dacint people, coming down here in her finery and airs, talkin' and wheedlin' around. If brother Jake had beat her enough and made her tuck up her curls and gone to the corn-field as we had to do, it might have give her some sense; but he was always too good, and let her walk right over him. Pore man; but he has had to suffer for his humerin' such a no count thing. Why, the stingy old cat would not even loan me her nice dress to go to church in. What she has is too good for her *betters*; I'll show her. If brother hadn't had a fool for a wife, he might be a rich man to-day and had a home, and not leave his family for us pore wimmin folks to take care of for her while she flaunts around over the country. And now that we have got them raised and large enough to work, here she comes with all her high notions of *education* and *books* and *finery.* If brother Jake would do right he would drive her away from here and send ye children to the plow and make ye good for something. Why, yer ma don't even know how to card a roll, the lazy, good for nothin' thing."

With such an education as this, could I wonder the children avoided me. They had all come now, and I saw by the sidelong glance Harriet gave me that I was not welcome there. She had opened the doors and busied herself about the room while I received and talked with the rest of my children, and now we proceeded to the door.

"Come in," said Harriet, "if ye can get in for the muss and dirt. I'm all in my dirt and rags, but we wimmin have to work here; we can't spend our time afore the looking-glass a primping like *some* can do." Yet there was hardly a mirror in the house one could

recognize oneself in, or large enough either. Then
in an undertone to her sister:

" Brother Jake loves the very ground that woman
walks on. He would stick his head in the fire to get
her back again. I'll show her! We'll see who is boss
this time, if she cuts up."

This to Ernest: " Ernest, you little lazy rascal!
Get some wood this minit for yore pore ole aunt that has
had hard enough time awaiten on yer, you scamp!"

The poor, pale child crept away in obedience to her
command.

Stella met me coldly and did not express any pleasure
at all at my return, though she had begged me with tears
to come back when I visited them in the spring. Now
she was perfectly indifferent, and I could not draw her
out or make her confide in me. I occupied her bed with
her that night, and by much coaxing and persuasion late
in the night she confessed that her aunts had taunted,
scolded and abused her on my account until she could
not bear it, and did not dare to want me or even mention
my name in their presence. She was glad I had returned
though, as that would get them out of their trouble
soon.

Mr. Roderick came in and was very agreeable and
pleasant and anxious to please me. Ready to do anything, commanding the children to wait upon me, and
falling into all my plans for the new home and for the
children.

Even Harriet's evil suggestions were not heeded. I
saw I must use a great deal of tact and discretion with
Mr. Roderick in order to make any advancement in their
life. Some time later I unwisely mentioned Miss Grov-

esnor's offer to take Stella in her school near Marion.
Like a match in a powder-keg Mr. Roderick flashed into
a rage, smashing chairs and dashing them across the
floor, slamming and beating doors and raving:

"That is your game, is it?" he said, standing by the
door rattling the knob and shaking it furiously. "A
mighty fine lot you'd make of them taking them from
work and sending them off to boarding-school."

I saw at once I was right in my belief that he was not
changed, but all the old evil nature lay dormant in him
still. But too late for me now. I had made the sacrifice
and must go on. I had returned to the old life, to live
with him whom I believed to be insane. The thought
was horrible, but to be with my children was comfort.
The unsettled life, the suspense of waiting, was unbearable
longer, together with that sickening feeling of loneliness.
Just so it was children and home, no matter what and
where, it was better than the world. That lonely, desolate feeling was particularly oppressive in churches
amongst strangers. If only they would not be forgetful
to "entertain strangers," what good they might do.

> "Not one could tell, for nobody knew
> Why love was made to gladden a few,
> And hearts that would forever be true
> Go lone and starved the whole way through."

The future we cannot see. The sacrifice I was making may not gain the desired end. I may not be the
means in God's hands of saving the souls of my children,
yet I prayed that though my life go out in this effort, it
would not be without its fruit for good. My faith in
God was strong. I believed, and there must be a
reward.

During my absence Mr. Roderick had been unfortunate in speculation and lost his town property; also one farm, so only the original farm his father had given him was left him now, and on this he had some time ago begun a new frame house. Not a room was finished, and we had to remain with Harriet until the house could be put in habitable condition. No furnishings prepared either; so we were soon very busy quilting and making up all the goods I had brought them. Harriet was extremely jealous of me, and did not want me to return and usurp her place over my children; so she made the two months we stayed with her interesting, to say the least. It took that time to get the kitchen prepared during the busy season of ingathering of harvest. Often when Mr. Roderick or the children were talking to me, planning for the new home, Harriet would eavesdrop at a crack in the wall, and often go away laughing a hard, bitter laugh, using sarcastic expressions, and always trying to get the children not to obey me.

Feeling my time was precious, I at once began to teach and train the children into better ways of living, better manners, and religious habits, as well as thorough instructions in their books. No one approved of this— not even the children.

One day vainly endeavoring to inspire my youngest daughter Celeste with some ambition and love for study (she was the most impressionable of them all), I was shocked to hear her say:

"I do not want an education; what's the use of it?"

"Why, my dear, you would be better fitted for life and——"

"What! You want me to git an education and then

run off and leave my husband and children like you did," she interposed. This was as she had been taught—the erroneous impression they had tried to give every one.

Harriet opposed my having all the children—one must stay with her and one with Rachel; but I overruled at last, and finally we settled down in the unfinished house, which had been weather-boarded but not plastered or ceiled. Four very small rooms in all, including kitchen.

With an ox-cart Ernest removed our new quilts, bedding, wearing apparel, etc., which we had been so busily engaged in making while waiting for the house. In the dreary month of November we took possession of our new home, on the eighteenth anniversary of our marriage, though we had November weather, too, cold and rainy. Marie was quite indisposed, having recently had the measles, and now taking a severe cold. I did not intend she should come out, and was surprised to see her late in the evening slowly creeping over the hill, enveloped in her father's old overcoat, whose tails dragged upon the ground as she walked, and an old hood upon her head, drawing Ernest's little toy wagon filled with all her dolls and presents my friends had sent them, soon followed by Bertha and Celeste in another direction, with a similar load. A comical picture they made as they slowly wended their way homeward—to home and mother at last. "Why did you venture out in this weather, my child?" I said to Marie. "Oh, mother, I could not, could not stay away; I wanted to be here, too, with the others." So that night we gathered all our little ones together at the family altar for the first time. I had persuaded Mr. Roderick we could not start our home without God's blessing. Little voices joined in the hymns,

and Mr. Roderick seemed happy, and peace for once
reigned in our home.

> "Jesus, Master! whom I serve,
> Strengthen hand and heart and nerve
>   All Thy bidding to fulfill;
> Open Thou mine eyes to see
> All the work Thou hast for me."

CHAPTER XII.

DARK DAYS.

"List! how the sad wind is moaning,
  How gruesome and dark is the sky,
And see! how the mad waves are tossing,
  How the billows roll up mountain high."

Many pleasant days we spent in planning and arranging our new home. Busy, hard work was the order of the day, indoors and out of doors. The week passed pleasantly, but Sunday's visit to the country church near by was an unthought-of trial, in that so many critical eyes were turned upon us. "The runaway wife had returned." The children were closely scrutinized and every article of dress noted. Such a change in their manners, frocks and general appearance elicited many a comment, and friends praised while enemies scoffed. Every eye was turned upon me as I joined in the songs that were sung, and every movement watched, but I felt God was with me and that I was in the right, so was brave and strong and independent of the world's opinion.

After services many came forward with a friendly greeting, inviting me to take a Sunday-school class and join the choir. This was for Mr. Roderick's sake, as it was his church, and now that his wife had returned they wanted to encourage him by welcoming me.

I set aside a portion of each day for the children's lessons—indeed, all the time it was possible to get away from their work. The habits of years were to be changed, and that rather unwillingly on the part of the children; consequently scarcely any change was evident for a year or more. Oh, the discouraging, trying work of it! Often I bowed my head in bitter despair as I saw my efforts ran contrary to by their aunts, and sometimes in a moment the work of weeks was undone. No one knows what a task I had before me, and often so discouraging! The two older girls, Stella and Marie, were harder to control or convince of the error of their ways, so set were they in what they had been taught and the only life they knew. Mr. Roderick's people opposed education, and said I was spoiling them. Ignorant little things! The two youngest, eleven and twelve years of age, did not know their alphabet, and none of them knew how to sew or do much else but drudgery work in the fields. Yet they showed in speech and manner that they mistrusted me, and had been told by their aunts to " beat " me should I attempt to control them.

The three eldest had seen the hardest life and been most unhappy, but the younger ones, Bertha and Celeste, were the most ignorant children it had ever been my misfortune to meet. They had almost run wild, and would ask questions a child of three ought to have known. Yet they were gentle, delicate in appearance, with golden hair and pretty faces. Ernest was small and frail, gentle in his manners and naturally refined in feelings ; was also strictly truthful and free from any evil habits, though had of course fallen into the customs and ideas of those around him. The children now began to tell me all the falsehoods which their aunts had told them about me, trying to disgust and make them hate me. Stella told of the abuse and neglect she had endured until her health was ruined. Every effort she made toward self-improvement was cried down, and she was quarreled at and abused, saying she was trying to be like her " stuck-up ma." She had gone through rain and cold, bare-footed and thinly clad, when already ill, to attend her aunts' cattle, often sitting for hours on the cold, wet ground, not caring to live and longing to die. Her nerves were unstrung from the many shocks she had suffered from her father's raving mad fits and altercations with her aunts. In summer they helped in the fields, and at noon, when all took their dinner and rest, they were required to pick berries, which they sold to pur-chase their winter shoes, cotton and calico dresses. Overwork had proved too much for Stella, and her health could not withstand the shock.

One awful incident the children related confirmed my belief in Mr. Roderick's insanity. Stella and Ernest had occasion to go with him to some place of work, and were running ahead when a strange noise behind them made them hastily return, and to their horror they discovered their father fallen upon the ground in a fit, frothing at the mouth, and groaning and making most horrible sounds, his eyes rolled, his teeth set in a terrible grin, and hands clenched. Stella could never recall the scene without a shudder.

Later, when sitting with the children with their books and sewing, often we would look up and discover Harriet standing in the doorway scowling down upon us. She had slipped in upon us, and now such a scolding we would get! These outbursts of passion we endured quietly, the one thought being for the benefit of the children. Mr. Roderick now began to have those awful bursts of passion quite frequently, and vented his temper upon the children at first, requiring most unreasonable things of them, driving them out into all kinds of bitter weather, quarreling about their studies and clothing.

One bitter cold winter day, the wind driving the sleet in fearful gusts, Mr. Roderick became enraged at poor little Ernest and determined to force him out into the weather on an unimportant errand six mile away. Twelve miles exposure in this terrible gale would kill him.

"Get up from there and go, you little lazy rascal! I'll teach you how to tender yourself up this way! Go, this instant! Don't stand there talking back to me! No, you shall not have a coat! Go just as you are! You shall not have a wrap!"

The pale, trembling figure disappeared from the doorway out into the storm. I waited almost breathlessly for an opportunity to slip out of the room, and soon followed with wraps. On, on, I ran through the blinding sleet and rain, at last discovering him getting on a horse at his Aunt Harriet's. I called. He saw me and waited. I shall never forget the feeling of joy as I wrapped up that boy! So thinly clad, he was now wet and shivering. Just in time to save you, my darling boy! For further exposure in that severe weather would have been his death.

In another fit of temper Mr. Roderick compelled all the children to go out in a cold spring rain to gather the cockerel out of the wheat; would not permit them to wrap up, and they soon became chilled and wet in the sleety rain. Their hands were all frosted and swollen next day so they could scarcely use them. Many a scheme I had to invent in order to get them out of that rain. I took an umbrella and went into the field. Standing upon a stump I began talking pleasantly with them all, lightly jesting, trying to get Mr. Roderick into a good humor. After talking for some time I at last got down, and said to Marie:

"Come with me, dear, I want you for some work I must complete this evening."

Mr. Roderick looked his surprise, but as I smiled back at him, saying:

"Now, you are not going to leave me all by myself, are you?"

He said, "Go along, you two good-for-nothings; we don't need you."

But they stayed and stayed, and I suffered such anxiety about their health I could not bear it any longer. So again I went to my old stump and perched upon it. I talked and talked, laughing and jesting, until when I said I wanted Bertha and Celeste, he reluctantly let them go, soon himself following with Ernest. Thus I had to scheme to save the children's health, though they did suffer for some years after from the ill effects of their father's cruel treatment. This constant interference to save them finally turned his temper upon myself.

During the first year of my return my health bore up quite well, considering the heavy tasks and mental strain and anxiety, together with insufficient food, for Mr. Roderick only provided the coarsest of food, and my weak stomach soon refused it. Through this continued state of semi-starvation and hard work my newly acquired strength gradually waned, and night after night I tossed on my bed, racked with intense pain in spine and eyes, many times sitting up or walking in the moonlight in the yard to relieve and cool my fevered brow. I now missed the letters from my friends; as my physical being became weak, I longed for and needed their comforting sympathy. But no letters came as they did the first year, and the presents that followed my return were missed—the loving attention more than the articles themselves; though I provided quite well for the family by raising fowls, sheep, etc., selling eggs, butter, and managing well in every way to help the children with their crops. Yet I suffered from want of proper food, for now, although I could help provide it myself, my stomach had become so diseased by much fasting that it would not digest it, and I could not eat.

I suffered greatly from insomnia, and one night I had tossed and endured the pain until I could not lie there longer, but sat up on the side of the bed sobbing softly, my body trembling with nervousness. Mr. Roderick awoke, immediately flashing into a passion at finding me weeping, began raving and calling me names. To escape him I slipped away to the window, not daring to open my lips in reply. He dashed wildly from the bed, throwing his arms and screaming. He hissed curses between his teeth as he came towards me. I sprang through the half-open window and ran with all my strength; but he came through the window, ran after me, caught me by the collar and dragged me to the door, shaking my body until I almost dropped. Bringing his fist down at my cheek and then beating upon the door (which probably saved my poor body, he vented his anger upon it.

He called loudly to Stella to open the door, which she quickly did, slipping in between us, holding me close to her while she begged and commanded him to leave me alone.

"You know mother did not do anything to you! Stop! Father, father, stop! Leave mother alone!"

What with persuasion and command she got him away. Still loudly talking and shaking his fists, he finally settled in a corner of the fireplace, growling and groaning, until at last he became quiet and subdued.

These scenes now followed each other so frequently that I became terribly weakened, and at times utter despair and desperation would seize me and I would go away into the dark woods and throw myself upon the ground and weep and pray until a measure of peace came into my soul, and strength was given to go back and continue the work before me. Indifferent as to my life now, I cared not if he should kill me. I resolved for the children's sake I would bring about a change for the better if I died for it.

One time I accidentally knocked a bucket from a shelf. Mr. Roderick was in the yard, and seizing a rock he ran towards me saying, between his clenched teeth, "I'll teach you how to throw buckets round, madam," he drew back to throw the rock, but I quietly walked into the house, when he snatched the door from its hinges and rushed at me. I turned calmly towards him with strength born of desperation and said, "Strike, if you like! Finish your work, and then you will be hanged for murder!" So differently I met him from former times that he was stunned with surprise. I did not run and show fear as in years gone by. His arm dropped at his side. My words convincing him that the law would hang him if he murdered me, he went out muttering to himself, looking all the sagacity of a cunning maniac. At another time he happened to overhear me speaking to the children of their resemblance to my father's family. "How dare you," he screamed, "compare *my* children to those infernal Canadians! If anything *I* had looked like them I would crush the life out of it! The wretches! The low-down scoundrels! How I hate them!"

He scowled, grasping me by the shoulder, shaking me violently and knocking a glass out of my hand, which fell in atoms on the floor. He then rushed out into the yard and cut a stick, saying, "I see what I have to do. I see what my duty is, and, though I hate to do it, I will have to. Just you come here, madam!"

I stood in the doorway unmoved, filled with indignation and desperation. Indeed, I cared not for my life, I was so miserable. If he had seized the axe lying near by—and I thought he would—and crushed my life out with it, I should have received it without an effort at resistance. I had not the slightest desire to save myself. The children rushed between us. Brave, Stella! With the strength of will and self-control that commands armies, she could sometimes reduce her father to a state of at least sullen quiet; and now she came to the rescue, commanding him to go away, talking as fast as she could, while she gently pushed me into the room and locked the door. Mr. Roderick spent his fury in the open air, and gradually subsided into sullen silence, would not speak to any one, and perhaps the next day would be on

the other extreme, and be too kind and good for anything.

Another great grief came into my life at this time—
my mother was now an inmate of an insane asylum. Ill health and my sad fate had partially dethroned
reason, and my mother had long been lost to me. My
poor, poor mother! Her condition was a continual
source of grief, and now that she must be amongst
strangers was worse. But dear father had exhausted
his strength in caring for her, was getting old and worn-
out and could not keep her as was necessary.

My mind was somewhat diverted by trying to get
Stella into school. I realized that this was the one thing
absolutely necessary for her now. Although she was
my main protector and shield at home, of course I could
not sacrifice her for my comfort. I approached Mr.
Roderick with great caution, and after many disappoint-
ments and fears, he at last, in a fit of good humor, agreed
to let her go, and all arrangements were perfected.

When her aunts discovered our plans they sent for Mr.
Roderick, who remained over night with them, and returning next morning said to me, "Write that old school-
marm that Stella can't come." Her aunts' jealousies
were aroused over her brightened prospects and they
were determined to bring her back to her old state of
submission to their cruel will.

Very soon after this another opportunity was offered
Stella—that to enter Greenville Academy under my former teacher, Miss Hattie Grovesnor. I felt that new
scenes and association with people of culture and high
character would develop her strong and sincere nature
into a fine, noble woman.

When I again pressed the matter upon Mr. Roderick, to my intense joy and surprise he yielded a ready consent. Hasty arrangements were made, and we kept it so quiet, hiding the garments we worked upon when her aunts were about, until all was ready.

The morning of her departure came, and I hastened her off, almost holding my breath with fear that Mr. Roderick would at the last moment retract and not let her go, and drew a breath of prayerful relief as the vehicle vanished out of sight bearing her to the railroad station. One object accomplished! one prayer answered! God knows with how thankful a heart I knelt at his altar that night!

I had now gained the perfect love and confidence of my children. Stella was so careful not to do anything to displease me, and the sincere grief she felt at parting proved her true and loving heart. The despised sorrowing mother, who had hungered and yearned for their love with unspeakable longings, was at last accepted and loved as ardently as ever mother was loved. Little surprises of affection were now ever coming into my life, such as occurred the next day after Stella's departure. Ernest came to my side and confidentially said:

"Mother, father shall never strike you again if I can help it. Do not feel bad because Stella has gone; I will protect you now."

Marie took Stella's place in the housework and performed her duties faithfully and well so as to save me all the anxiety and care possible.

Gentle little Bertha was extremely fond of flowers and always kept a bouquet on my table and a nosegay pinned at my throat, expressing her love by these quiet deeds and not in words. Celeste was more demonstrative and talked much, planning and helping in every way, showing her devotion to me—so thoughtful and willing to obey. At last they had awakened to the fact that I had been greatly wronged and persecuted, and in a measure realized how intense had been my sufferings.

One bright glowing shower of happiness was soon poured upon me in the conversion of my three daughters, Marie, Bertha and Celeste entering the church and giving their souls to God.

> "Behind every storm-cloud and shadow
> Is the light of His glory and love;
> And 'mid the loud roar of the tempest,
> Sweet music I hear from above."

Faith and prayer indeed have their reward, and oh, how they strengthened me then.

Mr. Roderick now began building a large new house upon a high knoll with a lovely lawn of trees, grass and flowers. The view was grand, and altogether it made a beautiful home. Myself and children planted and cultivated the flowers and spent many happy moments with them. Another source of comfort for me was my Sunday-school class. Three of my children also were in my class, and many were the happy lessons we learned. Then, too, I found pleasure in writing for the papers and journals, defraying all the expense of our reading-matter.

Notwithstanding our rather isolated location, we had a great many visitors, more of Mr. Roderick's relations than mine, as he was surrounded by his, but mine were far away. My brother and his wife came and my father and a few others, but Mr. Roderick's friends had seemingly become my friends, and all treated me well. Alas,

17

only one family of these new friends now remains true, so great was Mr. Roderick's influence in the community. And, indeed, I am not surprised, for he was the most double character I ever knew. Mr. Roderick in society was quite a different man from Mr. Roderick at home, and no one would believe me if I had told them of how he treated us. They would think it impossible for a man of such pleasing, affable manners, such a church leader, and Sunday-school superintendent! All was grace and politeness in company. So cordial, easy, gentle and generous! Who could clothe him in the character of a tyrant and a lunatic?

Ah, there was no use to speak of it to them. They could not conceive of such a change. Beside, I was ashamed for the public to know our private life.

One instance as an illustration. A Mr. Tolbert and family, one of the first families in that community, were good friends of mine and on pleasant terms with Mr. Roderick. They came to spend the day. Mr. Roderick had been somewhat vexed with Mr. Tolbert in some business matter; at least had raved at home about him being a "black liar," "hypocrite," "thief," etc.

Now he met him with a bland smile and hearty handshake. Did all he could to entertain and make himself agreeable and invited Mr. Tolbert out to see his bees. Inadvertently Mr. Tolbert started through the kitchen, turning he apologized. "No, no, that doesn't matter. Come right on. An old friend like you is certainly welcome here *anywhere*. Come right through, my dear sir, etc.

After their departure "That blundering blockhead daring to pry into my things! Run headlong into one's kitchen—the prying, black-hearted rascal! How *dare* he come imposing upon me in this way."

This we listened to, as often before, in astonishment at the sudden transformation of the gentleman into the unreasonable, raving, ill-tempered "man about the home."

"To say well is good, but to do well is better,
 Do well is the spirit, and say well the letter;
 If do well and say well were fitted in one frame
 All were won, all were done, and got were all the gain."

A glorious autumn morning! The sun rose in a clear sky, sparkling jewels on every flower and shrub and "tips with fire the needles of the pines," as Whittier so inimitably puts it, I stood in the doorway drinking in nature's loveliness, and chatting to the family within. Turning I espied coming up the walk to the house a gentleman and a beautiful, bright, happy looking girl.

"Stella! Stella! can it be you?" As we opened our arms to receive the school-girl home again; but no longer the sad-faced, sick-looking girl that had left home one year ago. Health bloomed upon her dimpled cheek, and happiness glowed from her deep blue eyes.

"Mr. Lyman, my mother, father, sisters, and little brother," she said, and then designated each child by name. We had glanced in surprise at the stranger, but now took a more careful survey of the gentlemanly, refined young man and gave him a warm welcome as Stella's friend. As we went into the house, a scene a year ago flashed into my mind. Stella, standing where I had stood in the doorway, had remarked.

"I wonder what my future husband will be like ? Wish I knew what he is doing now, and where he is. If I am to marry at all, I know he is living somewhere in this wide world, as he must have been born long ago."

Mr. Lyman coming in this way had recalled the scene, and I glanced at him, wondering if this was indeed the introduction to her future husband. The interest had already been aroused by her letters and I naturally felt curious to see him.

Mr. Roderick met them, kissing Stella, and warmly welcoming Mr. Lyman in his most cordial manner and all during the visit was so agreeable and nice, that afterwards when Stella told him of her father's cruelty he could not believe it, but said, "I thought I had never met a more happy, congenial family."

Indeed Mr. Roderick appeared the most indulgent and generous father and husband he had ever seen. We soon surrounded Stella with eager questions about her school and every one she knew. She expressed herself so happy in all but the one worry that I would not escape her father's wrath, and that thought of our unsafe condition at home often brought a cloud over her otherwise bright, calm sky. Mr. Roderick, learning of Stella's engagement, was very much pleased as Mr. Lyman had property, but to let her return to school was out of the question with him. She wanted another year or two in school but her father would not hear to it at all, so the poor girl had to give it up. Now, for seven months she remained at home, performing her duties and making preparations for her wedding.

During this time I made a visit to my mother in the asylum. I found her better. The physicians had discovered the seat of the disease and had greatly improved her condition. I took Marie with me, but did not introduce her as my child. Presently mother looked up at me and said:

"Ah, Edna, you cannot deceive me, that is one of your own little girls."

She was delighted to see us and appeared her own natural self, and it seemed wrong for her to be there. I really enjoyed my visit when I heard from others how my mother's Christian influence was felt. The physicians and others spoke of her beautiful character and for her sake gave me every attention possible. She was in the "sane ward" and was comfortable in every way, surrounded by flowers, music, birds, nicely carpeted rooms, each little room, as well as the ward, being carpeted and nicely furnished. Everything was neat, clean and attractive, and was made bright and cheerful for them. Sometimes most horrible scenes were met with. In the dining-room they were often uncontrollable, dashing dishes, laughing, screaming, talking. Often the attendants have to take them away. The dining-room accommodated five hundred persons. I sat with mother at the "sane table" one meal. It was neatly furnished with white linen cloth and napkins, but at the other tables only tin cups and plates and spoons could be trusted in their hands. The grounds were beautifully kept. Entertainments, even dancing, games, etc., for the benefit of the inmates, were frequently indulged in. But sad to say, many of these poor unfortunates were left to the asylum's care entirely. Their own people neglecting and perhaps never seeing them again. I found Dr. Murphy a kind, efficient physician and Christian gentleman. A good corps of physicians assisted him. All seemed in deep sympathy with the poor inmates and did all in their power for them. Little Marie soon became a favorite with them all and was often loaded with presents and tokens of esteem.　They called her "the little darling," and I had to watch her to keep her out of dangerous touch.

I was sad at the thought of leaving my mother, yet it must be, as she was not yet permitted to leave the asylum. Good-bye is said and a parting kiss, and mother and I parted once more.

Home again with its pleasures and pain.　Pleasures with my children and in Stella's happiness, though that was often clouded by her father's insane fits.　One night he screamed and raved so loudly that a clergyman staying over night at Rachel's, a mile distant, inquired who it was screaming so.　Though Rachel knew who it was, she answered:

"Oh, an old drunken man, half crazy with delirium tremens."

Another time I passed by his nephew's house and his wife, recently married, inquired:

"What is the matter up at your house?　Often I hear Mr. Roderick screaming and slamming things around and making most frightful noises.　What is the trouble?"

Mr. Roderick's sister Lizzie, sitting near by, said:

"I can tell you what is the matter.　It's brother Jake in one of his spells.　I know all about it, I have seen a many a one.　It's like fits but not fits."

I did not answer but could not refrain a smile.

"I never heard anything like that," Mrs. Dobbs answered.　"I hear him down here every day."

I moved away without further words.　It was a subject I could not discuss.　One time I did mention it to Albert, Mr. Roderick's nephew, a young minister, who

Love is a strong influence, and ruleth with a constant and lasting power.

asked me why I did not call on them for help, or come to them.

"We all know about those awful spells he has," he said, "and you ought not to stay there with him at those times."

He was Caroline's son and had obtained a good education through great opposition. There was a sympathy between us, and often he was kind and would have done anything to relieve us. But Mr. Roderick grew worse as the winter advanced, and Stella advised me to take some step for our safety, saying:

"I can never go away and leave you here. I can never see a moment's peace if you stay."

The months wore on and the day of her departure drew near. Mr. Lyman had visited her frequently and had endeared himself to the whole family. Though young, he was a most exemplary man and worthy of highest esteem. Stella had become converted but had not yet entered the church. Nearly all in the fold now. My *prayers answered again*, as they were gathered in "one by one." One left—Ernest—but he would come soon I knew.

All my children were now perfectly devoted to me. No sacrifice was too great for them to make for their mother. Love is a strong influence over a child, and ruleth with a constant and lasting power. No rod, no fear, no other power can rule over the heart of a child and endure to life's end as pure, sincere love.

> "A mother's love, how sweet the name!
> What is a mother's love?
> A noble, pure and tender flame
> Enkindled from above."

Our days were filled with many duties now, as the wedding day approached. Stella was happy in all but leaving me to endure her father's mad fits and cruelty.

Because of the small house (Mr. Roderick had not yet finished the larger one) we could not invite many people to the wedding, and my strength had been exhausted in having so much of the providing to do, as well as so much work.

Christmas day, the day of the wedding, dawned bright and clear. We had sent Miss Tolbert word to come and spend the day, but not to say anything about the wedding. As she came by Harriet's she stopped for a while.

"Well," she said, "I will be going. I brought my knitting along and thought to spend the day with Mrs. Roderick."

"Why, didn't you know thar's a wedding over thar? Some of Edna Roderick's grand doings. Never even invited us girls. *Stella!* that *chile*, marryin'! She'll be sorry fer it yit. Bless me, what does she know? About as much "stuff" as her stuck-up ma does. Will wonders never cease? What does she know about that *boy?* I would not trust any man, and she'll be sorry for it some day. Too good to have her pore ole aunts thar ; but none sich can prosper. She'll come down yit."

To my great pleasure my father happened to come down on a visit, though he did not know of the wedding. I had not extended any invitations, as would have to invite both sides if I did, and I disliked to mar Stella's happiness with the presence of curious and critical enemies.

Rev. Mr. Seymore, Miss Hattie Grovesnor's husband, whom she had married about three years previously, performed the ceremony, and his son Albert (by his first wife) was groomsman. Stella looked very sweet and pretty in her bridal attire, and Mr. Lyman's youthful face looked so earnest and devoted, I felt I had entrusted my child into good hands, as afterwards proved.

Marie and Albert, and Sadie Tolbert and Ernest were all the attendants. The scene was a very impressive one. Love pushing the frail bark of youth and beauty out into life's sea, perhaps tempestuous and rough, perhaps calm and serene. Serenity seemed the guardian spirit to-day, however. Even Mr. Roderick was in one of his most bland, contented moods. Tears would come to my eyes as the uncertainty of life and thoughts of all the awful past, tears of happiness, too, for so happy a release for Stella from the wretched life she had so long led. Glad and thankful indeed I was to place her into the hands of love and comfort, and one so worthy. Sadness would come, though, as we knew this was the beginning of the end of our life in the old home Changes are sad always and hearts are made to ache over the uncertainty of life. Part of my reward had come in the accomplishment of a partial education of one daughter and her happy marriage; but, above all, her conversion and consecration to God. Should I not indeed shed tears of joy?

Never again were we all together as we had been in the past. Soon other separations and long years of waiting. Were we not to be gathered again into a home of our own?

"I am glad that He knows, that He sees it all through
What I meant to have done, and the thing I did do,
And over my mistakes His sweet charity throws,
I am glad that He knows."

"I am glad that He knows all my wavering trust,
I am glad that He remembers that I am but dust,
What force of temptation I have to oppose
I am glad that He knows."

" The bird from the nest is flown, the good-byes said, and we are lonely without thee, my child, but happy in your happiness."

"I miss you, my darling, my darling,
The embers burn low on the hearth,
And still is the air of the household
And hushed is the voice of its mirth."

CHAPTER XIII.

HORROR.

"Oh, wild grows the tempest and wilder
The night draweth nigh; and so dark,
And all the wild waves and the billows
Roll over my frail, trembling bark."

The wind howled around the house. The sleet and rain blew in torrents against the window pane. I woke with a strange foreboding of evil. I must work before it was too late! must plan some means of escape from our present dangerous life. To the asylum I felt Mr. Roderick's people would not let him go, and though I did not wish to leave him only in peace and good will, yet for the safety of myself and children we could not remain in his power. I proposed to him that myself and daughters go into the millinery business in the city of Asheville. As it was to make money he acquiesced to our plans very readily, and we began to make preparations to open the business. When all was in readiness, he seemed to just realize that we were leaving him, and positively refused to let us go. Father witnessed several exhibitions of Mr. Roderick's fits of madness while he was visiting us at Stella's marriage, staying three weeks thereafter. One in particular I will mention. Father was seated by the fire one cold morning when Mr. Roderick came in. Flashing into a passion at the sight of us, he turned upon

me with the most violent gesticulations, calling me vile
names and raving in the wildest, most demoniacal rage.
Father slipped out of the door and picked up a rock and
waited to see if he would strike me.   He would have
killed him if he had.   But Mr. Roderick was too sagacious
for that and dared not strike.   Father afterwards said that
he needed no further proof of his insanity, and would do all
in his power to get him into an asylum.   He left us with
that object in view, giving his own affidavit and getting all
others possible.   But his letters to me were intercepted,
and for weeks I heard nothing from him, though he wrote
repeatedly.   He was taken ill with pneumonia fever, to
which he seemed doomed every winter, so seldom he
ever escaped.   He left me upon a bed of sickness, quite
worn out with work before Stella's wedding, and then
exposure since she left trying to provide for and teach
the children.   Cold on my lungs, fever and rheumatism had me in their grasp, and I lay upon a helpless bed
of suffering.   My hands became drawn with rheumatism
so I could not use them.   So all the comforts I had provided were exhausted.   The house was left cold and
cheerless, and the food brought me I could not eat.   The
children had all started to school except Celeste, the
youngest, who remained with me.   Mr. Roderick had never
liked Celeste, and had no patience with her; and worse
than all were his strange and horrible actions while the children were absent at school.   Stella and father gone, and
only frail, timid Celeste and myself to meet his wrath.   I
could not bear that the children should lose any opportunity of school, so begged Celeste not to give way to fear,
but bear up bravely until the weather brightened and my

father and myself recovered sufficiently to have some steps taken to save us.

Mr. Roderick was looking bad—pale and more haggard than ever. He would now rise in the morning groaning, muttering, and quarrelsome, or else sullen and contrary. Immediately after breakfast, when Celeste and I were alone, the other children gone to school, he would often come into our room and burst forth with a tirade of abuse in a most shocking manner, coming toward us with head thrown back, face livid, eyes rolling and glowering murderously, his arms raised to strike. I would look undaunted right into his eyes, which would seem to arrest him, and he would turn away muttering some blood-curdling threat, cursing and jerking as he walked. Celeste clung to me, pale and trembling, not for fear for herself but for me; and though I begged her to leave me at those times, she never would, saying, "Mother, if father strikes you, he will strike over my body. I will die to save you."

A fearful blizzard swept over our section of the country, and the board roof having warped from sun and rain, the snow and sleet blew in in great quantities, so that the children's beds, standing near the warm chimney, were saturated with the melting snow, which froze from the intensely cold wind blowing in almost as fast as it thawed.

The children awaking and finding their beds one mass of ice, snow and wet clothing, the wind howling outside, while snow and sleet beat wildly in their faces, called me, alarmed at their condition. Their father, aroused from his sleep, bade them lie still—a command they could not obey, and they begged me to come to them. Mr. Roderick, infuriated beyond control over their persistency, threatened and screamed in madding passion. His threats forcing the children to tears, who were groping about in the dark and the snow, afraid to come down and unable to be quiet, I quietly slipped up stairs to bring them down to the fire. The snow lay about in piles over the floor and bed. After examining Ernest's little room and making it more comfortable for him, I started with the three trembling girls to face Mr. Roderick. Unfortunately my foot slipped on some snow at the top step. Falling, I caught with one arm in the balusters, but the entire weight of my body gave it such a strain I had to sit down and moan in agony, while the children huddled about me in the dark and cold, weeping in terror and grief. Mr. Roderick's voice rose above the storm without, in threats and names, shaking his bed and jarring the house, striking and beating with his fists in the violence of his passion, making a scene never to be erased from the minds of those participating in the agonies of that horrible night. In the morning we found the children's bed buried in snow and ice, and the snow measured four inches on the floor.

Not only was he cross and cruel to myself and the girls, but Ernest was often subjected to the same mad, horrible treatment. Happening to speak discouragingly about the crops one day, Ernest brought down his father's wrath in torrents on his head. Having to work so hard and receive nothing in return, not even his clothes, it was quite natural he should feel discouraged. His father raved in a most frantic manner, calling names and threatening. Seizing a stick he began to beat Ernest, who quickly got out of his way. Such scenes as these served me as they did Stella before she left—so unnerved her that she would drop faint upon a chair unable to move or speak. My nervous system was shocked almost beyond endurance, yet what could I do? I thought of the sad fate of a young wife in our community, and an old friend of mine, tortured and abused by her husband, until in the despair of her heart she forsook her young babe and went and hanged herself. Could I go and do likewise? Was it not a temptation, with my daily life a curse to me? Tortured into ill health and almost madness, could I help thinking of this one means of escape? Madding, indeed, the thought! Reason would say, no; mother-love, no; and, above all, the Holy Spirit of God within my soul, *no*; calming the passion, the despair of human frailty, and I was saved from a wrecked mind and suicide.

> " My soul crieth out in its anguish
>   Lord, carest thou not that I die?
> When lo, o'er the storm-driven billow,
>   My Saviour himself draweth nigh."

With this message, " Let not your hearts be troubled, ye believe in God, believe also in me," etc. Over and over again I drank in these words and it calmed and saved me. Daily seeking God's guidance through prayer and his Word, I often arose at midnight to calm my wounded spirit with his peaceful, sweet comforting words. Aye, and there in that dear book can all so tempted find solace and healing for every wound. If every suicide had read with faith God's Word the moment before he took his life, there would be no suicides, not with sane people. This one chapter in particular seemed to bring me sweet peace, the 14th chapter of St.

18

John. This was my comfort and saved my soul from despair. I had never indulged in any habit of morphine or opiates, and was not tempted in that way—not even taking anything to alleviate bodily pain and to give sleep, which so often left me being determined no habit should become my master. And those who seek such habits to drown trouble, as they say, only add fuel to the fire, when if they had only turned to the source of all blessings, such beautiful peace would have filled their souls, and they would have counted it all joy that they were permitted to suffer with those who have suffered, aye, more than it is possible for human heart to endure. It is not the history of the saints that have passed through this life "on flowery beds of ease," and our sufferings here must fit us for a higher sphere of life hereafter. It is an honor to us that God counts us worthy to suffer.

> "Oh, fear not in a world like this,
> And thou shall know ere long,
> Know how sublime a thing it is
> To suffer and grow strong."

My children's pleading faces, that now so seldom smiled, were continually calling me back, back to their rescue.

Mr. Roderick kept a sly watch upon my every action, slipping about with his catlike tread, and peering in at doors and windows with a cunning, sharp look. His small, deep, piercing eyes flashing in wild restless eagerness, with that sinister, malicious, evil expression on his face which so often excited our dread and fear. Often a mirthless cackle of a laugh as he discovered us, or with jeering taunts he would turn away. To be caged thus with one acting like a maniac filled me with such horror that all the old fear and dread that I had when I first discovered him insane returned. One day of horror Celeste and myself hid all day from Mr. Roderick, and watched him from dark corners as he worked, talking and muttering to himself. I felt some immediate step must be taken for our safety. The roads were filled with ice and snow so Stella could not come and I could not send to father. So I decided to go to my friend Mrs. Tolbert for protection, and tell her my fears and condition and ask her assistance. Celeste was daily growing thinner and paler, her appetite failed and her pale face haunted my sleeping and waking hours. Through the child's entreaties I had stopped the children from school to be with us. Mr. Roderick immediately objected and forced them back to school, but they would hasten home in the evenings in alarm and terror for our safety.

Celeste's condition grew worse, her smiles ceased altogether and a great shadow fell over her young life. The weather became so bad I could not get word to my friends—the severest weather we had yet known in the South. The rigors of a mountain winter were upon us, and we were shut in from our friends, alone with a maniac. Celeste was now counting the days until school closed, so great was her terror. She watched her father's every movement, and when he came near me she determined to risk her own life to save mine. This constant care and devotion won my deepest love and appreciation and was never forgotten.

When the weather brightened Stella made us a short visit, advised us to leave, saying she would render any aid in her power. " Go to some of the neighbors and stay, and write me your plans and I will do all I can to help you." One week more of school, then I proposed to Mr. Roderick that he, Celeste and myself, spend some time with one of our friends. He gladly consented and we spent a few days with Mrs. Heard and others. No trace of Mr. Roderick's evil, insane nature was now visible; his "company manners" on as usual. He caressed and pitied Celeste, and talked of the children, and I was "my dear."

But I told them privately how he had been acting and our fearful condition at home. They replied that they had occasionally noticed at church the wild look in his eyes and now knew I must be right—that he was insane.

When Mr. Roderick said he must return home, they urged him to permit Celeste and myself to remain a few days longer. This they did to give me an opportunity to go to Marion and consult doctors and lawyers as to the proper course to take.

I thought now I would not receive much opposition from Mr. Roderick's people, as only a short while before they, having heard his screams at home, I said to them that I thought he was insane. They answered, "Yes, his spells are worse, and as he grows older he may become dangerous. You must come to us when he gets bad, come to us for protection." So I thought they might sustain me in the step I was taking.

Arriving in Marion, I found my physical strength less than I had calculated upon and could scarcely walk the streets without tottering. I consulted my lawyer, Colonel Clair, who advised me to get out a warrant for insanity and have Mr. Roderick brought before the physicians of the city for examination. Then I applied to the county physician, who promised to put him in the insane asylum if

I gained the consent of as many as two of his relatives. I had kept the matter as quiet as possible and requested them not to mention it. Returning to one of our neighbors, I spent the night. Next morning I was surprised and distressed to see Marie and Celeste coming to the house in tears.

Sobbing convulsively, they told how their father had already heard of my business in the city, and that I had a warrant issued for his arrest, and had sent them after me to return immediately.

As we passed the school Ernest came out and accompanied us home bravely intending to defend us if within his ability. The children stated that their father flew into a passion and uttered many threats against me. I well knew what to expect. Imagine my surprise when I reached the house. Mr. Roderick received me pleasantly, but sullenly. After talking a while he said : " I understand that you have sworn out a warrant against me for insanity. I am aware of the fact that something is the matter with me, and perhaps it would do me good to be treated, so if you will give me a few days I will prepare to go."

Innocent of any scheme of evil, I promised him two weeks' time in which to get ready, not knowing that his people had made this plot in order to defeat me. The children afterwards told me that his sisters and his nephews had been there talking a long time out in the yard with their father, and they feared the worst. I determined to do my duty and to tell Rachel all about him and my great fears, hoping to reach a tender chord in her heart to save my children. I could leave, but it was for them that I must enlist their sympathy. She advised me to go if I felt unable to bear his treatment, but the children, she said must stay and take care of their father. She charged Bertha and Celeste not to say one word against their father, commanding them to obey her. No, I said, I will not do this under any circumstances. It is for the children I suffer, not for myself. Mr. Roderick now raved incessantly. No letters were permitted to leave the house without his inspection, and the children were not allowed to carry any for me. My brain seemed on fire with the horror of our situation. What could we do? What step could we take? My father had recovered his usual health and now wrote me what he thought best for us to do and that he would come with help. The postmaster was a friend of Mr. Roderick's and reserved the letters, giving them only to him, who opened and read them, never delivering them to me. The children were forbidden to carry any letters to or from the office, and all were intercepted ; thus all communication with my friends was cut off. Mr. Roderick and his nephews, two strong, powerful men, now rode all over the country making fun of and making many false statements about me. One, that I had stolen valuable mail from the post-office, and the postmaster even came to the house accusing me of it, saying that I would have to go to the penitentiary, and tried to make me acknowledge that I had robbed the mails; their object being to frighten me into owning to some wrong-doing that they might have something that would weaken my evidence in court. Of course I knew nothing about the mail, nor had any opportunity to do so, or to even cause any suspicion. The postmaster who helped in this slander afterwards lost his position by being charged with the same offense he tried to accuse me of. Marie, just verging into womanhood, being sixteen years of age, wept piteously over

these accusations against her mother, whom she felt was
all that was expected of true womanhood. Often she
would stand over me as I lay upon the bed, too sick to
sit up, saying, "Mother, how can I bear it! To have
my pure, true mother so talked about! I cannot endure
it." My only reply was, "The Lord is my helper and I
will not fear what man can do unto me."

Mr. Roderick was daily more cruel. Would not permit the children to come near now nor wait upon me, nor
show any kindness whatever, talking and trying to turn
them from me; he talked to Ernest and told him such
awful falsehoods to turn him against me; they did anything
and all they could do, that they might take my children
away from me. But the children never answered a word,
nor for a moment doubted their mother. Mr. Roderick
would get the Bible and compel them to read, then
he would get up and preach sermons and make sarcastic
remarks about us all in the same breath; groaning, moaning, gesticulating wildly, laughing that dry, hard laugh,
and looking 'so thoroughly the cunning maniac that the
children were frightened into tears and often made sick
by these severe nervous shocks, they became deathly pale
and grew thin and nervous, shuddering when they heard his
footsteps approaching. Harriet's angry face would often
peer in at us from door or window, with loud threats
and abusive language, adding to our wretchedness.

Not a friend's face shadowed our door, not for days
and weeks; not even hearing from Stella, as my letters
to her were intercepted. Ah! those terrible days of
longing for one kind familiar face, one word of hope
of comfort! One evening after supper, Mr. Roderick's big, burley nephew, together with his sister Har-

riet, came in, presumably to sit until bedtime. The real object of their visit was soon apparent when Mr. Roderick began taunting and quarreling at me about getting out a warrant against him. The others joined in, and soon I was in a perfect Bedlam. They had their victim surrounded and helpless. Mr. Roderick now took the floor and said, "Now, madam, you have had your way just as long as I am going to permit it! I'll show you who is boss in this house and of these children! Books, fine clothes and all such *folderol* is at an end, do you hear? I'll teach them some sense. Send them to the field to work, where they ought to be clearing land and doing something that will make them some account. They shall work and take care of me, every one of them, until they are twenty-one. Do you hear that, madam?" he screamed. Dancing around the room, he seized his old hat and began slashing me across the head and face, calling names too malignant to repeat, the nephew and aun, urging him on. This was the scene they had planned and they were gloating over it. Their "brother Jake should beat such a wife as that."

Celeste trembling crept to my side and sat down, determined to shield me if she could. This only infuriated her father, who roared at her to go away, the others joining in the command. But she looked them bravely in the face and sat still until I, fearing for her safety, requested her to leave the room. He now stood over me beating me with his hat until his nephew, seeing his infuriated passion, came to the rescue and took Mr. Roderick out into the yard, where they had a long consultation. Next day I told Mr. Roderick that I would withdraw the warrant. He promised to do better. I thought the withdrawal would be some protection from him, but not for long as was soon proved. If possible he grew worse. I could not get away now; I was too sick to walk. The children could perhaps save themselves by running away but they would not leave me. Prayer alone was the only solace. Not a ray of light seemed to brighten our pathway. I begged the children to pray. Pray continually, I said. God alone is our helper. Each day they would take their Bible and steal off into the woods and pray, returning they would try to comfort me with the assurance that they knew their prayers would be answered. Especially was Marie confident that help would soon come. Ernest had become melancholy and nothing seemed to comfort him, and would often sit with his head in his hands and not say a word. He seemed in depair. When his father had attempted to beat him some time before he had declared he would run away. I had begged him out of it, as he was our only protector now. Spiritual-minded Marie was a great comfort with her perfect faith and love.

Mr. Roderick's sister Jane came and began discussing the warrant business. I said to her: "You are all now trying to prevent my proving your brother insane, but if he should murder one of us in his fits you would then do all in your power to prove him a raving maniac and save him from hanging. Remember, if such is the case, that I said to you that I did not want him hanged, not if he kills every one of us, *for he is at times insane*." She answered not, for she knew the truth of my words.

The children were kept under strict surveillance and not allowed to speak of me, not even to mention my sickness. I grew so much worse that I at last give up and wanted them to leave me to die.   What had the future for me, chained to a maniac, or go away again to hospitals, to the hard world I disliked so much. Even though kindly treated at the hospitals, it was not *home* nor *pleasure* to be there. I wanted my children and home—did not want to give them up ; be it ever so humble, it was a shield from the world.   Out into the world it was a struggle for shelter and food; and also for friends; a *homeless stranger*, doomed to walk and sit alone ; subjected to cruel criticisms, rebuffs and persecutions, trying to get people to believe my story and see things as they really were ; to believe, to trust me! Oh it would be so sweet to die, and rest—rest in Jesus' arms—rest in heaven—rest in the quiet grave.   Oh! let me die! I begged my children to cease their urging me to make further attempts for them and my life.   Let me die! Let me pass away even in all the horror of dying friendless, despised, persecuted, and neglected, in the hands of an apparent maniac. It was death I longed for, death I craved! My children could then run away--they were young and now could manage. My poor girls became wild with grief and sobbed in anguish. Celeste bursting forth in passionate weeping, alarming to hear, "Mother if you die I shall kill myself; all hope will be gone from us forever! Mother, all plead, we rather have you alive, even if separated from us, than all the world beside! Mother, go away and live for us! Do not give up, we beg, *beseech* you to leave us, and live for our sakes!   Do not remain to certain death !   What will we do without our mother ?"

Bertha said that if I would only go away and save myself and her sisters, she would sacrifice herself stay and bear it to save us. She was less sensitive than her sisters and ever unselfish and strong.

Before she was the first child to want to go with me, and now ready to sacrifice herself to save the rest of us. But I seemed lost to their presence and pleading, and looking beyond, felt unequal to again take up the burden of life. Worn, wearied spirit, longing for the heavenly shore ! The presence of Christ and his angels hovered o'er me, and I felt a perfect peace and a lifting up above the horrors of our situation. Knowing now that God had heard our prayers, I felt submissive to his will; whatever that might be, I knew it would be well. Remain, die, and leave the children, or go away, live and struggle on. Thy will be done, O Lord. The question was settled with me, and left in the hand of the One better able to direct it. A complete resignation to the divine will, and I was lifted in my Savior's arms to realms of light and bliss, known only to those who have suffered such anguish as mine and the following lines formed in my mind:

> Only in Jesus' love are we blest
> Only in Jesus hope we for rest,
> Only with Jesus, there ever to be,
> Savior of sinners, O! hide us in Thee.
>
> Only with Jesus burdens we share,
> Only our Jesus truly doth care,
> Only can Jesus feel every woe,
> More of our Savior we're longing to know.

In reply to my children's anxious questioning, I said "I am resting upon my God and await his will." Longingly they waited, watched and prayed, hovering about my bed (in their father's absence) with loving words and tender caresses; they felt it right for me to go and believed God would open the way. "Mother" cried Marie, one day, "the way is opened. See, Stella and Mr. Lyman are coming! Now you must go! Will you not? God hath sent them in answer to our prayers, and you must go." I could not doubt but this was his will and the right course to pursue ; for their sakes I made ready.

Stella, after a long suspense and waiting, had at last received the letter I had sent to the post-office by Bertha. Pinning the letter in the waist of her dress, the placid-looking child passed unsuspected to the furthest post-office and posted it. This letter Stella received and came at once.

Away from the children I knew I could not write and receive letters without their father's inspection, so we agreed upon certain signs and letters that we only could understand and their suspicions would not be aroused.

Thus we could keep each other informed all about ourselves; then, too, Stella would visit the children as often as possible until I was able to attend to having Mr. Roderick sent to the asylum, or get them away from him.

The parting was indeed distressing. My heart was torn with terrible emotions at leaving these helpless, weeping children at the cruel mercy of their father. Although they wanted me to go, they could not control their grief at the parting. Mr. Roderick was restrained by the presence of Mr. Lyman, and thought I was only going to the hospital; knowing I would return if he kept the children. He came out into the yard, however, and stated if I went it was against his will and he did not approve of it at all. I bade Ernest—pale sad-faced Ernest—to look after his sisters' welfare and protect them with all his strength. The dear boy promised to do all he could. "Oh my darings I go for your dear sakes. Trust to God,—he will keep you. Study all you can. Read your Bible and pray always! Hope in Jesus, and trust to my love and untiring efforts in your behalf. Good-bye, my darlings, good-bye!"

> " In the midst of wild tossing billows
>   Is *one* place of sweet perfect peace,
> Where the dear Loving Master *abidest*,
>   The storms and the tempests *must* cease.
>
> So I walk by the still quiet waters,
>   Even tho' the dark billows may roll,
> If only my Lord is beside me,
>   If only his peace fills my soul."

CHAPTER XIV.

THE BEGINNING OF THE END.

"What can it mean?   Is it aught to Him
That the nights are long and the days are dim,
Can He be touched by the griefs I bear,
Which sadden the heart and whiten the hair?
Around His throne are eternal calm,
And strong, glad music of happy psalms,
And bliss unruffled by any strife.
How can He care for my little life?

And yet I want Him to care for me,
While I live in this world where the sorrows be,
Where the lights die down from the path I take,
Where strength is feeble and friends forsake.

Where love and music that once did bless
Have left me to silence and loneliness,
And my life-song changes to sobbing prayers,
Then my heart cries out for a God who cares.
He lifts the burden, for He is strong,
He stills the sigh and awakens the song;
The sorrows that bowed me down he bears,
And loves and pardons *because He cares.*"

H, my children, how can I leave you so?
Oh, my children! My heart seemed breaking, and I turned for a last look at the
four dear faces watched by the gloomy,
stern one beside them.

Three bright, golden-haired girls, too timid and delicate for their hard life, and a boy of a mild and peaceful

spirit, strangely unlike his father, all left without one friend to whom they could turn in any emergency. Entirely helpless—no earthly aid; only in God could I hope for their safety. I also felt sorry for Mr. Roderick, whose demon of insanity had wrecked the lives of all belonging to him, and who in some future time would suffer entire separation from those who could have been his chief comfort. I had approached him with kind words at parting, but the evil spirit within him prompted a cruel reply; and thus we separated in coldness.

In Marion I did not even mention the subject to one person, for the men knew Mr. Roderick's side only, and while they knew it an uncongenial marriage and probably did not blame me for leaving, yet they were generally in sympathy with Mr. Roderick as regards the children. I felt, too, that anything I said then might reach Mr. Roderick's ears. The only safety for the children was to keep down those mad fits of his. I was altogether too weak and ill to discuss the matter, was physically unable to do anything yet, and skillful medical treatment and rest were necessary first.

Stella and her husband paid me every attention, as did also my friends Mr. and Mrs. Seymore. Resting with them I soon recovered enough strength to proceed to Asheville to physicians for skillful treatment to restore me to health, with letters of introduction from Mrs. Seymore to many of her friends and physicians in Asheville; also a good letter from Bishop Cheshier, who gave me a high recommendation and introduction to Mr. Dubose and the people of that city. I had appealed to a minister and one or two business men in Marion for a letter, but they refused, saying I ought to go back to my husband—not knowing but one side. So where Mr. Roderick's influence could be felt, I could accomplish but little. His was the most perfect double character I ever knew.

Soon after my arrival in Asheville I received a letter from my dear mother, which impressed me very much. Some extracts I give below:

"You think me a true prophet. You know my prophecy of old did come true. Well, here I say again, only trust and all will come to pass yet. Read 37th Psalm. You know how often you and I have read it together. Don't talk about dying. You will not die—you must not die. You have not accomplished your mission yet. 'Call her not hence with mission unfulfilled. Oh, leave her here and give her time to do thy holy will.'

" What would become of your children and me? Why, you are the central figure around which all my earthly hopes and wishes revolve. What do you suppose God raised you, as it were, from worse than death? Surely for a purpose, and his purpose will be accomplished. He has seen fit to let us suffer more still to purify us as he sees we need it for that purpose, and if, with all this suffering we are saved and our loved ones, it is well. I worry less and less about my children and theirs. I think and trust they will be saved. Christ suffered to atone for our sins. What fearful sufferings you and I have passed through! What was it for? Yours were unmerited. I was not entirely guiltless in your case, and of your great sacrifice. Perhaps it was all designed ; we know not. God and you, dear child, forgive me, for I can never forgive myself. I think He has forgiven me, I have prayed over this so much; but no one can take away the sweet peace from our souls, or our hope of eternal life. 'If God be for us, who shall be against us?' This helps me to bear up under affliction.

"I am glad your children are enjoying religion. Dear children, how I long to see them! Daniel calls upon God to plead his cause, you must do the same."

My friends at Old Fort were kind and sympathetic. I stayed a week at Mrs. Tremont's, and at church all my old friends came and warmly welcomed me. While at Old Fort a singular incident occurred in my receiving several letters from different parties in which they referred me, as mother did, to the 37th Psalm, and I often opened the Bible at the words "as thy faith is, so shall it be unto thee. All things work together for good to those who love God." These things impressed and encouraged me, so after locating with my brother Bradley in Asheville, I took up the thread of life with more hope. Arrangements were made to take me into the hospital for treatment. Health must be restored first. While there I succeeded in gaining a promise of my children's admision into schools, provided I could get possession of them, either by law or otherwise. A deep interest was soon manifested in my case among the physicians and prominent clergyman and church people, as well as the Masonic Fraternity. The leading physicians of the city, from my description, pronounced Mr. Roderick an insane man, or at times insane—probably an epileptic maniac. They said that if this was the trouble, it was dangerous for any woman or child to be left in his power, and advised me to take some immediate steps to rescue my children. My brother wrote letters and did all he could to assist me. I had come to Asheville with faith

19

that God would restore my children to me, and now it seemed the way was opening, though many would say they were unable to see how I could succeed, yet I believed all would come, and knew God was all powerful and felt his daily presence was with me.

The biography of my life, which I had begun several years before had been left in my brother's care. I now took it up and began writing again. Ever since I had thought of writing this book, I had felt when working upon it I was doing the thing God would have me do; when I gave it up I seemed to be neglecting a duty, and felt less hopeful. When by prayer and suffering I was drawn near to Him, I was always impressed that this was the work He had for me to do. Its influence for good to my fellow-beings I hoped and prayed might be felt, and thus I might be of some service to them and "make the world all the better for my having lived in it" and suffered. I did not want to go to heaven empty-handed.

> "Must I go, and empty-handed,
> Must I meet my Savior so?
> Not one soul with which to greet Him,
> Must I empty-handed go?"

Every letter from the children rent my heart afresh as they recounted their father's cruelty—not in words, of course, as their father read every line they wrote but by signs and letters we had agreed upon, they let me know their condition, until their letters stopped altogether, forbidden to write at all I suppose. In one letter Marie enclosed a rosebud and deep down in its petals, entirely hid from view, I found a little slip of paper in which she told me their sad state and sent her love and prayers for me. Each letter was such a shock to my nervous system that I became sick and weak and unable to sit up for some hours, so overcome was I by fear and sorrow for those dear children. Stella often said while I was with her that she feared for their lives ; that the life of one of them might have to be sacrificed yet, before that community would be convinced of the truth, and we both felt it would be Celeste, my dear youngest born, because her father disliked her on account of her quick perceptive mind, bright piquiant ways, and her devotion to myself. I feared this was only too true and received each letter in breathless horror, dreading to open it, and when the letters ceased coming at all the suspense was almost more than I could bear. I had to put my *whole* trust in God, and trust to Him in perfect faith, or my reason would have been dethroned. In this way strength came, faith lifted me above the situation, and I believed God would protect them. To God would I turn constantly, and often would open the Bible to passages which gave me such perfect assurance that it calmed and conforted me. My brother was again in poor health, and he could not give all the assistance necessary for me to make the effort to procure my children. A suit had to be brought, if Mr. Roderick could not be put into the asylum; if both failed the children would have to run away, and I would put them in school, and Mr. Roderick would *have* to bring suit then, and the matter be settled by law. This latter was the most difficult, because of the strict watch kept over the children by Mr. Roderick and his people. It would be almost impossible for them to slip away from him now that his suspicions were aroused. Money must be raised to aid in the work, so I resolved to try to borrow it. I went to the superintendent of the Vanderbilt estate, and his wife kindly loaned the amount sufficient for present expenses. I had left the hospital much sooner than I should have done, but I could not stay there a moment longer after I had strength to go away and be at work for the rescue of my children. Armed with letters from prominent clergymen addressed to the judge, also from physicians, schools and friends to the physicians of Marion, I returned to Stella's to begin the fight for those three girls and boy waiting so patiently for me. I found that Stella had not heard from them and had been too sick to visit them at all. I could not bear the suspense and urged her to accompany me. It was absolutely necessary that I should see them, tell them of my plans and give them money to bear their expenses in the event they had to run away.

I knew it was a dangerous visit, for Mr. Roderick's suspicions perhaps had been sustained by reports of what I was doing, as there is always some one ready and eager to carry news. The weather was intensely hot— about the middle of July. Stella not well, and myself still sick and weak, we were scarcely equal to the hazardous trip. As we neared the neighborhood we met a woman who, recognizing us, began talking about "poor Harriet," who, after all her trouble in raising the children, had had them taken away from her. I knew from her words what the opinion of the whole neighborhood was. Late in the afternoon we drove into the lane leading to the old home. As we neared the house we saw a golden head peep out from among the shrubbery, then dart into the house, and all three came running out to meet us. "Oh! Mother, we are so glad to see you, but father has threatened to kill you and you must not stay a minute. We dare not let him know you are here. He says he will surely kill you!" they exclaimed with bated breath and frightened looks, watching to see if he was coming. "He has been just as bad, if not worse, than when you were here. We have had a terrible time but you must go before he sees you." But I felt no fear, and stepping from the buggy I told the pale, frightened children that I *must* come or nothing would ever be accomplished. "Come in, I want to tell you my plans," and I soon told them of all that happened and what I wished to do. Bade them to wait one month longer, until the fall court; then if they heard nothing from me, they were to take their first opportunity and run away. I had previously enlisted the interest and sympathy of the conductors on the train who promised to take care of and deliver them safely to their journey's end.

I gave them their money and letters, with careful instructions to hide their money, and prepared them in every way for the escape. Even giving them an anesthetic to reserve for their father if he refused to sleep and watched them too closely, this to be used only as a last resort. if they could not "slip off" in any other way. A mild dose would put him to sleep long enough for them to make good their escape, and a physician had advised and given the exact amount, so I knew I was doing no wrong.

Fortunately I had found the children alone, for we had not a moment afterward. They told me of all that had happened since I left. How their father had beaten Marie until her face was black with bruises for a week, *because she was sick* and slapped Celeste so violently that the marks of his fingers appeared in bruises on her face next day.

He would pray and quarrel almost in the same breath, and would often hide the food not allowing them enough to eat. They had worked in the rain, and had been forced to work when so sick and tired they could scarcely stand. Indeed, Marie said she felt she must die at times she was so faint and ill (a modern Pharaoh in all his hard-heartedness and cruelty). They also said that Ernest had kept the promise he made me and did all in his power to protect and care for them. That he was still sad and talked but little.

In the time of our conversation some of them would continually keep watch, fearing their father's approach. Scarcely had the above been told before he came. Stella arose to meet him with all the pleasantness she could summons. I too spoke cordially and began telling him of some incidents of the past summer, then inquiring about things on the farm, about his bees, stock, etc. Then we jested wittily on different topics until the sullen expression wore into a smile, though occasionally I noticed a sinister, evil look flash from his eyes. Soon we were out in the yard with him looking at the new house and taking a general interest in everything; this we must do to keep him in a good humor. Ernest came in while we were at supper, but I had no opportunity of seeing him alone. All went pleasantly that evening with the exception of that sardonic look, which would come into Mr. Roderick's face, then he would hastily leave the room; several times he did this, and a dreadful foreboding filled my mind. I could not sleep, and arose unrefreshed next morning. I wanted to speak to Ernest alone and give him his money, but Mr. Roderick's sharp eyes watched my every movement. The children were at work and I was standing before the mirror combing my hair when Mr. Roderick came in; walking to my side, he gave my dress a violent jerk and made some sarcastic remarks. I foresaw the storm in his face and turning, smilingly said, 'Why, I thought this pretty black and white wrapper would please you." Scarcely were the words spoken before he fastened both hands into my hair and jerked and pulled it furiously, screaming, cursing, calling names, a perfect torrent of abuse. Ernest heard him and ran to my assistance. He finally loosened his father's hands and I slipped out into the yard. Jerking away from Ernest he ran and caught me (though I did not run) and snatched a handful of hair out of my head, screaming and dancing, saying I will kill you! "I mean it! You shall die!" Again Ernest interfered, and I walked away into the house. He rushed after me as I was in the act of taking up my Bible lying upon the table. "How dare you touch that book, you vile creature! Put it down! It is too sacred a thing for your vile *hands* to pollute," with a slap that sent me across the room against the door. I opened it and went off to the kitchen; he followed and rushed upon me again, beating me back into the corner and with his fist pounded my head and body, screaming through his clenched teeth that he would kill me, "stamp the life out of you." His murderous white face glowered down upon me in threats and curses too horrible to mention. His looks verified his words; murder was written in every line of his face as he continually cried, "I'll kill you! I mean it! You shall not escape me this time!" Ernest constantly tried to hold his father but was knocked to the back side of the room, saying, "You dare interfere, you young scoundrel! I'll cut your throat from ear to ear if you do not let me alone."

As the blows fell thick and fast with terrific force, I felt that I had but a short time in which to live. My jaws were nearly knocked from their sockets and my temples bruised and head bleeding, where my hair had been torn out. Was I to die such a death at last at the hands of this madman! After all my efforts for my children was it to end here? "Ernest! Ernest! Will you let your father kill me?" I saw Marie weeping in a corner, Celeste had run for a neighbor, Bertha was away from home, as was Stella. Ernest again sprang forward at my words, and succeeded in pushing him away for a moment. Then Stella returning, cried "Father! father! Stop this, or I shall die. Stop I tell you." She wept aloud and continued her entreaties until she and Ernest succeeded in getting him away. I could not weep nor cry out. The agony of the awful situation dazed and overwhelmed me. At this instant Celeste came in followed by Mr. Bob Crowley, a friend of Mr. Roderick's. Mr. Roderick turned to Mr. Crowley instantly dropping into his bland, cordial manner, then began telling him of me, charging me with all kind of misdemeanors. Mr. Crowey tried to quiet the weeping children by saying you need not fear, children, your father is too good a man to harm any of you, and your mother is in no danger, and he turned to leave the room. Stella ran out after him and entreated him not to go, "do not leave us until mother can be got away she cried. He will kill her if you do." I added my entreaties to hers but to no purpose. He only replied that Mr. Roderick was too good a man for that, there was not the least bit of danger.

"You do not care if he does" I said ; "you would like him to do it, and you have all been prejudiced against me and do not know what you are talking about. Can

I Will kill you! I mean it; you shall die, and murder was written in every line of his face.

you not see ?   See that I will be murdered by a cunning madman !" I said.   But our pleadings were of no avail; he left us, and Stella returned to her father, who was still raving in the room, crying, "Father ! father ! *you must not do this* ! I cannot bear it; I beg you to get my horse and buggy and let us go!   I shall die ! I shall die ! I implore you, let us go!"   She sobbed violently, and all the children cried silently in fear.   In the meantime I made hasty preparations to leave. Mr. Roderick following me, sneering, hissing, and would thrust his face right up into mine with a most awful maniacal expression; trying to make me acknowledge I was in the wrong and must ask his forgiveness, saying, "Madam! you shall not stay in this house another minute unless you apologize and promise me to be obedient hereafter and submit to me more than you have ever done before !" I had nothing to say, no apologies nor promises to make, and kept on with my preparations, trying to escape him by going out into the yard and away from him, but he followed.   Ernest soon had the horse and buggy ready, and Stella and I proceeded to get in. Mr. Roderick came up threatening to murder me and looking right up into my face. "I will drag you right out of here and kill you!" he said, clenching his fists and grinding his teeth. Stella's cries and constant pleading kept him down somewhat until we were safely in, and started away. The three weeping girls were sent to gather beans in the field although it was Sunday morning, and Mr. Roderick afterwards went on to Sunday-school where he was superintendent.   So I had to leave without saying good-bye to them. Mr. Roderick continued to follow us for some time, walking beside the buggy, raving and threatening, and I momentarily expected to be dragged from the buggy and stamped to death. Ernest followed unseen by him, slipping from tree to tree. but watching his father, so that if he did attempt to do us harm he would be near to protect us.

His father had driven him back when we first started, but he followed on the sly and kept a watch on him.

Grief overcame me as I thought of the unhappy result of this trip and leaving the children in still greater danger, but I knew I must arouse myself to the work of getting possession of them.

Scarcely a word passed between Stella and myself through that long tedious drive. In Marion I stopped at a drug store to get some medicine and met Dr. Armstrong, who inquired into the cause of my bruised up appearance. I told him all about it, then showed him the letters I had from Asheville. He at once said Mr. Roderick must be insane and said he would make an effort to have him put in the asylum and would himself see the other physicians of the town and the county physicians. This he did, but the county doctor declined to do anything. Then I went to him myself, imploring justice at his hands, but he refused with harsh, unkind words. I consulted several other physicians in the community, and all thought alike that Mr. Roderick was insane, but without the approval of the county physician, who was Mr. Roderick's friend, nothing could be done. So this plan had to be relinquished; no other course could I pursue but resort to law. With the assistance of Mr. and Mrs. Seymore, who so kindly aided me in every way they could, I notified my parents and brothers to attend, and then came the long waiting as is usual upon the courts. Suspense so wearing I could scarcely bear it.

What might not happen to the children while the slow arm of the law meted out its decisions to its subjects. Waiting was all for me to do now, and the following lines forming in my mind spoke my heart :

WAITING.

Waiting, dreaming, waiting, by some flowing mystic rill,
Waiting, hoping, waiting, strong desires my spirit fill,
Waiting, restless waiting, Oh'! could I join the busy throng,
Waiting, patient waiting, for right to triumph over wrong.

Waiting, weary waiting, as the hours creep slowly by,
Waiting, sadly waiting, unnoticed by those passing nigh.
Waiting, daily waiting, with fire alive in heart and brain.
Waiting, yearly waiting, tho' seeming but to wait for pain.

Waiting, striving, waiting, wisdom's goal I fain would win.
Waiting, weeping, waiting, ever bearing Adam's sin.
Waiting, vainly waiting, the race is for the swift and strong,
Waiting, sighing, waiting, pouring forth my grief in song.

Waiting, fearing, waiting, while the shadows gather deep,
Waiting, doubting, waiting, down the rocky cliffs they creep.
Waiting, longing, waiting, for man's promises not filled,
Waiting, trusting, waiting, Jesus speaks and all is still.

Stella was very ill, the result of the shock she had received at her father's, and was unable to be present at court, so her affidavit had to be taken by a magistrate from Marion. Among a few staunch faithful friends I found refuge during court weeks, most of them were old citizens of the town, who had known me since my girlhood, and a deep sympathy was manifested by many dear women. Unfortunately for me a very exciting criminal case was on trial, which occupied the entire time up to the very last day. It rain steadily, the streams rising and flooding the country, and the streets were almost impassable. From a window overlooking the court-yard I saw Mr. Roderick affectionately patting the men on their shoulders and walking with them, or with arm around them walking about the yard in earnest conversation. Ernest he had brought with him, but kept such a strict surveillance over him that he only had an opportunity to slip in and see me once or twice to assure me that he would speak the truth fully when called upon in court, and no fear of his father, or, indeed, of any one, could make him swear a falsehood. Once I saw them take him into a lawyer's private office, and I knew he was then going through the trying ordeal of cross question. From the faces of the men I read their displeasure at Ernest's answers. The criminal case and the severe rains had prevented the magistrate going for Stella's affidavit. Also my father and brothers had been water-bound so they could not come, though Harry met me at the beginning of court but had to return for father's affidavit and for others, and now could not reach the town because of the heavy rains. Mrs. Seymore had returned home with the intention to come back for the trial, but the flood and sickness detained her. Mrs. Tremont's baby died, so of course she could not attend. Mother's affidavit had not arrived, and the magistrate's and lawyer's entire attention was absorbed by the criminal case. And as I looked out of my window, with all these barriers to our success absorbing my mind, and looking would behold Mr. Roderick in pleasant conversation with the men in the court-yard, apparently on good terms with all, my heart would faint within me. Oh, the anguish of my soul as this suspense wore on day after day! I could not eat nor sleep, would walk the floor and wring my hands in agony at the thought of failure and of the hourly peril my children were in. Would they escape ? Oh, my heavenly Father, pity us! As things now stood, so far as human eye could see, no ray of hope was in view. Then a promise from the Bible would flit through my mind just as if spoken words, so vividly they impressed me that God was with me, and they gave me faith to persist and be brave. " Put your trust in God and He will bring it to pass" rang through my head continuously, and " Cast all your care upon Him, for He careth for you." These and many more similar ones kept alive the faith that had for years enabled me to rise above the waves of woe that so often threatened to overwhelm me.

The day before the trial the sun came out bright, and clear, and nature smiled joyfully through the tears of sparkling raindrops and many rushing streams.

About 10 o'clock that morning brother Harry's arrival first gladdened my heart and aroused slumbering hope, as beside his strong presence he brought money and father's affidavit. A magistrate had gone for Stella's affidavit and the morning's mail brought one from my mother, with a certificate from her physician as to her improved health, both physically and mentally, and her perfect ability to swear truthfully to such a paper. The noon mail brought encouraging letters and affidavits from Old Fort friends. Brother Bradley came with the affidavits and money for lawyer's fee. My Marion friends seemed now thoroughly aroused to a realization that now was their time to come to my aid if ever, and sent me strong affidavits and said and did all in their power. Mr. and Mrs. Seymore and Mr. Lyman came in bringing

Stella's and their own affidavits. At last all was in readiness for the final struggle. Only the children's presence was wanting, and they had been summoned. Would they come? was the question uppermost in the hearts of all us watching ones. Would they brave their father's anger by disobeying him?

Over and over I cried in my heart, would they come? "Wait on the Lord." "Cast all your care upon Him, for He careth for you," echoed in reply, and hope and trust would still the tearless, terrible anguish and suspense. Next morning I was up before light, waiting and watching for the children. I felt they doubtless would have to run away, as their father would not let them come to swear against himself. I walked out upon the streets I thought they would likely come. Up and down, back and forth, peering into every corner, but no children. Entering my door in sickening despair, with hope dying in my heart, I looked back and what did I see—the sight I so longed for—my darlings were coming, Ernest piloting the way; each with a bundle came hurrying in. They had risen long before day, slipped away from their aunts and walked nine miles, walking on the railroad track. Their father had been watching also, but at the time of their entrance his attention was engaged in conversation with a party near him, and though he was in full sight of the door he did not see them, neither did he know I was in that house. Taking the children we ran through the wet corn, climbed a barbed wire fence (though I received a fall in my effort) and ran through a lane to a friend's house, who had promised to hide the children until the decision of the court was given. The children and myself had resolved that whatever the court's decision

What did I see? The sight I so longed for ; my darlings were coming, each with a bundle, Ernest piloting the way.

we would let nothing again separate us, but would make good our escape that night away and out of the country. They said "no law, no person, should tear them from me." They would die first, pale weeping children!

The case was called before the judge, and Mr. Roderick and his lawyers learning now I had possession of the children, and hearing all the good evidence my lawyers presented, became frightened, and after much consultation among themselves, to our great joy and relief they agreed to give up the three girls, while to our sorrow Ernest was to return to his father; but not without a secret understanding between he and I that as soon as opportunity offered he was to run away and come to me. Although it cost me great grief to give him up even for a short time, I joined in this agreement, and Ernest came, without his father's knowledge, and told me good-bye. Mr. Roderick coming in to sign the paper turned to the three girls and made a most frantic, wild speech of all kinds of advice to them; losing his self-possession, he became excitedly insane in his manner and speech. When he left the room one of the lawyers came forward and said:

"Mrs. Roderick, I see you are right. I had believed you mistaken, but I understand it all now; *he is insane* No sane man could act and talk as he did."

All was arranged, and bidding my kind, hospitable. Marion friends good-bye, we accompanied Mr. Lyman to his and Mrs. Seymore's homes. With hearts full of gratitude to God we joyfully went with our friends, expecting soon to send my daughters to school. Stella was improving, and now mother was so much better and her mind restored that I was humbly grateful for all God's goodness to me.

At last the beginning of the result of all my hard work and prayers, with a ray of hope that would glitter and be a guiding star to the end. Hope was now firmly planted in our hearts and training our hands, and it was not with an unforgiving spirit that I left the Rodericks. For all their ill treatment and abuse I forgave them, and felt a deep pity and sorrow for Mr. Roderick. I went my way bearing no malice in my heart, leaving them in the hands of their God. At last four saved and Ernest would soon come.

REST HAS COME.

Father, before Thee I am kneeling in gratitude and love,
Sad, weary years I sought, appealing for succor from above.
My cries seemed wild as unavailing before thy chast'ning rod,
My spirit in the strife oft failing to trust Thee, Oh my God.

When floods of sorrow o'er me sweeping thy hand I could not see,
Then thou, when heart and strength were yielding, bade me to
    cling to Thee,
Strength from thy promise gave endurance to stem, to cross the
    flood;
I thank thee, rest in blest assurance of Jesus' cleansing blood.

CHAPTER XV

REWARD OF FAITH.

"Leave behind earth's empty pleasure
Fleeting hope and changeful love,
Leave its soon corroding treasures,
There are better things above."

AFTER a short stay with Stella and Mrs. Seymore I started the children to schools in Asheville, Marie to the "Normal and Collegiate Institute" in charge of Dr. Lawrence, Bertha and Celeste to "Pease Institute" to go from thence to the Normal as soon as sufficiently advanced. It was a happy day for me the day I saw them put upon the train bound for Asheville. Now I turned my thoughts to Ernest. His school opened a month later, and as he was not permitted to visit or communicate with me, it was quite a difficult matter to make the necessary plans for his escape. I wrote an open note. I thought he would understand, and sent it by a wagoner. It was so worded that no one but Ernest himself could understand my true meaning. The little ruse succeeded and he sent a portion of his clothes by a wagoner under the supposition that they were to be sold by me. I expected a note to be hidden in the clothing stating what day to look for him, but was disappointed. After some delay

I decided to write a private letter and trust it to a Mr. Lanier, whom I thought to be an honest, trustworthy man. Soon after the letter had gone, I again searched the clothes Ernest had sent, and discovered the expected note securely hidden away in an inside lining. It ran thus:

"Dear Mother.—I will come, and go to that school, but I am in great need of clothing. You may expect me on the day school opens. Will take the train that day, so father cannot get me back. I am writing this in the dark.   Your devoted son, Ernest."

This note gave me such relief and joy that I trembled with pleasure and anticipation at the thought that soon I would have all the children in school and doing well.

A few days of suspense and the morning of Ernest's arrival came. I had not slept for anxiety for him and arose before light and walked out on the road, hoping, fearing, lest he could not come. The minutes and hours dragged —nine,—ten,—eleven. Oh, would he not come? What had happened? Oh Ernest! Ernest! Where are you now, my darling boy? One hour more and your train for the school will have come and gone! What shall I do if you do not come? On! On! the minutes flew now. How I would hold you, as Joshua bade the sun stand still, you precious time, that my son could arrive before that train! I wrung my hands in anguish as the shrill whistle of the "express sounded in the distance and no Ernest could be seen anywhere. I trembled so, my weak and tottering limbs would not bear my weight and went in and sank on the bed as I realized it was now *too late;* Ernest would not come. Some dreadful thing had happened to him! My poor, poor boy! What can I do to help you! Oh, what am I to do? What am I to do? Truly my heart could respond in the "Oh Absalom! my son, my son!" of King David of old. My brain seemed on fire! For days and weeks I heard nothing from Ernest, and walked the roads, for I could not bear to be caged in the house. The nights were spent in sleepless tossing until exhausted nature would sleep only to dream some terrible dream of him. Heavy rains set in and the streams rose, making it more difficult for me to get word from him now. Only a mother's heart could realize the anguish of those hours. I longed to fly to him, but knew this would only make matters worse. My suspense became unbearable until one morning, to divert my mind, I went to a clergyman's wife, Mrs. Paxton, a dear friend whose husband had performed our marriage service, and began reading the Bible again, as had been my custom. I asked her to pray with me; that I could not bear this waiting and must have help from on high. We prayed long and earnestly and again opening the Bible I read from the 91st Psalm "for he shall give his angels charge over thee, to keep thee in all thy ways. They shall bear thee up in their hands, lest thou dash thy foot against a stone." This seemed a direct answer to our prayers, and that whatever Ernest's dangerous position God would take care of him. Often in the night I would arouse from some horrible dream and worry over Ernest's condition, when these words would again come almost as if spoken "for he shall give his angels charge over thee" etc. They whispered comfort and sweet peace, and I would drop off in peaceful sleep and thus learned to trust as a little child all to my Saviour. A few days later a short note came from Ernest saying he could not come, and that he was going to

Rutherford county to school. This was all. Disappointed I was indeed, yet I hoped it must be for the best, and
felt thankful to know he was safe and would be in some
good school even though not the one I had provided for
him.

It was some months later I discovered that the letter I
had sent by Mr. Lanier had never reached Ernest but
was delivered into the hands of Mr. Roderick. The scene
that ensued was never recounted to me. Ernest would
only say "I was into it down there." What with threats,
expostulations and promises he was induced to promise to
go to the Rutherford county school instead of coming to
this one. I had bought him a new trunk and made him
some clothes and remade his old ones. These I could
not get to him and feared he would suffer, as his father
never provided him anything, but for this I could have
been somewhat satisfied. I now turned my mind to mission work. I had returned to my father's for a visit while
I wrote letters and made arrangements for the work I
loved so much to do. A friend wrote me of a position in
a "Home" in Georgia and wished me to take charge of it.
The way seemed all opened when to my horror my eyesight failed and I again lay almost helplessly blind.
The severe, mental and physical strains 1 had suffered
were too much for my eyes; again I must pay the penfal-
ty in suffering blindness. I was unable to wait upon
myself, helpless for all that winter, and was tortured with
the thought of how I could possibly care for myself and
children now beside all the agony of blindness and constant
excruciating pain. Yet the messages would come. "Trust
in the Lord and do good, and verily thou shalt be fed."
"Wait upon the Lord and he shall bring it to pass." "All

things come to those who wait." These and other passages were sent, while the following beautiful verse rang over and over in my mind, as if spoken:

> "My Father is rich in houses and land,
> He holdeth the wealth of the world in His hand,
> Of silver and diamonds, of rubies and gold,
> His coffers are full, He has riches untold.
> I'm the child of a king, the child of a king,
> With Jesus my Savior, I'm the child of a king."

All prospects for my earning anything were now taken away. But thoughts of the little poems which I had composed when blind before kept coming to me as the *one thing* I could do. My father whose mind was well stored with knowledge would often divert me with readings, recitations, and anecdotes of his early life, and would calm and soothe with hymns and psalms of praise. Often in the still, lonely watches of the night I would hear his voice repeating in low accents some beautiful verse or passage of scripture. The moon shone in softly upon us and gleaming stars spoke in louder tones than his of a God who sees and cares. I had relinquished the work of writing the book of my life. Now during that long winter it haunted me constantly. "But," said I, "how can I write a book; I am now blind and ill; how can I do it?" "I will provide a way," a voice seemed to answer! "I will give you strength." "But I have been criticized for thinking of writing my life, again I objected." "What! write your own life! I thought that was something people tried to hide, to protect from the public eye." "Too sacred for a stranger's gaze! This is what people say to me." "True," answered the voice, "yet if your life shows out of what depth the power of faith can bring one,—the efficacy of prayer, the influence of Christian example, the Christian's forbearance; if in any way, be it ever so small, you can benefit your fellow-man and let the light of the gospel of Christ shine forth to the world, should you not do it?" "Ay! verily, but, where is my means to publish a book. Every gate is barred with gold and opens but to golden keys. I would have to overcome so many obstacles and no strength, nor health, nor sight, and no money." "My strength is sufficient for thee," came the comforting promise.

The impression was so strong that I felt that the means would be provided, and the amanuensis also, if my sight should never be restored, and all that was necessary, in his own good time.

"Why had my life run in such a channel? Why such fiery trials, such sad experiences? And why left at last blind and ill?" The answer, To show I am God and by faith are his children led, I will reward those who put their trust in me." Forget the things which are behind, and press on to firmer grasp and fuller reception of Christ and his joy, and I believe my life's sufferings had been for some good purpose. My parent's income was scarcely sufficient for their own comfort and my staying there was depriving them. My brother was in good health but had a delicate wife and several children depending upon him. The brother in Asheville, Bradley, had lost his health and had some business failures and could no longer give me any assistance. My children must be helped and I could not give up. Truly, I had to be up and doing, go to Asheville, get my little book published and try to sell it for my own and children's support. I left my father's and went to Stella's where I remained two months recuperating my health and trying to regain my eyesight. I found upon my arrival a dear little angel had flown to this home-nest to brighten and gladden their hearts. *"Grandmother"* now, how aged I felt! All winter letters had come from Ernest, but they were very unsatisfactory, as his father read them before they were posted, and of course he wrote reservedly. A sad tone throughout made my heart ache, but I was still unable to help him. Letters from the children in Asheville spoke of their returning health and strength, contentment and happiness, and progress in their studies. Letters from their teachers were very gratifying, speaking of the children in highest praise.

I could not expect Mr. Lyman to take the burden of myself and children; and not until their education was completed and they were grown, could I expect to relinquish my effort in their behalf. So, early in April I left Stella's, seeing enough to walk about but unable to use my eyes but a few moments at a time, they were so extremely weak. At Bradley's in Asheville I had the sweet pleasure of beholding my three daughters—bright with rosy health and glow on their cheeks, happy and contented, so unlike the pale-faced, sad-eyed girls of a year ago. I was nearly smothered with kisses, and Bertha had brought her apron full of flowers and all had so much to tell and to show me how much they loved me, that I felt indeed I had not suffered and toiled in vain; only the thought of poor Ernest made us unhappy. A cloud would come over each bright face at the thought of that dear boy's lonely, sad life. He had only been permitted to remain in the Rutherford county school a few weeks. Mr. Roderick had put him there just to keep him from coming to me, and took him out as soon as he dared, and put him to work. Poor Ernest! He was having a hard, lonely life. With assistance from my people I succeeded in getting my little book of verses published and began the new and strange work of selling it. The humiliation of the work—being such a small thing to do—has always made it repulsive to me. My heart was not in it, and only that God gave it to me and necessity forced me to do it, gave me courage; yet I was remarkably successful and received much encouragement, particularly from Masons, real, true Christians and friends. One peculiar thing about my selling this book was that it required daily prayer to make it sell. If I left home without first asking God to bless and prosper me that day, it certainly was brought to my remembrance before the day closed. Generally I was received with great kindness by the Asheville people, but often discouraged, footsore and weary, I would climb some long flight of steps only to be coldly received and perhaps rebuffed, with distrustful cold looks. Weary, faint and sick, I would turn with a heavy heart to seek another and perhaps have nearly the same experience. "The Lord is my Shepherd I shall not want," and much of the twenty-third Psalm ran through my mind and healed the wound that human heartlessness had made. "Bless the Lord, O my soul, and forget not all his benefits," would arouse my sinking heart to action and renew my strength.

> " Though the rock of my last hope is shivered
>   And its fragments are sunk in the wave,
>   Though I feel that my soul is delivered
>   To pain, it shall not be its slave ;
>   There is many a pang to pursue me,
>   They crash, but they shall not contemn ;
>   They may torture, but shall not subdue me,
>   'Tis of Thee that I think, not of them."

I soon made arrangements to have Ernest admitted to the Boys' Farm School for one or two years. I met the President of the Weaverville College and arranged for him to enter there after the term at the Boys' Farm School. He would board in the family with the President, and would be under the highest influences. I was exceedingly gratified and appreciated all this goodness to me most highly. So much more than I could have hoped for! "More than we can ask." "Prayer must be based upon promise, but, thank God, his promises are always broader than our prayers."

I had saved up money enough to provide clothes for Ernest and to defray his expenses; and the one thing necessary now was for me to see him and get him into this school. So I left Asheville for Stella's. I then wrote to Mrs. Tolbert and asked if she would deliver a letter to Ernest secretly so his father would not know of it. She answered that she would see it safely into Ernest's hands, and thus I sent it. I only wrote that I wanted to see him at Stella's, for him to come at once. Mr. Roderick, thinking I was still in Asheville, finally listened to Ernest's requests to visit his sister, and reluctantly gave his consent. He came sooner than I expected, and I was startled one day as I sat in the room when a voice behind me said, "Good evening"; and I turned to see a strange, tall, pale looking boy standing in the doorway. He had grown so since I left—run right up to a tall, pale-faced boy. I scarcely recognized in him my little Ernest. "Ernest, my dear, dear boy!" I exclaimed, clasping him to my heart, and clung to and wept over him. He too saved would be the drop to overflow my cup of bliss. But he had to return for his clothes and help gather in the crops, hoping to realize something from his summer's labor, but was disappointed. We did not know the exact time of the school's opening, and I had to find out and inform him by private letter. The greatest difficulty in the way now was the getting his clothes from his father's. He could make good his escape by running away, but how to get his trunk? The harvest gathered, but to his great disappointment not a cent of money was allowed him. So all his labor and time was lost. While Ernest was doing all this I made a short visit to my mother, having forwarded the school letters to him through Mrs. Tolbert. I found my mother much improved in health. She seemed to have risen above all her trials and troubles, and now lived in a higher, more spiritual atmosphere.

At last the day of Ernest's arrival came. Much to my relief he came early, but so haggard and tired that he dropped down upon a couch, and I made him comfortable and left him so he could have a few hours' sleep, while I kept watch, fearing Mr. Roderick would discover his escape and follow. I requested some negro workmen on the farm to work within hearing distance, so if anything happened I could call them, as Mr. Lyman was absent from home. But nothing occurred, and Ernest awoke quite refreshed after several hours' sleep. He now related to me how he escaped from his father. At supper the evening before he had requested his father that he might go fishing with some of the neighbor boys, which request was granted him, saying, "I think I will go over to your Aunt Rachel's and spend the night while you are fishing, as you will not likely get in before morning." This was as Ernest had hoped. So after his father left for Rachel's, he returned home instead of going fishing. (It was the custom there to fish at night for a certain kind of fish.) Procuring a horse from the stable, he took his small trunk and a very large bundle, which things he had previously packed and made ready, and rode a distance of seven miles; then dismounting he secreted his trunk and bundle in some tall weeds near the road, then mounted the horse and returned, replaced the horse in the stable, went to the house and wrote a short note to his father saying he was not contented and had determined to go to mother and enter the school she had provided for him. Leaving this upon the table he again retraced his way to where he had left his trunk, walking the seven miles. He arrived there about one o'clock a.m., so tired and sleepy he could not but drop upon the ground for a short nap. Arousing himself he shouldered his trunk and walked two miles to Marion. There leaving it with some kind friends he went back and got the bundle; as he entered the town day was breaking. He left his things with kind friends and came on to me, walking six miles to Stella's. No wonder he was too exhausted to speak. That evening Mr. Lyman took Ernest in his spring wagon and returned to Marion for his trunk, and to purchase him some clothes for school. Not returning at dark as we expected, I feared Mr. Roderick had captured Ernest and his things by law and would force him to return with him; so I lived over again that awful suspense, waiting from six till ten o'clock before the wagon drove up, and, thank God! Ernest was there with Mr. Lyman, all safe and sound, and his trunk with him. The relief made us all very happy, and we laughed and talked joyfully all the evening. Now I had all my children.

At last, at last! after all the anguish, the waiting and suspense, the prayers, hopes, and fears; and after all human efforts that had looked so hopeless had been made, my blessing had come and my prayers were answered. "God is good," just as the letters had said, that had so often passed before my blind eyes in the long ago. They had been sent to me then to show He was with me and would not forsake, though the way had so often been hedged by difficulties insurmountable to frail humanity. Only in his strength and wisdom had they been over-come. Thankfully I poured out my heart in prayer that night, saying, "God is good, God is good."

Next day we hurried preparations for our journey to the school, and were in readiness by the noon train, which we caught at a crossing by flagging the train down. Unfortunately some person had set the trunks down too near the track, and as the train came up it struck the trunks, knocking both under the train, and then some ob-stacle gave them a crashing blow that sent them out again down the incline on the other side just in time to save the train from a fearful wreck. The trunks were recovered, tied up so as to keep the things in, and soon we were speeding on our journey. Ernest looked very happy enjoying the trip. At Swannano a stationwe got off for the school. Vehicles were there to receive the boys, and Ernest was stowed in one and soon arrived at the school. Now at last he was safe and beyond the reach of his father, as only by a lawsuit could he recover him; and I knew he would not attempt that, as we had too strong evidence against him, besides Ernest was so determined that he could not retain him any way. He would have been made tired recovering him by law, as

he said he would keep running away until they left him
alone.

Mother soon wrote a joyful letter at my good fortune,
from which I submit an extract: "The good news of
Ernest going to you and being in school was glorious.
God's hand was in it! Did I not prophesy it all? During
those terrible years, even when my heart was like lead in
my bosom, and the clouds were so dense over us you nor
I could see a ray of light in the dark horizon of our
lives, yet I would not despair, but kept up my courage
and yours too, until my health gave entirely away. It
has all come to pass just as I said it would, though I
doubted myself after; yet it seemed to be an inspiration
to talk as I did to you. I could not see how it could be,
yet felt it through all. Now let me prophesy again to
you: You will yet be a prosperous and happy woman,
with a home and comforts. God has brought you
through all this for some purpose to work for and live
for his glory."

> " Pour out your song before Him
> To whom our best is due;
> Remember He who hears our prayer,
> Will hear your praises too."

Now that the children were all safe and in schools
doing well, my friends advised me doing something to
improve my own condition and restore my sight entirely.
Though I could see to go about, I could not use my
eyes to read, or for any constant use, not even housework. I had sold my books all over Asheville, so must
now seek a new field. The question arose, Where shall
I go? I had friends in Philadelphia and Baltimore, but
did not like going North for the winter months. Had

21

heard much of the eminent and skillful oculist, Dr. Calhoun, of Atlanta, Ga., and the climate being so much warmer, all my friends advised my going there. But I left it for God to direct, and sought in prayer to be guided aright. Everything seemed more favorable for my going to Atlanta in preference to other places. I believed God was directing my footsteps in that way and thought it best to go. Masons gave me letters to the Masonic Fraternity in Atlanta, and Dr. Campbell, pastor of the First Presbyterian Church, Asheville, gave me a letter to Dr. Barnett, of the First Presbyterian Church, Atlanta; Dr. Felix, of the First Baptist Church in Asheville to Dr. Landrum in Atlanta; letters from the physicians to Dr. Calhoun, a letter of introduction to Dr. Thomas of the Christian Church, also one from a Methodist clergyman.

These, in addition to the one I had already from Bishop Cheshire of the Episcopal Church, gave me a pleasant introduction in Atlanta. I took rather a circuitous route in order to sell my books and make a last visit to my friends before leaving North Carolina, defraying my expenses by these sales and saving up money for my journey. Arriving in Atlanta I stopped at Hotel Marion. Next day Dr. Barnett called and went with me to see Dr. Calhoun, who advised me to go to the hospital. After a thorough examination of my eyes, he said I would likely never be able to use them much, and that with the improvement of my general health they would improve some, but that in time past there had been a great deal of inflammation, which had left deposits in the retina that could never be removed.

Arrangements were soon made for my entranocet the Grady Hospital. There were at this hospital as fine a corps of physicians as I ever met anywhere or in any hospital. They were skilled in their work and perfect gentlemen; also, a kind superintendent and efficient nurses. The ministers to whom I had letters called, expressing much sympathy; also, many ladies from different churches. I gained quite an exalted idea of Atlanta people and found many friends. During my stay at the hospital I endeavored to find in those who visited me an amanuensis for my book. Some one must write for me, and that one had not yet arrived. I had many promises and a little help, but it was all so discouraging I finally gave it up for the time.

Soon after I entered the hospital a reaction from the excitement and change set in, and I was completely exhausted with nervous prostration. At times I could not speak, and would sit or lie for hours alone with my face to the wall. My children were saved and now were all well and doing well, but what a wreck the effort had made of their mother! And my life was still lonely, for I had to be without them for the sake of their education.

> "O sorrowing one, each stroke of love
> A covenant blessing yet shall prove;
> His covenant love shall be thy stay,
> And covenant grace be as thy day."

Again so beautifully expressed elsewhere:
"When thou passest through the waters I will be with thee." Really and truly *with* you, even if the rushing of the waters seem to deepen and blind you for the moment so that you cannot see nor hear Him.

Mother's health had improved, and her letters, always a comfort, were doubly so now. A friend, in looking over some old letters, came across a copy of one mother had written her sister Mary, who had sent it to me. As it will be of interest here, I give the following extracts:

"MY DEAR SISTER MARY:—I have been thinking for some time of giving you a brief outline of some of my sad experiences for the last sixteen years, yet I know there are no words in the English language expressive enough to convey to your mind a correct idea of my real sufferings. Within the last ten years every member of my family, myself included, have passed within sight of the 'silent shore,' and poor Edgar passed over the river some years ago. At the time we came here our only daughter, a good, beautiful, and gifted girl, was just entering her sixteenth year, and was much beloved by our family and all who knew her. She was 'the apple of my eye,' the sole daughter of our house. I was never happy away from her, and she seemed always to prefer my society to that of others. In consequence I had great influence over her, she always listening to my counsels, and abiding in my judgment in every affair of her young life. Hence when Mr. Roderick, a merchant of our town, sought the hand of our daughter in marriage, I urged her to accept him, believing him a noble true Christian, he was so unselfish and loved her so devotedly. I really believed in him and thought I was right. She had many admirers, but I distrusted them all. I thought if she did not marry Mr. Roderick she might eventually become the victim of some sefish dissolute man. With these fears I encouraged her to receive his addresses,

telling her that I would probably die soon, and her father
was in delicate health, having changed climate for his
benefit. Also telling her that the feelings of gratitude,
esteem, and liking she entertained for him would in time
ripen into a warmer feeling. I thought in case of my
death he would be her shield and protector. These
were my motives. She listened to me, and they were
engaged. Yes, I freely and trustingly gave to this man,
a comparative stranger, my only daughter, my one pet
lamb! and she without a murmur calmly and quietly laid
her golden head upon the sacrificial altar of a mother's
wishes. 'She was led like a lamb to the slaughter, and like
one she opened not her mouth.' By this silence I was deceived. Had I known all I would sooner have died than
encouraged such a sacrifice, for her happiness and pros-
perity were the one desire of my heart. They had not
been married many weeks ere I feared that I had made
the mistake of a lifetime, and before many months had
passed I was sure of it. But I told no one, hoping I
might be mistaken; but I was not. The eyes of love are
sharp, and soon the scales fell from them and Mr. Roderick
stood revealed to me clothed in his true colors, with the
temper of a maniac, so unreasonable and cruel. I have
read somewhere that there is nothing more dangerous,
more subtle, and more armed with secret stings, than the
urbanity of a hypocrite or the cunning of a maniac.
Dear sister, can you imagine my feelings after a knowledge of these facts had burst in upon me? I did not enjoy one moment's peace or happiness. By the one act
I had brought ruin and misery to one I loved better than
anything on earth. I alone was guilty. I, her mother,
have been the chief cause of all her misery and her

wretched and darkened life. I have not only made her wretched, but heaped untold misery upon my own head. Sister, you have young daughters, take warning and never advise them to marry unless sure of their future happiness. I have prayed, oh, so fervently! to be forgiven, and if suffering could make atonement, have suffered enough to make full atonement for the great sin against the peace of my child; and I know she has never harbored an unkind thought toward me for all this. In her "Life History," written by herself, she has described the cruel treatment she has received at the hands of her insane husband. When at my own home I never felt for a moment free from anxiety, always expecting to hear that she was dead or bodily injured. Whenever a stranger appeared at the house I would tremble, grow cold and faint, fearing to learn his errand, and constantly feared that Mr. Roderick, in one of his insane fits of rage, in which he often indulged, would crush out the small spark of vitality yet remaining in her wasted and enfeebled frame. All these terrible years she lay blind and helpless and at his mercy. She was patient and gentle through it all, and I often wondered at her Christian fortitude. Through repeated shocks to her nervous system she was reduced to a fate worse than death in any form; and she lay perfectly blind and helpless for six long years. There are degrees of wretchedness which can never be described: such was the case now. I would often go to the woods where no eye could see me, no ear could hear but God's, and throwing myself prone upon the ground give vent to loud cries of anguish and despair. After spending a short while in this manner, would return to the house, resume my labors, having partially relieved my almost bursting heart. I often felt as if I was enclosed within iron walls, where no light nor air could ever penetrate, and these huge walls were slowly drawing nearer and would eventually crush me. This fearful agony and mental strain brought on a spell of sickness, from which I was not entirely relieved for some years. My mental vision was obscured and over-shadowed by a thick cloud of darkness. My visits to my daughter, when physically strong enough to go, were attended with the greatest distress. Oh, my sister, I cannot tell you how I felt, believing that in all human probability one, if not both of us, would cross to the other side before long, and that we might never see each other more in this life. My heart died within me as I looked upon the colorless face of my desolate and almost friendless child, as I feared, for the last time in this world. Before leaving I would kneel by her bed and pray to our Father in heaven to spare us, if it was in accordance with His divine will, and permit us to meet again on the shores of time. I kissed her good-bye and went away without once looking back, feeling as if my heart-strings were being rent in twain. The last view of her haunted me always—the poor bandaged eyes, the pitiful, sad ex-pression of the face, the colorless, emaciated hands, and helpless form, forsaken of all but God. I knew I had left this poor creature, this desolate, pitiful wreck of humanity, in the hands of a hard-hearted and cruel mad-man, this child of mine, who, only a few years ago, was a lovely and blooming girl! Oh my God! I cried, spare me to her! What has she left her but me? What will she do without me? Is it not my work and duty to spend my life in her service? to die for her if necessary? Have

I not, by one act of my life, consigned her to a fate ten thousand times worse than death? With these feelings I left her, knowing it was my only resource if I wished to live. After years God took pity on us, and to my great surprise I began slowly to mend. Yes, God in his infinite mercy put forth his hand and lifted me from this terrible physical and mental prostration. This awful nightmare of the soul which I had so long endured was fast leaving me, and I could smile again, but could not and did not shed tears for months. I was so happy! Oh, sister, no one, unless they have had the same experience, can realize how I felt. I almost think my face shone, and my heart went out in grateful thanksgiving to God and to my dear husband for his constant and tender care of me. The happiest thought of all was that I would spend the rest of my life in the service of God, bless His Holy name, and oh, joyful thought! my child was still alive. Thanks, too, to the many noble Christian ladies, I would see her again! and, still better than all, when we died, we would live together in heaven with our blessed Saviour. Oh, how thankful I was to God! I kept saying, 'God is good.'"

> "Yet in the madding maze of things,
> And tossed by storm and flood,
> On one fixed stake my soul shall cling—
> I know that God is good."

The treatment at the hospital soon improved my general health and I began to look about me for something useful to do until I was able to go out into the world again. The field was ripe unto harvest for the work of saving souls. The Christans amongst the patients joined me in prayers, songs, and readings, that soon interested

DEATH-BED SCENE IN GRADY HOSPITAL, ATLANTA, GA.

If indeed I had been an instrument in God's hands in bringing one soul to Christ it would more than repay for all those sad years of suffering.

the others, and often we had some very elevating soul-inspiring little meetings. One young girl seemed especially interested, and was at last thoroughly converted and sent home to her mother a Christian. Another, who was a very sick woman and had led a wretched, sinful life, was aroused to a sense of her guilt, and often listened attentively to us. One day she sent for me, asking for prayer and hymns. I saw she was very low and could not live. I called in others, and we read God's word and prayed for her. After singing a hymn in which the dying woman joined, she opened her eyes and, smiling, said: "O, I am forgiven! I am saved! God has forgiven me all my sins for Christ's sake! Thank God for sending you to tell me about my Saviour!" Later I sat alone with her. Accidentally no one happened in for a little while. As I watched the pale face lying there, so lonely, and now no friend, no relations near, my heart ached for her. But as I noticed the calm, peaceful expression, I knew she was not alone, for Jesus was there and comforted her soul. He can be all, all we need to fill our lives. It is an awful thing to watch a soul taking its flight for eternity, and oh, the many thoughts that crowded my mind as I now beheld this dying woman! dying to earth, but entering the true life above. I felt, oh, so thankful if indeed I had been an instrument in God's hand of leading one soul to him! It would more than repay me for all those sad years of suffering. The wan face became more rigid and the gasps shorter, then the soul took its flight and I was alone with the dead. Oh, the mystery of the grave! Then the thought, "By thy glorious resurrection and ascension," and *light* flashed into my soul.

> "Sing hallelujah! Light from heaven appearing,
> The mystery of life and death is plain ;
> Now to the grave we can descend unfearing
> In sure and certain hope to rise again."

As spring opened my physician thought a change in the open air would be beneficial; and, accepting the invitation of some dear friends, I bade good-bye to Grady Hospital, resolving now to make every effort to finish the story of my life and do the work God had appointed me to do; my faith unshaken in my belief in its mission for good, regardless of the many barriers and difficulties that had arisen to hinder it. Not that I felt that my life was of any consequence, but the power of Christ shone through it and the leading of the Holy Spirit. Perhaps that might lead some heart to believe and be saved.

Among other friends I visited Mrs. Vaughn at Bethany Home. Here I felt strongly the spiritual atmosphere of the place, and was led to deep meditation and prayer. Never had I consecrated my life so thoroughly to God as I did at this time. Children, parents, friends, all ties, all earthly love, I would relinquish and go to the further ends of the earth—*anywhere* where my Saviour called.

> "Oh let me know
> The power of thy resurrection.
> Oh let me show
> Thy risen life in clear reflection.
> Oh let me soar
> Where thou my Saviour Christ art gone before.
> In mind and heart
> Let me dwell always only where thou art."

At this time I received a letter from Marie stating her desire to prepare for mission work. She wrote: "I have wept and longed much for a father's love and care, but I now have our heavenly Father for my friend, and why should the daughters of a King go mourning all their day? I no longer grieve for the past, but shall follow Christ's bidding, 'Go ye, therefore, and teach all nations.' Mother, dear, I must work for Jesus." I had long since given my children to God, and felt honored that one of them had already been called. So my answer returned in the following lines.

THE GIFT.

God has called you, my Marie, and I hear the sweet voice
Of Jesus our Saviour; He would make you his choice
To work in his vineyard, to teach in his name;
He would give you the power lost souls to reclaim.

I give you, my darling, an offering to him,
Who died to redeem us, to save us from sin.
Be filled with His spirit, be strong in the strife,
Bring souls unto Jesus, in Christ there is life.

And when all is over and we meet on the shore
Of Heaven's fair Jordan, to part nevermore,
With Christ ever present to soothe away tears,
All pains we'll forget of those sorrowful years,

MOTHER.

I was sorry to leave my friends at Bethany Home, they were such true, noble Christians, but I must be up and doing. Dr. Calhoun encouraged me but little as to regaining my eyesight perfectly. He has a noble, unselfish heart and treated me with great courtesy. There was left nothing for me to do now but return to selling my little book of verses. With a letter from him and from many of the clergy of Atlanta, I again resumed "my burden," selling this book, so trying on nerve and heart, besides the great physical strain—walking, walking, day after day, until exhausted. I continually prayed that a different and more agreeable work might be given me and this trial removed. On one occasion I felt again a message of peace whispering in my ear. "You have trusted me," said the voice; "your hours of trial are nearly over, and my peace and rest shall abide with you and fill your soul, and my strength shall lift you from the dark places to brighter and happier days than you have known for years. Lift your head and look up, for I the Lord, having brought you through the deep waters, will strengthen, and will remove the burdens." I knew that Jesus was speaking, and his promises would not fail. Confident and resting in this new assurance, I trusted in the change I knew was coming.

As the days went by I kept an outlook for the one who was to finish my *life's history*. One day in a quiet retreat I discovered and formed the acquaintance of an artist, Miss Evelyn Noble, one whom I soon saw had suffered and borne with Christian fortitude the battle of life. Self-sacrificing, generous, and kind, we soon were in perfect sympathy with each other. I saw at once she could comprehend and sympathize with me in my life's trials, and was sure God had at last directed me to the right person. The work was taken up where I had left it, and it progressed rapidly, and soon some chapters had been copied by the typewriters.

Friends and Masons now became interested, and with their kind assistance it was all about ready for the publishers. God raised up many friends, who interested themselves in it and kindly offered their assistance, and I knew the way would open for its publication. Two great efforts of my life were now accomplished.

My children had been saved from ruin and were all converted (Ernest had given his heart to Christ during my stay at Grady Hospital), were 'in good schools, and were enjoying brighter prospects. Stella and Mr. Lyman had some time ago entered the church. *So all were within the fold.* The other effort, the book, was nearly written and ready for publication—the result only time can tell. God grant it may fulfill the desire of my heart in pointing some soul to Christ, and in its work may it glorify his holy name.

> " Though sometimes the way has been dreary,
>   And toilsome the path I have trod;
> Soon, soon I shall be where the chosen
>   Find rest in the arms of their God.
>
> How blissful will then be the meeting
>   Of the chosen ones of the Lord!
> Compared with its rapture how fleeting
>   The pleasures the world can afford.
>
> Oh sweet is the thought that I never
>   Shall leave the bright city above!
> I shall dwell with my Saviour forever,
>   Forever be blest in his love."

" The Lord shall give thee rest from thy sorrow, and from thy fear, and from the hard bondage wherein thou wast made to serve." Isa. 14:3.